Shutting Out the World

— A NOVEL —

Shutting Out the World

— A NOVEL —

JANICE WILLIAMS

Primix Publishing
11620 Wilshire Blvd
Suite 900, West Wilshire Center, Los Angeles, CA, 90025
www.primixpublishing.com
Phone: 1-800-538-5788

Published by Primix Publishing   01/31/2022

ISBN: 978-1-955177-73-3(sc)
ISBN: 978-1-955177-74-0(e)

Library of Congress Control Number: 2021924954

Contents

Preface

Once you get the soft, sugar-white sand between your toes, it stays with you forever. It beckons you back to the surf, sun, salt air, and scenic beaches of the Emerald Coast. The sparkling turquoise waters and sunny shores of the Florida Panhandle have become an adventurous playground for those lucky enough to visit or live along the emerald shores.

I lovingly dedicate this book to the early years of growing up along the snow-white beaches—a time when enormous, tall, sand dunes lined the emerald shores—a time before high-rise condominiums encumbered its pristine beaches when you could park your car and climb to the top of the towering white dunes and down to the water's edge. A time when you could take your transistor radio, spread out your beach towel, and listen to music as the tranquil sound of waves gently washed ashore. A time unimpeded by cell phones, computers, and I-Pads, which today constantly vie for our attention. For those of us fortunate enough to remember life as it was along the Emerald Coast, we share the memories of a time before others discovered the beauty of the place we call home.

The story, which follows, is fiction and not intended to reference established businesses or individuals. Instead, it depicts a snippet of life in the late 1970s along the Miracle Mile, as imagined in a romantic novel.

Chapter One

The sky was dark and ominous as gray clouds swirled menacingly overhead. Suddenly a bolt of lightning too close for comfort sent Jillian sprinting frantically inside to the safety of the inn. It was hurricane season. Like the other small towns dotted along the Gulf Coast of the Florida Panhandle, the community of Destiny Cove knew firsthand the sudden fierceness and devastation these storms brought with them. Those who resided along these beautiful sugar-white beaches were too familiar with hurricanes.

Closing the screen door, Jillian just managed to avoid the heavy deluge. Stopping for a brief moment, she looked back toward the beach. The heavens opened, releasing a sudden downpour of rain, thunder, and lightning. The waves appeared angry as they rolled ashore, leaving a deposit of foamy brine. Continuing inside, Jillian shivered from the sudden coolness in the air as she pulled her windswept blonde hair away from her eyes. Wearing a pair of cut-off denim shorts, she brushed the sugar-white sand from her tan, slender legs before walking into the lobby.

"Hey Jillian, Mom wants to know if the umbrellas and chairs were picked up?" Gracie questioned, sporting a headset that was attached to her new transistor radio. Gracie's long auburn curls flowed effortlessly over the counter as she leaned across the front desk.

Gracie, now almost sixteen, was only two years younger than Jillian. However, as siblings, they shared no similarities. Gracie was much shorter with a hint of red in her long curls, green eyes, and a sharp wit. It seemed her gregarious personality, even though popular with hotel guests, always kept her in trouble with their mom. Jillian was quite her sister's opposite. She was tall and slender. Her gorgeous blue eyes made it easy to see she was the beauty of the family. Jillian had inherited her father, Dimitri Demo's handsome Greek profile. Sadly, he had been lost at sea during a sudden vicious storm when she was only twelve. After the tragedy, she had grown up fast. Her life was on hold after graduating from high school. She had become self-reliant and independent at a young age and was the one her mother counted on to keep the Sea Oates running smoothly. Their mom, Daniella, now in her mid-forties, still looked young and vivacious despite the fact she was heavily in debt. Pulling her long blonde curls into a ponytail, she hid her stunning blue eyes behind her favorite sunglasses. Daniella ran every morning along the beach, trying to stay fit and trim. The early morning jaunts helped clarify how she would repay the loans connected to the small fleet of boats Dimitri had owned and operated before his death. Now, with only the Sea Oates to support her and her two daughters, life was hard.

Henry Johnson, now in his late fifties, worked for Dimitri. He had always been a loyal employee and shared a close connection with Daniella and the girls. The time Henry had spent working on the docks, and maintaining the numerous fishing boats, had aged him beyond his years. The fact he had never married and had no family of his own made it an easy decision for him to remain in Destiny Cove after the tragic event. Henry felt it an honor to stay and help with the inn after Dimitri passed. It seemed he was one of the family at this point. In addition, Henry had an uncanny way of recruiting locals to do odd jobs without pay whenever needed.

"Yes. Don't worry. Henry put them away earlier. Where's Mom?" Jillian answered, bolting up the stairs.

"Oh, she ran into town. She wanted to make sure we had enough batteries, just in case they're needed," Gracie answered, nonchalantly stuffing her mouth with chocolates.

"I'll be up in my room if you need me," Jillian yelled, continuing her sprint up the stairs. She was anxious to curl up on her bed with a good book. Hopefully, if they were lucky, the storm would narrowly miss them as it skirted along the Gulf Coast.

The Sea Oates had been a dream of Daniella's. She and Dimitri had discussed buying the inn after they married in June 1960. Finally, Dimitri surprised her by purchasing the dilapidated inn on their third wedding anniversary. After years of pouring sweat equity into the property, it provided a substantial income. The three-story structure had character. Tall pilings lifted it from the beach, allowing the onslaught of storm swells to pass effortlessly underneath its huge frame during hurricanes. Dimitri refurbished it with white shutters that trimmed the tall windows on each floor. Brilliant turquoise awnings covered each frame, complimenting the blue tin roof. Dark timbered shingles encased the structure, and each floor encompassed a wraparound deck that held an abundance of whitewashed Adirondack chairs and high back cane rockers. Dimitri had meticulously restored the inn to its fullest potential. Daniella's vision for its possibilities had finally transpired into a gorgeous inn where tourists spent long weekends leisurely on the beach. Now, with Dimitri no longer with her, she clung to the inn as her way of staying connected to him. It had been over six years since the tragic accident. The salt air had finally started to take its toll on the place. It was in need of repairs that were costly. Trying to maintain the inn in working condition was not going to be an easy task. However, with Henry's help and a booked calendar each month, Daniella planned to start by taking small steps towards the necessary maintenance. With a bit of luck, the storm would not be a direct hit, allowing those occupying the inn to remain.

Daniella finally returned. She had enough batteries to see them through the worst, just in case luck was not on their side. Hurriedly, she began unpacking the van. Then, noticing her dilemma of getting groceries up the steps to the main entrance, Henry came running over.

"Hey, Miss Daniella, hold on there. Let me help you get everything in before we get another downpour," Henry shouted.

"Oh, thanks, Henry. I could use your help. Did you manage to get the umbrellas and chairs stored?"

"Yes ma'am, not a problem," he answered with both arms fully encumbered with bags. "I think we'll be able to get it all inside without getting wet."

After several trips to the van, Henry finally placed the last grocery bag on the kitchen counter. Ava Albright, the chef for the Sea Oates, was busily preparing the main course for the evening meal. The appetizing aroma of fried seafood and hushpuppies infused the air. Stopping for a moment, she went through the bags, checking each item against her list of needed supplies. Ava was a stout woman in her mid-fifties. Wearing her gray hair pulled back in a bun, she wore a white apron to cover her large round belly and a short sleeve blouse with black pants. It was easy to see by her appearance that she loved food.

Ava had been a great addition to the Sea Oates. Her name was synonymous with a good meal. The locals and those fortunate enough to visit the Sea Oates never failed to recognize her talents in the kitchen. Ava had never married. She had devoted her entire life to her culinary skills. Working in one of the larger hotels in Atlanta for many years, Ava needed a change. She had always dreamed of relocating to the sunny shores of the Florida panhandle. As luck would have it, she answered an ad. It appeared the new owners of the Sea Oates, located in Destiny Cove, were in desperate need of a chef. With her impeccable resume and pleasant personality, it was easy for Dimitri and Daniella, the owners, to hire Ava. After working at the Sea Oates from the first day it opened, she was practically family.

"I think it's all here," Ava smiled, quickly returning to the stove.

"Henry, sit down. I will get you a cup of coffee. So what's the latest you've heard in regards to the hurricane?" Daniella questioned.

"Well, I think we might just get lucky on this one. Everyone hopes it will follow the same path as the last two storms. It looks like it will make landfall over in Louisiana."

"Here's your coffee. Be careful. It's really hot. I sure hope you are right. I could use a little luck around here," Daniella smiled, taking a seat across from Henry.

Suddenly Gracie bounded into the kitchen. It seemed the aromas coming from the kitchen had aroused her appetite. Running over to the stove, she grabbed two golden brown hushpuppies, quickly cramming them into her mouth.

"Child, you better stay out of those," Ava teased, handing her a piece of fried fish on a napkin. Mullet was a favorite among the locals. There was even a yearly festival named after it.

"Oh, Mom, I almost forgot. You had a call while you were gone. I think his name was Mr. McDermott," Gracie stated ravenously, devouring the warm fillet.

"Did he leave a message or the reason for his call?" Daniella asked inquisitively. Sitting down her cup, she looked up just in time to catch her daughter sneaking another piece of mullet from the stove.

"No. I'm sure if it's important, he will call back." Pouring herself a tall glass of iced tea, Gracie took her radio, placed her headset over her long curls, and ran outside to the covered porch.

"McDermott, that name sounds familiar," Henry recollected taking a sip of coffee. Then, suddenly, he sat up straight, putting his cup down. "Now I remember," he said, scratching his head. "Someone by that name was down at Brinkman's Hardware Store yesterday. I overheard Gene introducing him to some of the locals. Wonder what brings him to Destiny Cove?"

"Well, I don't know. Guess we will find out soon enough. Henry, would you like to stay for supper?" Daniella asked, watching as Ava filled a platter with fried mullet.

"Oh no, I better be going before this weather gets any worse."

"Henry, wait just a minute," Ava smiled, wiping her hands on her faded cotton apron. "Something for later," she mentioned, covering a large plate of fish and hushpuppies.

"Thanks. I sure won't turn it down," Henry smiled, getting up from the table.

"Say, Henry, if you hear anything further on Mr. McDermott, let me know," Daniella asked, holding the screen door open as Henry left.

"Oh, sure thing. If this ole place springs any leaks tonight, and you need me, you know where to find me."

"Thanks, Henry."

"Miss Daniella, please don't think I was eavesdropping on your and Henry's conversation but did I hear you mention someone by the last name of McDermott?" Ava inquired.

"Yes. Why do you know someone by that name?"

"Oh no, for heaven's sake. It's just the fact that the hotel in Atlanta where I was employed as a chef was constructed by someone with the last name of McDermott. If memory serves, I believe he built many of the high-rise hotels in downtown Atlanta. Just a coincidence, I'm sure."

"Yes. I can't imagine why someone of that significance would bother coming down to Destiny Cove. Ava, I know it's Friday evening, and our menu is primarily local seafood, but what did you decide to prepare for our guests who might not love our seafood dishes?"

"Oh, honey, don't worry. I've got you covered. I know it's Friday. I prepared a huge pot roast earlier this morning with all the trimmings, an apple cobbler, and a chocolate cake that is divine. I believe your guests will love what your menu has to offer."

"Thanks, Ava. I knew I could count on you. I think I am going to check on Gracie. The lightning is getting intense. I want to make sure she didn't leave the safety of the porch and walk down to the beach in this weather."

"Okay. By the way, if you find her, do you think she would mind lighting the candles on the tables for me? It's almost 5:30 p.m., and we start serving at 6:00 p.m."

"Not a problem. We might need those candles tonight," Daniella shrieked as the lights flickered. Thankfully, staying off for only a few seconds, it was a wake-up call to let Daniella know she should check the generator.

"On second thought, can you please see that Gracie comes inside? I'm going down to make sure the generator is in working order."

"Yes. Be careful on those old stairs," Ava warned with a smile, pulling a pan of homemade biscuits from the oven.

The intensity of the storm was getting worse. The dilapidated inn creaked and groaned as Daniella descended the steep rickety steps leading down to the lower level. Turning on her flashlight, she wiped cobwebs from the ceiling before inspecting the archaic generator. It was just another thing on her long list that needed replacing. Maybe Henry should have stayed over in the extra guest room, she thought. Kneeling, she took a closer look. Daniella did not need anything going wrong tonight or any other night for that matter. The Sea Oates was booked solid for the next two months, and she could not afford to jeopardize that fact. Suddenly, a loud thunderous bolt of lightning made her jump. Quickly checking the amount of fuel and oil the outdated equipment contained, she headed back upstairs. Unfortunately, her knowledge of such things was limited. Once more, she cursed Dimitri for dying and leaving her and the girls. The task of running the inn and now trying to keep up with the maintenance had become a daunting task. However, it was all she had and the only means of making a living for her, Gracie, and Jillian.

It seemed luck was on her side as she woke to blue skies and sunshine the following day. Destiny Cove had managed to escape the direct onslaught of the fierce storm. Sadly, those a little further down the coast did not fare as well. So it seemed the perfect opportunity to make an overall inspection of the inn. After creating an initial assessment of needed items, she decided to call Henry. It was finally time to make some much-needed repairs.

Chapter Two

Picking up the morning paper, Daniella was shocked to see the headlines. It seemed she no longer needed Henry to learn the identity of Mr. McDermott. On the front page of the Bayou Gazette for the entire world to see was his photo. John McDermott smiled as he stood next to Mayor Allen and a few city council members. He appeared astute as they shook hands. Taking a closer look, he was rather handsome, tall, thin, and probably in his mid-forties. A hint of gray in his black hair made him very distinguished. However, what got her attention was reading the fact that stated, *'McDermott Corporation to build high-rise condominiums.'* As she read further, it said his corporation had already agreed with one of the locals to purchase their beachfront property. It appeared the owners of the Break Waters Hotel were among the first to sell. However, the paper did not mention the price his company had offered. She braced herself, wondering if that had been the reason for his recent call. Picking up the article, she went into the kitchen. She needed a cup of coffee.

Placing the paper on the table, she poured herself a cup of coffee and sat down. Maybe this was the answer to her prayers.

"I suppose you've seen the headlines," Ava mentioned walking in. "So what would you do if he wants to purchase the Sea Oates? Oh, and by the way, that is most definitely Mr. McDermott, I was telling you about from Atlanta."

"Ava, are you sure? There are lots of people who happen to share that last name, and don't be silly no one has approached me in regards to selling."

"Oh, I'm sure of it. You didn't work in one of his hotels without becoming familiar with who he was and how rich he was," Ava laughed. "Didn't Gracie say someone by the name of McDermott called here the other day?"

"Yes, as a matter of fact, she did. I don't know what I would do. However, I'm facing some hefty repairs. It's all just a lot of speculation right now as far as the Sea Oates," Daniella scoffed, folding the newspaper. If you have breakfast covered, Henry is supposed to come over and go with me to an appointment with a roofing company this morning."

"Breakfast is all prepared. I got up extra early this morning and made blueberry pancakes. I have everything ready to serve at 7:00 a.m. I think most of your guests are checking out at noon, and I already have a start on the dinner menu for the guests arriving later this evening. If I need anything, the girls are here. Don't worry."

Hearing a loud knock, Ava smiled, seeing Henry at the screen door.

"Hey, Henry, come in. Would you like a stack of blueberry pancakes this morning?" Ava inquired, quickly pouring him a cup of coffee.

"I certainly wouldn't turn you down," Henry grinned, pulling out a chair. "See you've seen the morning paper," he quizzed, looking over at Daniella.

"Yes. It made the headlines. So what have you heard?"

"Well, it's certainly the buzz around town. I was down at the docks earlier this morning when the Wave Runner came in with her crew. It seemed to be the topic of conversation. A lot of them are sure skeptical about the McDermott Corporation. But, on the other hand, it surprisingly appears the owners of the Break Waters Hotel settled a little undervalue for their property."

"What? Who in their right mind settles below appraised values?" Daniella gasped in a state of shock.

"Well, I guess people have different reasons for deciding to sell. It seems the owner, Ed Carrington, was already planning to relocate back to Indiana. One of the men who works on the docks mentioned that his mother was in bad health. I think he had been planning to sell for a while. Guess McDermott just happened to catch him at the right moment," Henry mentioned, shoveling blueberry pancakes into his mouth.

"That's too bad. I sure hate to hear that," Ava mentioned refilling their cups with coffee.

"Yes. That's crazy. What else have you heard?" Daniella asked.

"Geez, it's all hearsay. Don't know how much truth there is to any of it," Henry replied, taking a huge gulp of coffee. "Some of the guys swear that Mayor Allen and the city council members are in bed with the McDermott Corporation. You cannot repeat a word I've said. It's all second-hand news, and who knows if there's a bit of truth to it." Finishing his pancakes, Henry pushed his chair back from the table.

"Wow. I tend to believe your sources. Even though it's pretty hard to believe, you're right. Most times, there is a bit of truth to the story," Daniella agreed, looking up at the clock. "We better get going. It's almost 8:00 a.m. Ava's got breakfast to serve, and we have an appointment downtown." Walking over to put her cup in the sink, Daniella grabbed her purse. "Please let Jillian and Gracie know that I'll be back in about an hour. Oh, one last thing, the gardeners are coming this morning to cut the shrubs and palms out front. I left a check for them under the register in the lobby."

"No problem," Ava smiled, folding a stack of ironed cotton napkins.

"If we hurry, I think we'll have just enough time to stop at Brinkman's Hardware," Daniella suggested as they walked through the foyer. "I need to pick up some new faucets for the bathrooms."

"Okay," Henry grinned, pulling a worn baseball cap from his back pocket. Putting on his faded blue cap with its depiction of his favorite fishing vessel, the Wave Runner, it perfectly complemented his red flannel shirt and distressed jeans.

Walking into the hardware store, Daniella immediately went over to look at sink fixtures. It didn't take long to find something suitable to match the bathroom décor. It was a cheap fix, and with some new paint, it beat the cost of a complete renovation. After choosing a light blue color and picking up brushes, she walked over to the counter to pay for the items.

"So, are you going to sell?" Joe Brinkman asked as he rang up the items.

"Sell what?" Daniella asked, suddenly caught off guard by his question.

"The Sea Oates," he queried. It looks like you're making a few upgrades to the place."

"What? Are you referring to the article in today's paper?" Daniella hesitated for a moment, looking up at him, then continued placing her items on the counter. "No way, I just needed to replace some worn fixtures and decided while I'm in here I might as well pick up a gallon of paint. News sure travels fast around here," Daniella smiled, reaching into her purse for her checkbook.

Noticing that Daniella had finished her purchase, Henry walked over to the counter. Joe and Henry were lifelong residents of Destiny Cove. Neither of them had ever lived elsewhere, except for the two years Joe had spent in the Navy. Joe was now in his mid-seventies. He was stout with receding salt and pepper hair. As always, he was wearing his trademark blue denim overalls. After his time in the Navy, he had returned and opened the hardware store. It seemed Brinkman's Hardware, and the local post office were the main two places in Destiny Cove to hear the latest gossip.

"Oh, I didn't mean to pry. I'll run over and mix the paint. Give me just a minute," Joe continued.

"Give me the paint. I'll run to the back and mix it for you," Henry offered, walking over to pick up the can. "We're sort of in a hurry," he explained.

"Thanks, Henry," Joe smiled, opening his cash register as he reached for a paper bag. "I heard McDermott purchased the Break Waters Hotel. The talk around town is that he plans to purchase a large number of our older hotels, tear them down, and build high-rise condominiums. Just imagine all those new people moving down here. What do you think about our little community being invaded by city folks who want to own a piece of our beautiful beaches?" Joe asked with a bewildered expression.

"Well, I'll tell you one thing for sure, he's not going to get the Sea Oates. I don't care how much he offers. He can keep his high-rises in Atlanta for all I care," Daniella responded with a stern look of determination.

Just at that moment, Henry walked back to the counter with the paint.

"Talking about McDermott Corporation, are you?" Henry smiled, sitting the paint down. "That man has sure stirred things up around here. Just look what happened a few miles down the coast at White Point. Those poor people cannot even get to their beautiful beaches without paying to enter a park. High-rise condominiums now cover their entire beaches as far as the eyes can see, and to make matters even worse, the traffic is terrible in the summer," Henry stated.

"Oh, I hear you. Don't get me started. I shudder to think what might become of our little community. Of course, those tourists' dollars would be good for business. But then again, if I'd wanted to run and operate a larger business, I'd never stayed in Destiny Cove," Joe chuckled.

"Henry, we better get going," Daniella suggested looking down at her watch. "Guess we'll all have to wait and see what happens. See you later."

"Let me get those for you," Henry offered as he picked up the heavy paper sacks.

After making her next appointment at the roofing company, Daniella was ready to call it a morning and return to the Sea Oates. It seemed the roofing materials were more expensive than what she had initially planned to spend, which meant continuing to patch the old roof. She could only hope and pray that Destiny Cove did not become the target of another destructive Hurricane during the upcoming storm season. Arriving back at the inn, Henry agreed to stay for a while and change out the fixtures.

"Well, let's just hope we don't wind up in the direct path of one of these fierce storms this season. But, if we escape, I think the roof should get you through a few more months," Henry remarked, carrying the bags inside.

"Why don't we take a break before you get started with those," Daniella suggested walking into the kitchen. "I'll get us a glass of iced tea."

Seeing her walk in, Ava came in from the porch where she had been watering plants. "You got a phone call while you were gone."

"Really. Who called?"

"You're never going to believe it, but it was Mr. McDermott. He left his number and asked that you return his call."

"Well, he can continue to call. I have nothing to discuss with him. Who does he think he is coming down here to our little community dictating policy to everyone?"

"Wow. He seems to have ruffled your feathers, and you've never even met the man," Henry chuckled, taking a sip of his iced tea. "Don't you think you should, at least, hear him out and see what he has to say? You know this ole place could sure use a lot more than a couple of new faucets and a roof."

"I think Henry's right. You should give him a call," Ava mentioned, making another pitcher of tea.

"Okay. I'll think about it, but I'm not making any promises. Henry, as soon as you finish your drink, I would like you to get started on those faucets. Hopefully, we can get them changed before our new guests arrive."

"No problem. I wouldn't worry too much about the roof. The weather forecast doesn't show any rain for the next few days."

However, that was not to be the case.

Later that night, after an exhausting day, Daniella retired upstairs to her room. Finally, the worries of the Sea Oates and maintenance left her as she drifted off to sleep. Only a short time later, Daniella woke to a familiar sound. Sitting up in bed, she cringed, listening to the sound of rain as it hit the tin roof of the Sea Oates. Darn, Henry and his weather report. It appeared a small front sitting off the coast had moved ashore earlier than expected. There was nothing to do but wait for morning and hope it did not bring news of more leaks. She had always loved falling asleep to the sound of rain when Dimitri was alive. But now, it only brought the problems of an expensive repair.

The following day as she sat in the kitchen drinking a much-needed cup of coffee, she waited anxiously to hear any news of a leak. However, it seemed she did not have to wait long as Gracie bounded into the kitchen searching for cereal.

"Mom, did you hear the rain last night? I hate to tell you, but there's a large brown stain on my ceiling near the window."

Gracie always loved playing practical jokes. It seemed her way of entertaining those around her. However, those whose fortune it was to be the focus or target of her sense of humor never seemed to appreciate it.

"Gracie, are you sure? Seriously, that's not funny," Daniella vented, quickly putting down her cup of coffee.

"Mom, I'm telling the truth. But, I think you need to go up and take a look."

Hearing her daughter's reply, she instantly felt sick in the pit of her stomach.

"Did you hear the rain last night?" Ava asked, walking in with the morning newspaper. "Henry was sure wrong about his weather forecast."

"Oh, Ava, not only did I hear it, the ceiling in Gracie's bedroom leaks," Daniella worried, rubbing her forehead.

"Well, I guess you better make that phone call," Ava grimaced, pouring herself a cup of coffee.

"First, I'm going to call Henry. He can take a look and let me know how extensive the damage is and what repairs would cost. Mr. McDermott can wait until tomorrow morning."

Later that afternoon, Henry came over. After Daniella had given him a good scolding on his so-called weather report, he climbed into the attic and finally up onto the roof. It seemed the news was not good. The cost of a new roof was well beyond her budget. She would return the previous phone calls from Mr. McDermott in the morning. However, she was still undecided about selling despite the looming repairs. Her close personal attachment to the Sea Oates and its memories were all she had left from her marriage to Dimitri.

Chapter Three

Waking the following day to clear skies and no further leaks, Daniella headed downstairs to the kitchen. She needed a cup of coffee before making the dreaded phone call to John McDermott.

"You think that's strong enough? I think you might need some liquid courage before you make that call," Ava chuckled, walking into the kitchen with the morning paper. "I have a special bottle. I've been saving it for a moment like this." It seemed Ava could easily read her thoughts.

"Oh, no thanks, but hang onto it. I might need it afterward. One thing is for certain if McDermott thinks he will purchase the Sea Oates as cheaply as he did the Break Waters, he might as well head back to Atlanta," Daniella frowned, taking a huge sip of coffee.

"It's none of my business, but the Sea Oates is all that you and the girls have left. I cannot tell you what to do, but how would you even begin to put a price on this place. To me, it's priceless," Ava worried as she stuttered under her breath.

"Ava, I know. Please don't worry. You will always have a place with Jillian, Gracie, and me. You are family. Trust me. He would have to offer a huge sum of money for me even to consider selling the Sea Oates."

"Well, the John McDermott I remember from Atlanta could be very suave and mesmerizing. But, of course, he was much younger back then and extremely handsome."

"Look, the last thing I'm possibly looking for is a husband, and he's probably married," Daniella scoffed, noticing the time. "Think I'll take a short run along the beach to clear my head before his office opens. I am going upstairs to change clothes. If Jillian comes downstairs, ask her if she would like to join me," Daniella added, putting her cup in the sink.

Returning from her usual morning run, Daniella sprinted back inside the kitchen for a tall glass of water on her way upstairs to shower and change. She was still confused about whether or not she would sell. However, she would return his call. It wouldn't hurt to hear what he had to say. Maybe her answer would depend upon his offer.

"So, did you get the clarity you were looking for this morning?" Ava inquired, pulling a large pan of warm cheese biscuits from the oven.

"Not really. But I'm curious. So I've decided to return his calls," Daniella replied confidently, wiping beads of sweat from her forehead. Then, after getting another glass of cold water, she ran upstairs.

"Good luck," Ava called out as she left the kitchen.

An hour later, Daniella returned with a perplexed stare. Pouring herself a cup of coffee, she sat down and crossed her arms.

"So, let's have it. What happened?" Ava questioned. Daniella's expression left little hope the call had been good.

"Oh, that," Daniella teased half-heartedly. "I spoke to him briefly. But, it seems Mr. John McDermott never talks business on the phone, so I'm meeting with him later tonight."

"Really. Where?" Ava stopped peeling potatoes to wipe her hands on her apron. Walking over to the coffee pot, she poured herself a cup of coffee and refilled Daniella's cup. "Honey, you seem awfully worried and confused," Ava questioned, taking a seat at the table across from Daniella.

"Oh, the Whales Tail at 6:00 p.m. this evening. Well, in a weird way, I'm confused. I had hoped to get a feel for the reason he called earlier. However, he never once even mentioned the Sea Oates. Can you believe his audacity? However, he's sending a car over to pick me up."

"I'm sure he's a busy man and thinking back, I don't remember him being very friendly when he came to the hotel where I worked. So I would not read too much into the conversation. You will have your answers soon enough. Don't worry. I'm sure it's about him wanting to purchase the inn," Ava reassured her as she quickly finished her coffee. "I've got dinner to prepare, and we have a full house this evening."

Welcoming her guests as they checked in kept Daniella's mind off McDermott and busy taking care of their needs. The Sea Oates had a full occupancy this evening, and she would ensure their stay was pleasant. Hopefully, as guests, Ava's delicious home-cooked meals along with the beautiful warm waters of the Gulf would guarantee their return and soon bring them back. Gracie was busy with school, leaving only Jillian to help provide the personal hands-on experience that the Sea Oates had built its reputation around.

It seemed the afternoon had flown by, leaving only an hour for Daniella to shower and dress before meeting with John McDermott. She would soon be face to face with the one person who might hold the key to her financial struggles. That is if she decided to sell, and at this point, she was still determined to hang on to the inn despite its much-needed repairs.

"Miss Daniella, I think your car is here," Ava shouted as she watched the limo drive up to the front entrance.

"Thanks, Ava. Please let the girls know that I am leaving. I shouldn't be out late."

Racing down the stairs, Daniella stopped briefly to take a quick peek out the front windows before she exited the lobby. A luxurious, sleek limo was waiting for her.

"Good evening. I'm Carl, Mr. McDermott's chauffeur. He will join you at the restaurant," Carl explained, opening the car door.

"Thank you," Daniella answered, flashing him one of her beautiful smiles as she stepped inside the car. She looked elegant, having chosen a simple black dress with heels.

As the car entered the highway for the short drive, a million thoughts were racing through her mind. However, what she could have never known was the shrewdness of the man she was about to meet. John McDermott never made appointments or invited clients to dinner without first learning everything possible about the individual. His business strategy was like a game of chess. He was always one move ahead. He loved the art of the game, and knowing his adversary gave him an advantage. John knew before even seeing her that she was in a crisis in regards to the Sea Oates. He knew her probably better than she knew herself at this point. However, knowing she was a widow somewhat softened his heart and feelings toward her. Regrettably, even this fact would not become a detriment when it came to closing a deal. Unknowingly, he was about to meet a woman whose inner strengths and tenacity would take him by surprise.

Entering the Whales Tail, Daniella immediately noticed a tall, distinguished man walking towards her. He appeared to be in his mid-forties, extraordinarily handsome and fit for his age with a hint of gray in his jet-black hair. As he came closer, his charm, gorgeously sculpted profile, and captivating blue eyes quickly caught her attention. The fact he had a perfect five o'clock shadow made him even more alluring.

"Good evening Mrs. Demos. I'm John McDermott. I've reserved a table for us in the back where it's quiet," he smiled. "I'll show you to our table."

Touching the small of her back, he ushered her towards a candlelit table at the back of the restaurant. It faced a wall of windows, which revealed breathtaking views of the beach. Pulling out her chair, he seemed friendly and not the ruthless, overbearing CEO she had suspected.

"Welcome to the Whales Tail. I am Kevin, and I will be taking care of you this evening. Would you like a glass of wine to start?" the waiter inquired, handing Daniella a list of beverages.

"Yes, please," she replied, reaching into her purse for her reading glasses.

"May I take the liberty of suggesting a great wine for dinner?" John inquired, staring intensely into her beautiful blue eyes.

"Yes. Thank you."

Daniella was having difficulty finding a reason to disdain the attractive man sitting across from her. But, of course, the night was young, and there had been no mention of his motives regarding the Sea Oates.

"We would like two glasses of cabernet sauvignon," John stated after quickly reviewing the list of available wines.

"I'll be right back with those," the young man replied, picking up the beverage menus.

"Thank you for returning my calls and agreeing to meet with me this evening. I was beginning to think you were trying to avoid me," John smiled once more, giving her another intense stare.

"Well, Mr. McDermott, I was a bit hesitant after reading the newspaper. And to be honest, I don't think everyone in Destiny Cove approves of your plans for revitalizing our beautiful beaches."

"Please, call me John," he smiled. "I certainly hope you don't believe everything you read," he teased charmingly. "Let's order dinner before I explain my reasons for wanting to meet with you this evening."

Briefly glancing through her menu, Daniella removed her reading glasses after looking over the menu. "I'll have the braised red snapper with rosemary and new potatoes," she smiled, looking up as the waiter returned with their wine taking their orders.

"I'll have the Maine lobster with grilled zucchini and mushrooms," John added.

"Great choices, the waiter smiled pleasantly after picking up the menus."

"Thanks again for accepting my dinner invitation," John grinned warmly, picking up his glass.

"You can call me Daniella," she smiled, somewhat unsure of his motives.

Taking another sip of wine, Daniella studied John's face noting a small scar slightly above his right cheek. It seemed barely noticeable. However, it appeared to work in his favor. It added to his alluring persona.

"So, how long have you lived in Destiny Cove?"

"Oh, I'm a native. I have never lived elsewhere. Immediately after graduating, I married my high school sweetheart, Dimitri Demos. He relocated to Destiny Cove from Greece along with his father after his mother passed away. He was only ten at that time, and being an only child, he was close to his dad. After we married, he worked with his father on his fleet of fishing boats. Unfortunately, they were lost at sea during one of their fishing expeditions. An unexpected storm capsized their boat, sinking it within seconds, taking the whole crew with it. I still miss him terribly. Thankfully, I have my daughters, Gracie, and Jillian, to keep me busy along with the inn."

"What about your parents?" John inquired. He was acting reserved while merely playing a game. He already knew everything there was to know about her. Taking another sip of wine, he continued. "Do they live nearby?"

"Sadly, my parents were killed in a horrible traffic accident along with my sister not long after Dimitri and I were married," Daniella explained somberly.

"I'm sorry to hear of your loss. It seems you've had more than your share of heartbreaks and tragedies."

Returning with their meals, the waiter sat piping hot plates of seafood in front of them. Not a moment too soon, he thought. John had endured enough small talk for the evening. He was ready to eat and get on with more important things, like purchasing the Sea Oates.

"Let's eat, and then we'll discuss why I invited you here. I ate here last week with the mayor, and it was delicious," he mentioned cutting into his fillet of mahi-mahi.

As she finished her last morsel of fish, Daniella was beginning to find herself intrigued by the handsome man sitting across from her. She needed to know more about him. What were his reasons for choosing to develop Destiny Cove? Daniella was not one to hold back her thoughts. She always spoke her mind regardless of the consequences that often followed.

"Before we discuss the reason you invited me here this evening, I would like to know more about you. Is there a Mrs. McDermott?"

"We're divorced. My line of work has always taken me away from home for long periods. Regrettably, my career is not very conducive to a great marriage. We divorced after Matt was born." Daniella's blunt questions caught him off guard. Taking a sip of wine, he smiled. He did not like being put on the spot, so to speak, and asked such personal questions when meeting someone for the first time. However, he liked her tenacity.

Is Matt your only child?"

"Yes. Matt is majoring in environmental studies at Harvard. I believe he is coming down next week with some friends. After hearing about your beautiful beaches, nothing could keep him away," John added politely. He waited pensively for her next question.

"So, where do you call home?" Daniella asked without hesitation.

"Atlanta, Georgia. However, I was born and raised in New York." John seemed amused with her child-like fascination. "So I guess you're wondering what brought me down to Atlanta," he smiled.

"Well, since you've brought it up," she inquired demurely, returning his smile. Daniella already knew he lived in Atlanta. However, she continued wanting to learn more.

"I earned my degree as an architect from NYC University, and my first job happened to be in Atlanta. Would you like another glass of wine?"

"Yes. Thank you."

"I think we should get back to our reason for being here," John suggested motioning for the waiter.

Taking a few moments, he collected his thoughts.

"Daniella, I'm not going to make this long and drawn out. The Mayor of Destiny Cove, Mr. Allen, and the city council members chose my company, McDermott Corporation, to revitalize your beautiful beaches. A few members of the mayor's team came up to Atlanta, and I was lucky enough to get the approving bid to build high-rise condominiums. Unfortunately, it seems Destiny Cove has lost millions of tourist dollars over the past decade. Allen and the council members finally realized the urgent need to rectify their past mistakes of not incorporating high-rise multi-units into their long-term plans for your community. Our development will bring a substantial financial boom to Destiny Cove.

I am sure you heard I purchased the Break Waters Hotel. I have brought you here this evening because I am also interested in buying the Sea Oates. I am prepared to offer you full market value. I know you are looking at some expensive repair costs to keep the inn open, so I think you will be extremely excited to be able to walk away from those. With our gracious offer, you will no longer have those worries, plus you and your daughters will be quite comfortable. You'll be able to travel and live life the way you'd like without being tied down by the inn and its pending repairs.

My assistant will stop by the Sea Oates tomorrow morning with our offer. Please look it over and get back to me," John smiled. "Would you like dessert and coffee?"

"Coffee sounds great. I think I will pass on dessert. I will go over your offer. However, I am not making any promises. The Sea Oates might not seem valuable in today's market. But, you need to understand it's extremely valuable to me. My husband purchased it for me, and now that he's passed, it's all that I have."

John motioned for the waiter. It wasn't long before he returned with cups of coffee. Slowly sipping the hot beverage, it provided an awkward silence between them. John desperately tried to read her face for hints she might be willing to sell. Still, Daniella offered no emotions that would indicate her decision. She felt the ball was in her court for now. Whatever the offer, it was not something on which she planned to make a snap decision.

"This has been a wonderful evening," John smiled, looking down at his watch. "It's certainly been a pleasure meeting you. I will wait for your decision. You can reach me at my office," he grinned, handing Daniella his business card. "I look forward to working with you on the sale of the Sea Oates. I'll walk you out to the car. My driver is waiting to take you home."

"Thank you for dinner. I'll let you know my decision," Daniella smiled as he once again gently placed his hand at the small of her back, ushering her out to the waiting car. "I'll call you tomorrow," Daniella added as he opened her car door. Taking one last look at him, she found herself entirely captivated by his handsome appearance.

Watching as the limo drove away, he found her fascinating. He smiled, sensing a woman made of steel under her quiet disposition. John McDermott loved a good challenge. However, Daniella could never have known the lengths he would go to ensure the sale went through as planned.

Arriving back at the Sea Oates, Daniella walked into the kitchen for a drink, surprised to find Ava still awake.

"For heaven's sake, what keeps you up this time of night?" Daniella remarked, opening the fridge.

"What do you think? I want to know how the meeting went," Ava paused, putting her coffee down. Curiously looking up at Daniella, she was anxiously waiting for answers.

"Well, to be honest, he does want to buy the Sea Oates." Pouring herself a glass of juice, she sat down across from Ava.

"So what did he offer?"

"Well, that's just it. He's having his assistant bring over a package in the morning. However, he made it appear that it would be a great offer. He also mentioned the fact that he knows the hotel is in desperate need of repairs. He indicated his offer would be enough to sustain the girls and me. John said it would give us a second chance at rebuilding our lives without the worries of the Sea Oates."

"Wow. You're on a first-name basis, and that doesn't exactly answer my questions. You can read a lot into that statement. Sustain is a very subjective word. Guess we'll have to wait until morning," Ava muttered, finishing her coffee.

"I'm turning in for the night, and yes, you're right. I guess we'll have our answers tomorrow," Daniella replied, putting her glass in the sink.

"Honey, try to get some sleep. I'll see you in the morning," Ava whispered as she walked over, giving her a gentle squeeze. "Don't worry. The way I see it, the ball is in your court."

"Thanks."

Getting into bed, Daniella pulled the covers up to her chin. Ava was right. There was no need to spend the night worrying, and she did not have to sell. The Sea Oates had been her comfort and refuge since losing Dimitri. Maybe second chances were overrated. Burying her head into the pillow, she quickly fell asleep.

Chapter Four

Waking to the robust aroma of coffee from the downstairs kitchen, Daniella sat up in bed, rubbing her eyes. The morning sunlight streamed in through the curtains, immersing the room with its brilliance. Suddenly, Daniella looked over at the clock on the nightstand. It was almost 6:30 a.m. Quickly jumping out of bed, she headed immediately to the shower. Today was important. Hopefully, it would bring a second chance at a new life for her and the girls. Even though the Sea Oates had been a safe harbor after losing Dimitri, it was time to leave behind their memories and get a fresh start.

The warm water sent a tingle of excitement through her petite frame as she jumped into the shower. Lathering shampoo through her long blonde hair, she entertained the anticipation of a life free of repairs. The worries of maintaining a booked calendar, keeping her guests happy, and ensuring their stay at the Sea Oates resulted in a return visit would soon no longer be a worry. Daniella felt excited, inhaling the floral scent of the foaming shower gel as it covered her body.

Finally grabbing a large white bath towel, she stepped out of the shower running over to the closet. Today called for something special. Pulling her favorite gingham sundress from its hanger, she dressed quickly. Next, Daniella grabbed the hairdryer and hurriedly styled her hair, pulling her long blonde curls back with a floral hair clip. Afterward, she wiped the moisture from the bathroom mirror before applying make-up. Lastly, grabbing her favorite heels before running downstairs, she was finally ready to start the day. The expectancy of John McDermott's impending offer was overwhelming. The only thing missing was a jolt of caffeine to start the day, she thought as she headed down to the kitchen.

"My, you look stunning this morning," Ava complimented, immediately pouring Daniella a cup of coffee. "I'm sure you probably need this. Did you get any sleep last night?"

"Yes. I fell asleep as soon as my head hit the pillow. There's not anything I can do now but wait for the offer." Taking the hot cup, Daniella grabbed several pieces of bacon before sitting down.

"I made a huge stack of buttermilk pancakes. Let me get you a couple to go with your bacon," Ava laughed. "You certainly seem to be in a great mood this morning."

"Well, it's the excitement of the offer arriving. I have to say I have a good feeling about it."

"Have you told the girls?"

"No. I thought I would wait until I've seen it and thoroughly scrutinized it before I tell them," Daniella smiled, cutting into her pancakes.

"Geez. Your excitement is contagious. You've got me feeling a little hyped and curious," Ava mentioned, pouring herself a cup of coffee.

Just at that moment, everyone heard voices coming from the lobby. Daniella's heart stopped contemplating thoughts it could be John's assistant. Instead, watching as Henry walked in with Jillian, she felt disappointed.

"I love the smell of bacon," Henry grinned.

"Hey, Henry, sit down. I'll pour you a cup of coffee and get you a stack of pancakes with bacon," Ava smiled. "Jillian, are you ready to eat breakfast?"

"No, but thanks. I am just going to have a glass of juice this morning. Hey, Mom, I didn't see you last night before I went to bed. Ava said that Mr. McDermott invited you to dinner. You haven't mentioned the fact that you were seeing someone."

"It's nothing like that. It was a business meeting."

"Really. What's going on?"

"Well, I was just waiting until I received the offer before I said anything to you or Gracie?"

"What offer?" Jillian curiously demanded as she sat down with her orange juice.

Henry instantly stopped eating, looking up at Daniella.

"You received an offer?" Henry inquired with a perplexed stare.

"Okay. I guess since you're all here, I might as well let you know. I met with John McDermott last night at the Whales Tail. He wants to purchase the Sea Oates."

"Mom," Jillian exploded. "How could you even think of selling without first letting me and Gracie know? The Sea Oates is our home. Gracie and I love living here. My fondest memories of Dad are here. He bought this place just for you, and it is all that we have left of him. How could you?" Jillian raged.

"Jillian, calm down. Nothing has happened yet. I was going to tell you, but I was afraid you and Gracie might overreact. The Sea Oates requires some expensive repairs. Just ask Henry. He'll tell you."

"Oh, so you're in on this too?" Jillian fumed, staring at Henry.

"No. I swear. I don't like that man, but I would never tell your mom what to do. She didn't even tell me she was meeting with him," Henry interjected. "We talked about him buying the Break Waters Hotel and that he might be interested in purchasing the Sea Oates. I mean, we did talk about all of that, but trust me, I didn't know that he had made your mom an offer," Henry answered sternly.

"Listen, I've not seen the offer yet, and I certainly haven't made any decisions regarding whether or not I will sell. The Sea Oates needs a new roof. We have a few plumbing issues, and the bathrooms' décor needs updating. Those things aren't cheap. But, Jillian, this could be a new beginning for us. It could provide us with enough money to get you and Gracie through college. Heck, we could take a trip to Greece," Daniella countered excitedly.

"Why don't you all just calm down," Ava reprimanded as she walked around the table, refilling the coffee cups. "The way I see it, your mom is at a crossroads with this place. It hasn't held up well through the last two hurricanes, and who knows what this season will bring. But, Sweetheart, you need to trust your mom," Ava recommended sitting the coffee pot down, giving Jillian a tight squeeze.

Suddenly, startled by the loud sound of the bell sitting on top of the desk in the lobby, everyone jumped.

"This must be your offer," Ava announced, looking over at Daniella. She seemed transfixed as if she had not heard a thing. "Daniella, your offer, I think it's here," she repeated.

"Thanks. I'll be right back," Daniella smiled eagerly.

As she walked into the lobby, Ava, Henry, and Jillian waited anxiously for an indication that it would be a good offer. One that would easily give Daniella the money she would need to start over, making life comfortable. It seemed they did not have to wait long.

"Oh, hell no," Daniella screamed, forgetting the full occupancy of the Sea Oates and their sleeping guests. "Hell no," she vented loudly.

Turning to stare at each other, Ava rubbed her forehead as Henry got up to pour himself another cup of coffee. It was apparent Daniella was not happy. The news could not have been good. The only glimmer of a smile seemed to be coming from Jillian. Only someone as young and naïve as Jillian could find a reason to smile under such difficult circumstances.

Storming into the kitchen, Daniella tossed the manila envelope containing the offer on the table.

"Well, that man is completely crazy if he thinks I would ever agree to that," she vented. "He must think I am an uneducated, ignorant woman with no sense of the value of this place. Oh, you just wait until I talk to that man. Who does he think he is? What gives him the right to come down here from Atlanta thinking we'll just give our places away," Daniella steamed.

"Honey, sit down. Let me get that special bottle I always save for occasions like this," Ava said, getting a step stool.

Reaching into the top cabinet, she brought out a bottle of Cognac.

Opening the bottle, she poured three small glasses with the strong drink. "Here you go, Sweetheart. There's more here if you need it," Ava mentioned handing Henry a glass as she downed her entire drink in one large gulp.

"Maybe one more," Daniella instructed, wiping her mouth.

"Oh hell, keep 'em coming," Henry demanded.

Oblivious to the fact Jillian was even in the room, the three of them consumed several drinks before slowing down, not realizing the early hour of the day.

"You want another?" Ava grinned, looking over at Daniella.

"No. I think I had better stop. I want to be in my right mind when I speak to that arrogant ass," Daniella scoffed.

"Mom, please. Are you okay?" Jillian asked, putting her arms gently around her mother.

"Oh, yes, Honey, I'm fine. At least, I will be as soon as I tell that man where he can stick that offer of his."

Ava and Henry roared with laughter, hearing the words fly out of Daniella's mouth.

"That's what I want to hear. That's my girl," Ava interjected.

"So, what was the offer?" Henry smirked.

"The offer was eight-hundred-thousand dollars. The Sea Oates was constructed in 1956. However, it has gained value since then. Yes, it needs a new roof, and the décor needs updating. But, hell, it's worth more than that. He must be crazy. He had me believing that I would have enough money to start over comfortably and maybe even travel," Daniella remarked, eyeing the bottle of Cognac. "In today's market, if I made all the necessary repairs and took into consideration the fact we've had no problems with our occupancy rate, it's worth over four times that amount. Plus, we have full access to the Gulf. But, hell, he is just going to tear it down. Oh, Ava, what am I going to do?" Daniella cried.

"Well, for one thing, you're not going to shed any more tears. McDermott is not worth it, and you do not have to sell. I am sure Henry can come up with a way to offset some of the costs of the repairs. Just try not to worry. We'll think of something. You look so pretty this morning. Why don't you and Jillian go into town? I've got everything here under control, and I'll be here when Gracie comes in from school."

"Please, mom, come on, let's go shopping. It will take your mind away from your problems. I don't like the fact that you are so upset, and besides, I need a new pair of sneakers," Jillian mentioned giving her Mom another hug.

"She's right. You need to get this off your mind. The roof has been patched, and thankfully it didn't leak during this past rainstorm. I've got your back," Henry smiled, reaching over to take Daniella's hand.

"Oh, Henry, what would I do without you? What would I do without any of you," Daniella replied softly, squeezing Henry's hand. "Okay, let's go shopping." Wiping her eyes with the back of her hand, Daniella picked up the worthless offer. "I'll just put this away for now. Let me go upstairs, and then I'll meet you at the car."

"Great. Mom, we'll have a good time. I'll get my purse. See you in the car, but I'm driving. Remember you had those shots of Cognac," Jillian reminded as they left the kitchen.

"Henry, I think you could use another cup of coffee after those drinks," Ava suggested, quickly brewing another pot.

"Sure. I feel so bad for Daniella. McDermott is the worst possible thing that could have ever happened to Destiny Cove. To hell with his high-rise condominiums and enhancing our lives around here. We were all doing just fine without him. He needs to head back to Atlanta, and the sooner, the better."

"Yes. I agree. I still have a little time before serving breakfast, and I cooked too much bacon. So help yourself," Ava mentioned sitting a huge platter of fried bacon on the table in front of Henry. "I think the coffee is ready."

The girls had only been gone about thirty minutes when the phone rang in the lobby.

"Let me get that. You never know. It could be important." Ava hurriedly set her coffee down before racing for the phone.

"Hello, is Daniella there?" a man's voice inquired.

"No. I am sorry. Daniella went into town with her daughter. May I take a message or let her know who's calling?"

"Yes, please. This is John McDermott. Make sure she returns my call. By any chance, do you know if she's had time to review my offer?"

"Well, since you've brought it up," Ava exclaimed. "How dare you," she scolded without a thought. "Who do you think you are getting her so upset? As she said, you must be completely crazy. I'll tell her you called, but don't expect her to return your call," Ava stammered, slamming down the receiver.

"Wow. What a piece of work," Ava muttered as she walked back into the kitchen. "You'll not believe it, but that was John McDermott. He sure has a lot of nerve calling after sending over that earlier offer."

Looking down at his watch, Henry noted the time. "Thanks for the bacon, pancakes, and coffee. I have to get down to the hardware store. I promised to pick up some paint for my landlord. He's giving me two weeks' free rent if I paint one of his rental units tomorrow. I better get going," Henry, explained putting his cup in the sink. "Oh, don't worry about Miss Daniella. I'm sure she'll find her way through this."

"Yes. I know. It's almost time to set up the breakfast buffet. I usually serve breakfast from 8:00 a.m. until 10:00 a.m. on Fridays and weekends. Have a good day Henry."

"Yeah, you too," Henry replied, walking out through the back porch.

A wicked grin overtook John McDermott as he hung up the phone. "So she called me crazy, did she?" he thought with a smile. He always got his way. He had not exactly been sure of Daniella the night before. However, she was intriguing, and he should have expected this. He knew when he wrote the offer it was low.

Nonetheless, the Sea Oates was a teardown for him. He never felt good throwing good money on something he only planned to demolish. There was no way he ever intended to open with a higher offer, even though his corporation needed the property. However, there was more money, a lot more, that he could incorporate into the proposal. It was like a game of cat and mouse, and he loved the fascination. He found Daniella captivating, attractive, and someone he quickly felt an attachment to after only one night. He smiled, fondly reflecting on their dinner meeting the previous night. After being given her whereabouts earlier on the phone, he had to see her.

Grabbing the keys to his Maserati, he walked out to the garage. Destiny Cove was a small town. Surely, there would be no problem finding her. Considering that she was with her daughter, it would only take a systematic method of checking places where a mother and daughter might hang out.

Parking along Main Street, it seemed all eyes were on him as he locked his car. He smiled, knowing the car to him was only transportation, a mere toy. However, it was evident that parking a Maserati on these streets was not a daily occurrence. Noticing a clothing store across the street that displayed the latest fashions for a town of this size, he immediately walked over. After thoroughly searching through the racks, it was quickly apparent they were not there. Next, he decided to check out the local shoe store on Main Street. It was his next guess, as women were notorious for shoes.

Once again, a glance through the store let him instantly know they were not there. Maybe they were eating an early lunch? It was a hunch. Walking back across the street, he took a quick peek into the Main Street Deli. Sure enough, his hunch paid off. He could easily see Daniella and her daughter sitting in a booth near the back. Not sure if he should make an appearance at this moment, he decided to wait. He felt like a stalker. However, that was not his intent. He simply had to see her and confront the issue of his offer. Lighting a cigarette, he paced outside, making sure they did not catch sight of him. After two cigarettes, he watched as they were finally given their tab and slowly made their way to the register. He would wait until they had exited the store and walked a bit further down Main Street before he approached. He was not about to pounce on them unexpectedly. Patiently waiting, he could see they stopped in front of a consignment shop. Deciding to make his move, he walked over.

"Daniella, didn't anticipate seeing you here this morning? What brings you out this early? Is she your gorgeous daughter," he asked reservedly. "I called the Sea Oates and was told you might be downtown. Did my assistant get to the inn with my offer this morning?"

"Oh, so, you're my stalker now too," Daniella steamed. "Yes. I received your offer if that is what you call it. How dare you? It is worth four times that amount, and even that would be giving it away. You will not rob me of the only livelihood I have left for my daughters and myself. How dare you? You have to be crazy. I can only imagine what you must have offered for the Break Waters. Those poor people, I bet you took advantage of them too. Why don't you do us all a favor and go back to Atlanta?" Daniella screamed.

"Hey, Sweetheart, calm down. You are not exactly helping my image by yelling at me. You will have everyone here on Main Street thinking I am the worst thing that ever happened to Destiny Cove. Not to mention they might start to question your sanity as well," John grinned coyly.

"Oh, how dare you call me Sweetheart? And, you're questioning my sanity? Wow. What nerve you have to say such vile things. Really, who do you think you are? I detest you, everything your corporation stands for, and to think we all thought you came here to help revitalize our community. Really. What was it you said about helping the good citizens of Destiny Cove put more money in their pockets by bringing in tourist dollars?" Daniella steamed, poking her manicured finger into his chest.

"Geez, sweetheart? That offer was only the first offer. You must not know a lot about real estate. I figured you might not be pleased. If I practiced real estate as you think, I would be broke by now. I needed to see where your head was at as far as price. I am not interested in saving the Sea Oates. It's simply going to be demolished by my company. I never intended to keep it. I need the property and access to the beach," he stated, attempting to keep his cool.

"There you go again. I'm not your sweetheart. How many times do I need to repeat myself?" Daniella fiercely snapped back. Her face was now beet red with frustration.

"Listen, I'm sorry. I need to apologize to you and your daughter. I never expected this to turn into a heated discussion on Main Street. Honestly, I never intended for this to escalate. Trust me. You will be delighted before our deal closes. I promise," he winked. "Why don't I pick you up later tonight, and we'll have a few drinks and continue our conversation. I don't want to air our business in public. What do you say? Give me another chance to redeem myself."

"Mom, I don't think you have anything to lose. You should take him up on his offer. I certainly don't want you to sell, but I guess it wouldn't hurt to hear what he has to say," Jillian suggested. "Mom, I think you should," she reiterated.

"Oh, alright. I must be insane for giving you another minute of my time. I suppose Jillian is right. Okay, pick me up at about 7:00 p.m. But you better bring your A-game and a lot higher figures, or our little meeting will be over before it even begins," Daniella heatedly responded. "You got it?"

"Yes. I've got it," he grinned. With a tender gesture, he reached over to pull Daniella's long blonde hair away from her eyes.

Instantly, she raised her hand to meet his pushing him away.

"Jillian, it was nice to meet you. Thanks for having my back," he smiled.

"Well, it was nice to meet you too. But, don't read too much into that," Jillian smiled as she turned around, taking her mom's hand.

They had only walked a short way when Jillian stopped to whisper in her mom's ear. "I think he likes you," she laughed. "He's quite handsome," she added.

After spending the next hour window-shopping and purchasing a new pair of sneakers for Jillian, they were finally ready to drive back to the Sea Oates. The morning had brought with it a roller coaster of emotions. Finally, arriving back at the hotel, Daniella felt drained.

"Jillian, I'm going upstairs to take a short nap. Please check to see if Ava needs any help with dinner this evening."

"Sure."

Walking into the kitchen, Ava was eagerly waiting to discuss the phone call she had received earlier.

"You're not going to believe who called after you and your mom left?"

"Let me guess, John McDermott," Jillian answered.

"How did you know?" Ava curiously inquired.

"Let me think for a minute. Perhaps, it was the fact you told him we were downtown," Jillian vented.

"Oh, well, you'll be glad to know I gave him a piece of my mind. How dare he get your Mom so upset? That man is nuts," Ava shrugged, taking a pan of hot cinnamon rolls from the oven. "Where's your mom?"

"She went upstairs to take a nap. He may be, but I think he has a thing for mom, and he's not bad looking either," Jillian remarked, quickly grabbing one of the warm rolls. "We ran into him while we were out. Mom almost lost it on Main Street when she saw him."

"What do you mean? Do you think he followed you?" Ava appeared stunned as she began the preparations for her favorite recipe, meatloaf.

"Well, I think it's more like you told him where we were. Mom accused him of stalking her," Jillian laughed, pouring herself a glass of iced tea. "I'm not thrilled with the idea of mom selling the Sea Oates. Just wait until Gracie hears about this. She is going to flip out. If you don't need any help, I'm going upstairs to change. I'll be down at the beach if you need me."

"Okay. I've got dinner well underway for the moment. So go ahead and enjoy yourself. I'm not sure if your mom told you, but I know John McDermott?"

"What? You know him?" Jillian stopped turning around to face her. "How in the world do you know him? He's not from Destiny Cove."

"I know. He's from Atlanta."

"Geez. I guess you do know him. But how?" Jillian enthusiastically inquired.

"He owned the hotel in Atlanta where I worked before relocating to Destiny Cove. He's well known in Atlanta or, at least, I should say his corporation. He is very wealthy. Did you know?"

"Wow. Mom never mentioned it." Surprised by Ava's fascinating bits of information, Jillian smiled. "You don't think there's a chance those two might start seeing each other, do you? Wait just a minute. He's picking her up tonight, and I encouraged her to go. Maybe, I just answered my question?" Jillian added with a demure giggle.

"Well, I guess stranger things have happened. I know one thing.

He didn't exactly get off to a great start with that offer this morning," Ava replied, grabbing a bag of potatoes from the pantry.

"Geez. That's something to think about. I am going down to the beach. Let Mom know if she wakes up. What time will dinner be ready?"

"In about an hour or hour and a half. Still have to peel the potatoes and bake the meatloaf. Have fun. Oh, I would not mention to anyone that your mom might sell. Let's just wait and see what happens."

"Okay. Any chance you might be baking one of your famous chocolate cakes later?" Jillian questioned.

"You better get out of here before I have you peeling potatoes," Ava chuckled. "I'll think about that cake."

The delicious aroma of meatloaf wafting upstairs from the kitchen stirred Daniella awake. Slowing, dragging herself out of bed, she walked over to the window pulling back the drapes. Removing a small stack of books from the comfortable window seat, Daniella sat down, taking in the gorgeous views of the turquoise waters. Tears welled in her eyes as she reflected on her marriage to Dimitri and everything he had gone through to purchase the Sea Oates. She had loved him more than life itself. However, it seemed fate had not been kind. Losing him was never part of her plan.

Deep in thought, she looked around the room. The Sea Oates was all she had that remained of him and their life together. Maybe selling it was not a good idea. Maybe Jillian was right. Perhaps the low offer was a sign that she should not sell. The girls loved it here. Since birth, it had been their home, and it would be difficult to start over. Getting another whiff of Ava's meatloaf instantly brought her attention back to the fact she was famished and that she had agreed to meet John later. Maybe tonight would give her better clarity about whether she should sell or stay despite the onslaught of upcoming repairs.

"Wow, Ava, nothing like the smell of your meatloaf to wake a person up," Daniella smiled, walking into the kitchen. "Did Gracie come in from school yet?"

"Nope. I haven't seen her, but Jillian said to let you know that she went down to the beach. Hand me a plate. No need to wait until later,"

Ava suggested, serving up a huge slice of her delectable dish. "Jillian said you were meeting with John McDermott this evening. Do you think that's a good idea?"

"Well, he cornered me on Main Street. It seems you told him we were downtown. He wants to meet later and discuss the offer. He said it was just a beginning offer. So I reluctantly agreed after Jillian suggested I should go." Pouring herself a glass of iced tea, Daniella took her plate and sat down at the kitchen table.

"I just don't want to see you get hurt, or worse yet, sell the Sea Oates to someone of his caliber and have nothing left to support you and the girls."

"Ava, trust me, I would never give this place away. He's crazy if he thinks I would ever accept that ridiculous offer. I have not made up my mind about selling. It depends upon many things. Mainly how high he would go. Let's just see how bad he wants this place. Don't worry. I know what I'm doing. Say, did you happen to make a chocolate cake for dessert this evening?" Daniella asked, smacking her lips.

"Oh, you girls, and your addiction to chocolate. Jillian already put in her request earlier. Guess there's no way out of it," Ava laughed. "I'll get one in the oven right after I finish the potatoes."

"You're awesome, Ava. One in a million. I could not possibly have hired a better cook. You are a huge reason our guests return. Who wouldn't want to come back and enjoy more of your scrumptious southern cooking?" Daniella bragged, giving Ava a giant hug as she put her plate in the kitchen sink. "I'm going upstairs and find an outfit for tonight. Wish me luck."

"Daniella, just be careful. John is an extremely handsome, powerful man. He always gets what he wants. Please don't gamble with your and the girls' future. Men like him are very alluring, and you are certainly an attractive young woman. Don't be putty in his hands," Ava warned.

"Oh, Ava, there you go again. Please give me some credit. I know what I'm doing, but I appreciate your motherly concern. I love you, don't worry."

"Remember, the ball is in your court," Ava added loudly.

It seemed the afternoon sped by quickly. Bounding down the stairs, Daniella was a vision of beauty dressed in a floral strapless sundress adorned with pearl earrings and a matching necklace.

"Wow," Henry complimented with a loud whistle.

"Geez, Henry, I didn't know you were here."

"Oh, I heard through the grapevine Ava was baking one of her famous chocolate cakes. Nothing could keep me away," he laughed. "I saw Jillian earlier. She said you were meeting with that crook McDermott tonight. Please don't tell me you're going to reconsider his offer," Henry frowned.

"Henry, you're as bad as Ava. Ya'll need to give a girl a little credit. No. I would never reconsider his offer from this morning. Are you crazy? However, I am going to meet with him. It was only his first offer. Don't get me wrong. I detest him. However, I believe he knows how serious I am. I will never sell unless I get enough money to take care of the girls and me. I have to go. He just drove up."

"Shouldn't you wait for him to come inside?" Henry asked, taking a quick peek out the tall window in the lobby.

"Henry, please, you're old-fashioned," Daniella laughed. Then, after quickly grabbing her purse and wrap, she eagerly ran out the double doors like a teenager on a first date.

"Did Daniella leave already?" Ava inquired, walking out from the kitchen. "I was going to let her know the cake was ready and that I have coffee brewing."

"Oh, she's gone. She didn't even wait for him to come inside. I'm worried about that girl?"

"Henry, she's a grown woman. Unfortunately, either right or wrong, she's determined to make her own decisions."

"You should have seen the fancy car he was driving. I don't think I've ever seen one exactly like it," Henry mentioned, scratching his head.

"McDermott is a wealthy man. You probably have not seen one like it. Who knows what it was. Come in the kitchen the cake is ready. You still want cake, right?" Ava smiled. "By the way, did I hear you whistling earlier?"

"Yeah, Daniella looked so pretty. It's a shame a woman that beautiful has been a widow for so many years."

"Come on, Henry, I think the coffee is ready."

Ava was not born yesterday, and Henry's comment gave her reasons to worry about Daniella. McDermott was wealthy, divorced, and alluring. On the other hand, Daniella was young, beautiful, and unattached. Henry was right. She had been a widow for far too long.

Walking around his car, John met Daniella outside the double doors of the Sea Oates. She almost melted at the mere sight of him. He looked handsome and debonair, wearing a pair of dark jeans mixed unexpectedly with a black sports coat, white dress shirt, and sunglasses. He appeared elegant yet casual. His sculpted facial features and jet-black hair made him even more alluring.

"Good evening Daniella, you look stunning," John smiled, opening her car door.

"Thank you." Entering the Maserati, the scent of the car's luxurious Italian leather interior was hypnotic and extremely comfortable. It left no doubt that he was a man of substantial wealth.

"The guys I work with rave about a quaint little bar called the Crab Shack. It's only a short drive and shouldn't be too crowded at this time. How does that sound?"

"Great. I know that place. It happens to be one of my favorites."

"Guess the guys didn't steer me wrong. Daniella, I hope you've forgiven me for earlier. It seems we've gotten our friendship off on the wrong foot," John reiterated, reaching over to take her hand.

"Alright, you're forgiven. But, you should know, I'm not giving away my only means of supporting myself and my daughters to watch your corporation tear it down." Then, turning to face him, she flashed him a stern look as she loosened her hand from his grip.

"Sweetheart, trust me, I didn't build my corporation by stealing from widows."

After an awkward moment of silence, her eyes met his, and they burst out laughing.

"Wow. That's my girl. I was beginning to think you hated me," he winked.

"Hate is a strong word. Let's just say I was trying to get my point across."

"Got it," he grinned. "I'm starved. I hope the Crab Shack's menu lives up to its reputation."

"I don't think you'll be disappointed."

After finding a place to park, they had finally arrived. Opening Daniella's car door, John took her hand and led her inside. Outwardly, the owners of the small bar built it to replicate a small shack. The décor was much the same as they walked inside. Aged wooden planks incorporated the walls as larger beams traversed the ceilings. Lanterns hung near the entry glowed softly, emphasizing an extensive array of fishing nets, boat oars, and Styrofoam life rings, which enhanced the walls. Its ambiance gave the patrons a warm nautical vibe. Finally, an overwhelming aroma of fried seafood infused the air. After a quick visual sweep of the bar, John asked for an open booth near the back.

"Well, it's certainly small and charming," he acknowledged, following behind the server.

"Don't judge it by its size. The menu is phenomenal," Daniella remarked after being seated.

"So, what do you recommend?"

"Well, everything is delicious. However, the Crab Shack is famous for its fried or raw oysters. So, of course, if you order them raw, I'd suggest covering them with tabasco sauce and downing them with beer," Daniella laughed.

After taking a few moments to look over her menu, she looked up.

"I think I'll have the fried mullet, along with hushpuppies, potato salad, and iced tea.

"Great. I think I am going to start with an appetizer of raw oysters. However, the seafood platter looks amazing. If everything is as tasty as you say, then I guess I can't go wrong, can I?" John grinned, looking up at her. It was evident Daniella was relaxed and finally appeared to be enjoying herself.

Once the waiter returned, John placed their food order asked for a pitcher of the local brew.

"So let's eat, and then we'll discuss business."

Soon, the waiter brought out a small platter of raw oysters sitting in their half shell, along with a pitcher of beer and Daniella's iced tea.

"Here you are, sir, our finest Apalachicola Bay oysters. The world's best, I might add."

He watched Daniella's expression as he covered one in Tabasco sauce and downed it, quickly chasing it with beer. She winced at the site of the small gray muscular creature. Little did she know, he was very familiar with the delicacy. However, wanting to amuse her, he decided to keep this fact a secret.

"You should try one," he suggested.

"I'm fine. I think I'll wait for my fish," Daniella grimaced, hoping that would discourage any further comments.

"Oh, come on, be a good sport. You have to," John laughed. Then, taking his fork, he handed her one of the small slimy mollusks.

Not wanting to feel obstinate, she reluctantly agreed.

"Okay. But first, you have to cover it in Tabasco sauce and hand me your mug of beer."

Quickly complying with her instructions, he passed the briny gray oyster dripping in hot sauce across the table. Watching her reaction, he tried desperately to control his laughter.

Daniella hoped not to taste the flavor of the oyster as it quickly slipped down her throat. She had not dared to chew it. Immediately, she took a huge gulp of beer to chase it. The expression on her face must have been horrifying as well as hilarious. Leaning over the table, he wiped the remaining hot sauce from her mouth. Taking advantage of the moment, he gave her a quick kiss. Caught up in the excitement of his unexpected kiss, it sent tingles throughout her entire body. She felt flush, hoping he had not noticed. After only knowing him for a short time and despite his earlier hostile words, she instantly felt attracted to him. She could only wonder if he felt the same.

After enjoying dinner, John ordered coffee.

"Well, what do you think?"

"Think about what she asked?"

"Discussing my offer to purchase the Sea Oates," he smiled, taking a sip of coffee.

The evening had been so exceptional that Daniella had even forgotten the reason for their being there. "How was that even possible?" she thought. However, Daniella knew. Surprisingly, she was beginning to feel an attachment to him.

"Excuse me while I run out to the car for a quick second. I have a new purchase offer in my briefcase, and I would like to go over it with you. After all, that is our reason for being here, isn't it?" he grinned.

"Yes. Of course. I will be right here. Waiting," Daniella added demurely. What a stupid answer, she thought. Of course, she would be waiting. Instead, however, she felt giddy like a teenager falling in love, and she had not even had a sip of wine. For the first time since losing Dimitri, she entertained thoughts of finding love once again.

"Alright," John smiled, returning with a manila envelope. "Let's get to it, shall we?"

"Daniella, I never meant to offend you with my first offer. But, seriously, it was just that a first offer to purchase. So here's my new offer," he smiled, slowly sliding the purchase contract across the table.

Taking a quick look, she gasped. "Is this for real?"

"I believe so," he teased.

The purchase line read *two and a half million dollars*. Reading the offer, she was shocked to see the sudden increase.

"You never gave me an asking price to start with, and I've had serious thoughts about you and your daughters. I know you cannot put a dollar amount on memories, but hopefully, this will help. I hope you will forgive me for the earlier offer. I was not trying to insult you," he explained, reaching over to take her hand. "Does this seem adequate?"

"Oh, John, I never expected the offer to be this high," Daniella replied, barely audible.

"Well, if it meets with your approval, I think we have a deal," he winked.

As their eyes met, little did he know she would have accepted less. Little did she know he would have gone much higher.

Chapter Five

After signing the purchase agreement, it was time to move on with her life. Finally, Daniella had made the right decision. The Sea Oates had been home for over a decade and held precious memories of her former life with Dimitri. However, the sale gave her the freedom to start life again with her daughters. In addition, she now had the financial means to relocate to a more affluent location that offered her, Gracie, and Jillian a few luxuries. After lengthy discussions and weeks of exhaustive house hunting, she found the perfect place, Greyson Beach Estates. The new development was only a few miles away and offered many amenities, tennis courts, an Olympic-sized pool, a gym, and a large centrally located clubhouse. The only drawback was direct access to the beach. However, the builder of the development had incorporated a lighted walkway to provide homeowners access to the beautiful turquoise waters. After picking out their desired floor plan, it was time to choose countertops, kitchen cabinets, flooring, and a multitude of other upgrades necessary to make a house a home.

"Ava, have you seen the girls? I promised they could help in choosing the upgrades, and I have an appointment at the sales office later this morning," Daniella questioned, pouring herself a cup of coffee.

Ava paused, wiping her hands on her apron. "Gracie came in earlier to get a bowl of cereal, but I haven't seen Jillian this morning."

Hearing a knock at the screen door, Ava sat down a huge platter of warm rolls and walked over.

"Hey Henry, what brings you over so early?" Grabbing a cup from the cabinet, Ava filled it with hot coffee.

"Maybe the smell of those biscuits," Henry teased, sipping the hot brew.

"What will you ever do after this place closes?" Ava shrugged. "Sit down. I've got some fried bacon and scrambled eggs to go along with those." Opening the fridge, Ava brought out butter and grape jelly. "You can't possibly have warm biscuits without these," she suggested.

"Henry, once this place closes, guess you'll have to drive over for breakfast or take a longer hike down the beach," Daniella laughed.

"Yeah, I'm sure going to miss this place. Are you sure you're doing the right thing by selling?" Henry frowned, reaching across the table for more butter.

"Yes. Henry, it was the right decision. You know Ava is moving in with us, and I am sure she will be cooking breakfast every morning. You know you're always welcome."

"Oh, I know. It's the convenience of this place being so close to my apartment. But, to be honest, I can't imagine life without the Sea Oates," Henry scowled, taking another sip of coffee. "Darn McDermott Corporation, I don't know why they had to choose Destiny Cove to redevelop. They should have gone a lot further down the coast and interrupted those poor folks' lifestyle."

"Change is good. You will see. Can I pour you another cup of coffee?" Ava interjected, walking over to the coffee pot.

"Henry, I certainly didn't mean to upset your life by selling the Sea Oates, but now I can afford to put the girls through college. Trust me. It wasn't an easy decision. However, it was the right one. This place holds too many memories for me, but it's time to move on. I can't live in the past forever," Daniella smiled, reaching over to touch Henry's hand. "It's going to be an adjustment for all of us."

"So, how long before you close?" Henry asked reluctantly.

"Well, I've decided to honor our reservations for this month. I didn't want to jeopardize any last-minute plans our guests might have. Therefore, we officially close on the first of next month, September 1st. It's a good time, school starts, and our reservations begin to slow down during that time."

"Seems like you've got it all worked out, but just for the record, I think you're making a huge mistake," Henry frowned, standing up to put his plate in the sink.

"Henry, I know you're just looking out for the girls and me. I appreciate your input. Honestly, I do. However, I have given this a lot of thought. We aren't moving that far. It is just a few miles from here, and you are welcome anytime. Trust me, you're not getting rid of us that easy," Daniella smiled, walking over to give him a big hug. "So, what are your plans for the day?"

"Oh, the Wave Runner came in with mechanical problems this morning. I promised to take a look at her. I hope it's an easy fix. The crew cannot afford any down days. Fishing pays the bills around here, but then again, I don't have to tell you. I'll stop in later for supper," Henry mentioned adjusting the brim of his weather-beaten cap.

"Okay, Henry, see you later. By the way, I'm making shrimp gumbo tonight," Ava informed him as she began washing the dishes.

After Henry left, Ava paused for a moment. Then, wiping her hands on her worn apron, she looked at Daniella, "You know, he's going to be devastated without the Sea Oates."

"Well, maybe, but I have to do what's best for the girls and me. So I'm going downtown to Hinson's to arrange the move, and later I'm going to the sales office. If the girls show up, please let them know. Jillian can use the van and drive them over to the sales office. I'll take the jeep."

"Alright. Have a good morning. Oh, please don't let anything Henry said bother you. He means well. He's just old and set in his ways."

"Oh, I know," Daniella smiled, pausing for a brief moment to contemplate Ava's advice. Deep down, it did bother her that Henry wasn't exactly happy about the move. She loved him like a father. He had always been there for her and the girls after Dimitri died. She had always felt it an honor to have him stop by the inn, and never once had she ever thought of charging him for meals. He was family, and Daniella had always treated him as such. However, what Henry did not understand was that she needed a change. Raising two daughters alone without the help of a husband had not been easy. However, she was still young, and the small windfall of cash would give her a new lease on life—a chance to enjoy life without the worries of running the hotel and the constant repairs. John was right. She would now be able to travel and experience life as never before. She was not getting any younger.

After arriving at Hinson's Moving Company, it took less than an hour to schedule all the details regarding the move. Leaving Hinson's earlier than expected, she looked down at her watch. She had an hour before her next appointment at the sales office. Noting the extra time on her parking meter, Daniella decided to walk down Main Street and enjoy a few minutes of her favorite pastime, window shopping. She stopped, strolling past the local travel agency with its vivid, colorful posters. Briefly, she entertained the dream of visiting one of the faraway places. She had always wanted to go to Greece. Dimitri had made it sound like heaven on earth or perhaps take a European tour. Maybe, it was time. Suddenly, her concentration was broken. She flinched feeling the gentle caress of someone's arm encircling her waist.

"Hey, Sweetheart, are you going to take my advice and do some traveling?" John smiled.

"No. What brings you down here this morning?"

"I had business to take care of at the bank."

Noticing she seemed captivated by the posters, he had to interject his thoughts.

"You know the posters are intriguing, but nothing can compare to visiting those places and experiencing the culture of each country. Trust me, I know. I've built hotels all over the world," John grinned, removing his sunglasses. "I have an idea," he whispered, pulling her close. "Why don't you pick a place you've always wanted to visit, and I'll take you. Consider it my way of saying, 'thank you.' I have a private jet parked at the airport. We could be anywhere in the world in a matter of hours," he winked. "You do have a passport, right?" he questioned.

"No, and I could never do that," she answered rather demurely without much thought to his question. "Besides, I have a huge move in less than a month and a new house to furnish." She knew she was only making excuses. There were many exotic places she wished to visit, and now with the sale of the Sea Oates, she might finally have her chance. Greece would always be her first choice.

"Sweetheart, I know, and that's exactly why you should agree to my offer. Listen, I will be more than happy to help with your relocation. I feel somewhat responsible for putting all of this on you so suddenly. So please let me help. After you're all moved into your new home, I'll take you away from here to any place you choose," John smiled, giving her an unexpected kiss on her cheek.

"Maybe, I'll think about it," Daniella answered. "I've got to run. I have an appointment at the sales office to pick out upgrades," Daniella freaked noting the time as she looked down at her watch.

"Wait just a minute. Would you mind if I tagged along? I could be of help. I think I know a thing or two about upgrades," he laughed. "After all, I am an architect," he winked.

"Oh, okay, but we need to hurry."

"Where are you parked?" John inquired.

"Down the street in front of Hinson's Moving and Storage Company. I'm afraid the parking meter may be expired," Daniella panicked.

"Why don't I follow you back to the Sea Oates, and we can take my car from there. Here take this," he laughed, handing her the change from his pocket.

"Okay, thanks. I will meet you at the inn. Hurry," Daniella insisted, giving him a quick hug.

Driving back to the Sea Oates, Daniella smiled, seeing John's Maserati in her rearview mirror. What was happening? Why had he so suddenly come into her life, changing everything? It seemed as if he appeared at all the right moments. She could not remember wishing on a star or any silly thing, which might have brought him into her life. Instead, he was just unexpectedly there, out of nowhere, as if it were kismet and she would not change a thing. Maybe it was Dimitri's way of getting her to move on with her life. Whatever the reason fate had brought him into her world, she finally felt herself falling in love again. After many years of being alone, it felt right. Maybe she would take him up on his offer of the trip. She needed to know more about him.

After spending almost two hours going over upgrades, Daniella was positive she had picked the most amazing embellishments to fill her new home. Unfortunately, it seemed the girls never arrived to give her their input. However, with John at her side, she never once doubted his recommendations. It was as if they were on the same page. Almost as if he were reading her mind, he gently guided her through the process of picking the right enhancements.

"Why don't we end the evening with dinner?" John asked on the short drive back to the Sea Oates.

"Well, I guess I can't argue with that," Daniella smiled. "But I'm not exactly dressed."

"Sweetheart, you're gorgeous. I wouldn't change a thing," he winked.

His words made her blush. "Would you mind if we made a quick stop at the Sea Oates? I need to let the girls and Ava know."

"Of course," he smiled. "I'll make reservations for us while we're there. I know the perfect place," he suggested.

"As long as they don't have oysters on the menu," Daniella teased.

"Don't worry. I think we can safely cross that one off our list. It was a little overrated."

Walking into the lobby of the Sea Oates, John took Daniella's hand as if by instinct. Jillian smiled, seeing them together. However, the fact they were together and holding hands didn't seem to bother her.

"Geez, Mom, where have you been?"

"Jillian, did you forget the appointment at the sales office earlier this afternoon? I was expecting you and Gracie to come and offer your opinions on the upgrades," Daniella quizzed. "Good thing I accidentally ran into John while I was downtown. He volunteered to tag along and help with the choices. So even though you or Gracie didn't make the appointment, you will be pleased with our selections," Daniella frowned, showing outward signs of disappointment in the girl's absence.

"Oh, Mom, I'm sorry. I forgot. We both forgot," Jillian apologized.

"Alright. You're forgiven," Daniella replied. "Where's Ava?"

"She's in the kitchen washing dishes. Oh, hey, Mr. McDermott."

"Jillian, please just call me John," he winked with a smile.

"Okay," Jillian blushed. "Wow, had he just winked at her. No wonder her mom was beginning to fall in love with him. Who wouldn't," she thought. However, she knew Ava would be more than skeptical.

Walking into the kitchen, it seemed Daniella and John had caught Ava off guard. Looking up, she gasped, almost losing her grip on the bowl she held. Ava had not expected to see the two of them together. Nonchalantly, she tried to hide her reactions. However, it was easy to see her disapproval from the expression on her face.

"So, what brings you both here?" Ava asked curiously.

"I wanted to let you know all the upgrades were picked out for the house and that John has invited me to dinner. You will love the white marble countertops, white cabinets, and oak flooring we chose for the kitchen. In addition, your bedroom and adjoining bath will be spectacular. Has there been any problems while I was gone?"

"Nothing much, just a stuck window that wouldn't open. Henry was here, so it was a quick fix," Ava scowled, appearing very cold and distant. She chose to be obstinate and unappreciative.

Daniella knew it was time to leave before John completely took a disliking to her. Ava could be very stubborn, and even though she did not have a mean bone in her body, you would never know from her facial expressions.

"I'll see you later. John and I will be on our way," Daniella explained. Then, taking John's hand, they left the kitchen and walked back towards the lobby. However, turning around for a quick second, Daniella stopped giving Ava a stern, threatening look. A look that implored her not to utter another word.

"Jillian, John needs to use the phone. Where is your sister?" Daniella asked, walking over to the reception desk.

"Oh, Gracie is up in her room. I will let her know you're here. But,

Mom, did you see Ava?" Jillian laughed, holding her hand over her mouth, trying to hide her smile. She knew Ava detested John. It was very apparent Ava had never gotten over his first offer and considered him a scoundrel.

"Yes," Daniella whispered, trying to avoid the topic of Ava's disapproval of John and hoping that he didn't overhear their conversation. "Jillian, I'll be back later this evening. Would you please let Gracie know? Oh, I almost forgot. Boxes will be arriving tomorrow morning. I need you and Gracie to start packing your rooms. Will you please let Gracie and Ava know about the arrival of the boxes?"

"Sure, Mom, have a great evening."

After a wonderful dinner, which did not include oysters, it was time to call it an evening. Returning to the inn, John parked under the front portico near the entrance to the lobby. Suddenly reaching over the console, he pulled Daniella into his arms.

"Sweetheart, thank you for including me in your day and saying yes to dinner," he lovingly whispered. Then, without another word, John kissed her. Surprised by the intensity of his kiss, Daniella fell helplessly into his arms. It was evident a tiny ember of love now united them.

Opening her car door, John reached for her hand, accompanying Daniella inside the lobby.

"I'll call you tomorrow morning," he mentioned, softly kissing her cheek before he left. "Oh, by the way, you should get your passport," he winked flirtatiously.

The following day found the girls busily packing their rooms. It seemed even Ava had finally gotten into the spirit of boxing up her personal belongings. Unfortunately, Daniella seemed the only one not caught up in the excitement of the move. Even though the night before had assured her that her feelings toward John were mutual, it was hard leaving the memories of Dimitri behind.

Walking downstairs to the lobby, Daniella felt overwhelmed with feelings of sadness. It was finally time to say goodbye. The inn represented a living history of their time together. As she slowly looked around the room, it was easy to see memories of Dimitri and their life everywhere. Maybe it was good that John's corporation was tearing it down. It would be next to impossible to drive past knowing her connection to this place, to Dimitri. Daniella walked over to the receptionist's desk. Slowly, she rubbed her fingers along the dark aged surface. It felt smooth and comforting. Tears gently rolled down her cheeks. For a brief moment, she felt the closeness of touching Dimitri's tan face. Her heart was aching for him. Feeling faint, she took a seat in his favorite high-back leather chair. Feeling emotionally drained and physically exhausted, she must have drifted off for a moment. There was no other plausible explanation. However, with every ounce of her being, she felt his presence.

"Sweetheart, it's okay. I'll always love you."

It seemed barely audible, a faint whisper, but distinctly Dimitri's voice. Maybe, she was having a nervous breakdown. Whether she was conscious or asleep, she would never know. She only knew the experience seemed real. It did not matter. It worked to give her closure. Many years later, she would mention the incident to John. She knew the power of love was strong, and nothing was impossible. Wiping tears from her face, she was finally ready to leave the Sea Oates and its memories. Daniella now had a new start in life for her and her daughters. She believed somewhere deep inside that Dimitri's love had been the guiding force, which had given her a second chance at life, at love. It was time to embrace a new beginning.

Chapter Six

The move had been busy but, oddly, cathartic. Daniella and the girls, along with Ava, had finally settled into their new house. At first, it seemed a bit strange, but it felt more like home with every passing day. It was a sprawling Tuscany-inspired single-story home. Tall stone arches welcomed you to the front of the house, and massive wrought iron glass doors invited you inside. Every aspect of the décor was European. Daniella had made sure of it. She had chosen upgrades, which emphasized its neutral wall colors. It was a spacious 4,000 square feet of opulence, which encased an open-air courtyard. Daniella had specifically incorporated a custom kitchen for Ava. It was a chef's dream containing high-end appliances within easy reach and an oversized granite island. However, Ava seemed to have a difficult time adjusting. It seemed she still missed the large ornate kitchen at the Sea Oates and preparing huge meals, which could easily feed a crowd. Ava was a chef at heart. She loved cooking and watching the excitement on the faces of those lucky enough to experience her cuisine. Ava also missed Henry's frequent visits. Daniella had an idea up her sleeve, but she was waiting to discuss it with John. Maybe there was a way Ava could continue her love of cooking. Undoubtedly, the new hotel would need a great chef. However, today presented a bigger problem. It was the scheduled demolition of the Sea Oates. Daniella was unsure if she was up to watching her former home become a heap of rubble. Hearing the phone ring, she ran to answer it.

"Hey, Sweetheart, have you made your decision if you want to come over and watch our crews demolish the Sea Oates?" John asked.

"You know, after giving it a lot of thought, I don't think I should. I can't trust myself. I might feel compelled to do something stupid like trying to stop the wrecking ball," she sighed.

"Daniella, I'll be there. Trust me. I would not chance that happening, but suit yourself. I completely understand. I will pick you up for dinner later this evening. How does that sound?" John suggested.

"I would love that. I can't wait to see you."

"Great. I will pick you up around 6:30 p.m. See you then."

"Oh, John, one more thing, please be gentle with her," Daniella insisted.

"Seriously, this is a demolition," John laughed. "I don't see how that will be possible. I'll have my crew take a moment of silence before we start if that will make you feel any better," he teased.

"Whatever, John. Please, don't make fun of me. Do I have to remind you that was my home?"

"Sweetheart, if I don't get off this phone, nothing is going to get done. So I'll see you tonight, and if you are up to it, I'll walk you over to the site after dinner."

"Thanks, John, I would love that. See you later," she answered, hanging up the phone.

Walking into the kitchen, she needed a cup of coffee. Finding Ava sitting at the island, she looked bored.

"Ava, John, and his crew are demolishing the Sea Oates today. I feel totally consumed with emotions," Daniella moaned.

"Oh, honey, sit down. I have just what you need," Ava smiled, reaching for her favorite bottle of whiskey, Jack Daniel's. Ava poured them each a drink. "Take this, and let's drink to the Sea Oates. Like a Phoenix, she'll rise from the ashes, even larger and better," Ava toasted. "You did say that John and his company decided to keep the name, right?" she asked.

"Yes. That was so sweet of him. But, Ava, you have him all wrong. He really is a nice man. You're the first person I've told, but I think I am falling in love with him," Daniella blushed.

"What? Child, do you even know what you are saying. I need another drink," Ava scowled, pouring herself another drink.

"Oh Ava, you don't know him as well as I do," Daniella mentioned pouring herself another round. "In fact, I received my passport today. We're taking a trip. We leave on Friday."

"Wow. You're just full of surprises this morning. Are you serious?" Ava vented, quickly downing her third drink.

"I am. I'll show you my passport," Daniella laughed, finishing her drink. "Ava, I think you've had your limit. Give me that bottle," Daniella insisted, watching as Ava attempted to pour a fourth.

"I just hope you know what you're doing?" Ava defiantly reprimanded as she reluctantly handed over the bottle of bourbon.

"I'm a grown woman. I've been to the rodeo, and it's about time I get back on that horse," Daniella laughed, somewhat slurring her words.

"Are you drunk?" Ava questioned. "Geez, Daniella, you've only had a few drinks. You certainly don't have a tolerance for alcohol. So where are you and John going on Friday?"

"I don't know. John is keeping it a surprise. Did you know he has a private jet parked at the airport?"

"Nothing surprises me about that man," Ava grimaced. "So he's not dropped any hints about the destination? Do the girls know?"

"Not yet. I'm going to tell them this week. I have talked a lot about Greece and wanting to go to Mykonos and Santorini. We discussed the fact Dimitri was born on Mykonos and still has relatives who live there. I have my suspicions. However, I'm totally open to any place as long as it's warm."

"Okay. I hope everything works out for you. I certainly agree it's time for you to get on with your life. But, please, don't worry about the girls. They will be fine. I'll make sure of it."

"Thanks, Ava. I don't know what I would do without you. I am not going to be here for dinner this evening. So you'll be cooking just for the girls and yourself," Daniella added. "Think I'm going to take a walk down to the beach. It always helps me clear my head. I feel consumed with emotions knowing the Sea Oates will no longer be standing after today. Today hasn't been easy for me."

"Oh, child," Ava frowned, walking over to put her arms around Daniella. "I can't imagine what you must be experiencing. I know that place meant the world to you. Henry has told me all the stories regarding Dimitri. How very much he loved you and the sacrifices he was willing to make to ensure your dream came true of owning that place. Sweetheart, I know you needed to sell, but some things in life are priceless."

Ava stopped abruptly with her remarks. She didn't want to heap tons of resentment on Daniella for deciding to sell. Further reminiscing would only make her feel worse about her decision. She knew that selling the Sea Oates was probably the best thing Daniella could have done for herself and the girls. Sometimes in life, you have to make choices, hard choices. She respected Daniella for being able to let go and move on. She knew it would have never been an easy decision. She needed to change the subject and help Daniella cope. Daniella had endured more than her share of heartbreak in life. She had lost her husband, her parents, and her only sibling.

"Child, you go ahead and take a walk down to the beach. However, promise me one thing, please don't be so hard on yourself. I am proud of you and your decision—no more sadness. I love you. I'm going to start dinner for the girls and maybe surprise them with one of my chocolate cakes."

"Thanks, Ava. I love you too. Sounds good."

Walking down the weathered boardwalk, Daniella watched as the turquoise waters sparkled and glistened, reflecting the brilliant rays of the sun. She loved living here. It didn't matter where John took her. Nothing could ever compare to Destiny Cove. Removing her sandals, she immersed her feet in the warm water as she strolled along the sandy shore. Suddenly, her emotions consumed her. Thoughts of losing the Sea Oates brought tears to her eyes. She felt weak in her knees just thinking about it being demolished. That part of her life with Dimitri would now be in the past. Walking over to one of the blue canvas chairs, she sat down, watching seagulls gracefully circling overhead. Resting her head on the back of the chair, it seemed her worries drifted away with the warm salty breeze as it gently wafted in from the water. Life was good, even if her former home was in rubbles by the day's end. After spending over an hour of solitude watching the waves wash ashore and inhaling the invigorating salt air, it was time to leave. The serenity was all the therapy she needed. She was looking forward to seeing John later that evening and enjoying dinner together.

Walking back to the house, she heard sounds of laughter coming from the kitchen. No telling what the girls and Ava were up to this afternoon. It made her smile. The sounds of laughter were cathartic.

"What's going on?" Daniella questioned, walking into the kitchen.

"Mom, I'm not sure you want to know," Jillian snickered.

"Gracie, what are you trying to hide?" Daniella demanded.

Just at that instant, a puppy wiggled out of Gracie's arms.

"Oh, Mom, we have to keep her. Oh, please, please," Gracie pleaded.

Looking down, Daniella had to admit she was cute. She was tiny, with jet-black curls completely covering her petite body.

"What kind of dog is she?"

"Oh, she's a teacup poodle. She will always be small. Can we keep her? Please," Gracie continued to beg.

"Where did you get her?"

"She belongs to my friend, Lexie. Her dad just got orders for overseas, and they can't take her. Can we keep her? I promise to take very good care of her. Ava even said she would help."

"Oh, so Ava's a part of this too?" Daniella remarked, looking around for her. It appeared that Ava had suddenly vanished. I will think about it, but you have to promise to take care of her. That includes walking her outside, or does she use puppy pads?"

"I'm not sure," Gracie mentioned.

"Okay, Ava, you can come out of hiding. It looks like you've been volunteered to help with the puppy when Gracie's in school," Daniella yelled down the long hallway, which led into the living room. "Alright, we'll keep her. What's her name?"

"Oh, it's Truffles," Gracie giggled, kissing her new friend.

"Girls, I have a dinner date with John tonight, so I'm going to take a shower and get dressed. Gracie, I don't want her running loose around the house. You make sure that she goes potty outside. I don't want her going inside on the new floors. Do you understand?" Daniella sternly warned.

"Yes, Mom, thank you," Gracie beamed, giving her a huge hug and kiss.

"Geez, Gracie, that seemed too easy. I think Mom likes her," Jillian laughed. "I'm going to my room and watch television. You better keep a close watch on Truffles."

"Don't worry. I'm not going to let anything happen," Gracie snapped back.

"Famous last words," Jillian teased.

Daniella was almost ready, wearing a mauve off-the-shoulder dress with matching heels. Finding her floral silk shawl, she completed her ensemble for the evening. Then, deciding to wear her long blonde curls swept up in the back, she held it in place with a silver comb. The hairstyle complemented her oval face. Then, after one quick spray with her favorite French perfume, she was ready.

Looking down at her watch, it was almost 6:30 p.m. John was always punctual. Not surprised to hear the doorbell, it announced his arrival.

"Ava, we're leaving now. See you later."

"Have a nice evening," Ava yelled from the kitchen.

Eagerly, Daniella ran over to open the door.

"Sweetheart, you're stunning," John smiled, giving her a quick kiss.

"Thanks," Daniella blushed. She had never felt comfortable receiving compliments.

Looking up, she found herself staring into his gorgeous blue eyes. Even though she was wearing her highest heels, he towered over her wearing a dark suit and tie. Just one look at his handsome appearance, and Daniella was utterly captivated.

"Are you ready to go? We have reservations at 7:00 p.m. at Bel Cibo."

"Yes. I've heard a lot of wonderful things about Bel Cibo, but I've never eaten there."

"Great. It reminds me of one of my favorite restaurants in Sorrento," John explained, taking her hand. "Bel Cibo means beautiful food. I think you will love it."

Walking her out to the car, John put his arm around her, pulling her close. The fragrance of his cologne seemed an amazing masculine mixture of sandalwood and bergamot.

"Oh, you're not driving tonight?" she questioned, seeing the limo in the driveway.

"No. Should I be?" he teased.

"It's just the fact, I hardly ever go by limo these days," she laughed.

"Daniella, I wanted to make tonight extra special for you," he winked, kissing her on the cheek. "Today had to be hard for you. I couldn't imagine all the emotions you've probably experienced knowing we were demolishing the Sea Oates. I could hear the sadness in your voice on the phone today. But, seriously, sweetheart, asking me to be gentle. That was a first. It was a demolition," he grinned.

After the chauffeur opened their car door, he took her hand, helping her inside the car. Pulling her close, Daniella leaned against him. As waves of emotions once again consumed her, she desperately tried to hide her tears.

"No more crying," he smiled, taking the handkerchief from his suit pocket to wipe her eyes. "Sweetheart, I've fallen madly in love with you," he softly whispered into her ear.

It seemed that hearing his loving words only made the tears flow more rapidly down her face. How was it possible on a day like today, when she had lost so much that someone like John could find his way into her heart and life?

Arriving at the restaurant, it was gorgeous, and the food was even better than he had described. The Limoncello was incredible. However, she had no appetite. She went through the motions of having dinner after excusing herself several times to withdraw to the serenity of the women's restroom. However, at this point of the evening, she only needed him—a place where the two of them could be alone for the night, shutting out the world.

Sensing that something was wrong, he reached across the table, taking her hand.

"Would you like to leave?"

"Yes, desperately," Daniella suggested.

Motioning for the waiter, John paid for dinner, leaving more than a generous tip.

Taking her hand, he escorted Daniella outside to the waiting car.

Once inside the limo, he noticed her tears. Taking his handkerchief once again, he gently wiped her moist face. He had an idea. Something that he hoped would completely take away her worries.

"How are you with spontaneous, impulsive ideas?" he winked.

"Unbelievable that you should ask. I can't think of a time in my life when I felt this unsure of anything," she smiled.

"Do you trust me?"

"Yes. Explicitly."

"My kind of girl. I was hoping that was your answer."

Asking the driver to stop before they left the parking lot, he exited the car. "Wait here. I'll be right back."

Walking back inside the restaurant, he called Stan. He was the corporate pilot, who happened to be on standby for the evening. Even at this late hour, calls from John were never a surprise. Billionaires like him traveled at odd hours, sometimes business-related, sometimes not. Tonight it seemed to fall into the latter category. He instructed Stan to contact his First Officer and the cabin crew, immediately informing them to arrive at the airport as soon as possible for the impending flight. Stan had to file a flight plan into Kennedy International. John next asked his chauffeur to drive them out to the airport.

"What's going on? What are you thinking?" she asked as John stepped back inside the limo.

"No more questions. Let's just say you're not going home for the evening," John smiled.

Arriving at the airport, John took her hand, escorting her aboard his private Lear jet.

"Really," she laughed. "Remember what I said earlier this evening concerning the limo," she smiled. "Well, I've never exactly flown on a private plane either."

"Great. It looks like tonight will be even more remarkable. Excuse me for a moment. I'll be right back."

Getting out of his seat, John noticed the arrival of the pilot, co-pilot, and cabin crew. Regardless of the time, day or night, they were always punctual when receiving a call from John. After speaking with the pilot, he assured the weather was great, and they would arrive at their destination on time.

Daniella felt totally out of her element. Maybe, this was a dream. She could not be sure.

"Good evening, Mr. McDermott," Stacie smiled. "Would you or your companion like a drink before we're airborne?"

"Yes. Champagne and chocolate-covered strawberries."

"I'll be right back with those. If you require anything else, please let me know."

"Thanks, Stacie," John smiled.

"Sweetheart, let me help you with that," John instructed, securing her seat belt into the tan leather seat. "Are you nervous?" he asked sympathetically. John knew that Daniella was apprehensive about her decision. However, he offered her unconditional support. Closing the window shade, he would later open it at just the right moment.

"I think I'm past nervous at this point," Daniella smiled, finally attempting to shed her earlier worries from the day.

She was trying her best to get a grasp on what was happening. However, it was evident powerful men like John were familiar with doing things their way regardless of time. She was beginning to get an insight into his world. Men of John's importance and wealth did not live by the hands of a clock. Daniella found this fascinating.

"Daniella, how are you holding up? We should be airborne soon. The champagne should help relax your fear of flying."

"Yes. I could use a drink," Daniella smiled. "If Ava and the girls only knew," she laughed. Morning would come soon enough, and she would call them.

"Stacie, this is Daniella Demos, my companion for the evening," John smiled as Stacie returned with their champagne and chocolate-covered strawberries.

"Daniella, it's a pleasure to meet you. I hope you enjoy your flight. If there is anything I can get you, please do not hesitate to let me know. Would you like a warm blanket or pillow?"

"Maybe later," John interjected with a smile.

"I'll check back with you as soon as we're airborne."

Daniella grasped John's hand as the plane taxied to the runway, squeezing it tightly. She appeared petrified.

"Babe, don't be nervous. I practically live on this aircraft. Well, maybe not live, but I spend many hours in the air. So you are going to be fine. You're with me," he laughed, trying to ease her fears.

Within minutes, the plane began a smooth, steady climb into the dark, starlit night. Leaning over, John gave her a long passionate kiss. Hopefully, it would alleviate her fears while the plane reached its cruising altitude. His kiss began to work its magic as she slowly began loosening her vice-like grip on his hand.

"Did that help?" he smiled.

"Help?" Daniella questioned.

"I mean the kiss. Did it help to ease your fear of flying?" he teased.

"John, that was sneaky, but yes, as a matter of fact, it did. I love you."

"What did you say? What were those three little words? I'm not sure I heard you correctly?"

"John, I love you," she repeated with tears running down her cheeks.

Wiping her moist face, he quickly kissed her once more.

"Sweetheart, I love you too. I would do anything to take away your worries. I hope this helps."

Tonight was turning out to be surreal. Did things like this happen to people? Looking around, she found it almost impossible to believe. Suddenly, she gave herself a quick pinch. She had to be sure. However, it seemed John noticed.

"Daniella, let me see your hand." Tenderly kissing it, he gently pulled it upward to his face. Then, slowly, he rubbed her hand delicately against his face. She could feel his day's growth of stubble. "Babe, I'm truly real. Now, look around you. I assure you, it's all real," he smiled with a wink.

"Thank God you are. Things are happening so fast. I was beginning to doubt my sanity."

"Take a sip of champagne. I think it will help."

Taking one of the chocolate-covered strawberries, he held it to her mouth.

"Take a bite, their delicious," he suggested.

"John, you're by far the silliest man I've ever met."

"Well, at least, you're not crying," he laughed, handing her another.

After several glasses of bubbly, it seemed the excitement from the day was beginning to ease as Daniella found it challenging to stay awake. Finally, reaching into the upper compartment for a blanket, he snuggly wrapped it around her.

"John, are you ever going to tell me where we're going?" she asked before falling asleep.

"Remember, I said no more questions. You will know soon enough. Sweetheart, try to get some rest."

Reaching for another blanket, he snuggled close to the beautiful woman who was now sleeping peacefully as she rested her head against him. It only took minutes before they were fast asleep, released from the worries of the day.

They slept soundly for almost three hours when Stacie gently nudged John awake.

"Mr. McDermott, sorry to wake you, but we're only one hundred miles out from the airport. Would either of you like breakfast or coffee before we arrive?" she inquired. "Warm towels. Would you care for those first?"

"Yes. Thank you, and afterward, we would like coffee. I will wake Daniella. I am not sure whether she would like breakfast now or later when we arrive at the hotel."

"Certainly. I'll be right back."

Returning with the moist steaming towels, Stacie handed them to John.

Taking one, John gently wiped Daniella's face.

"Sorry. It's time to wake up. We're only a short distance out from the airport, and we'll be landing soon," he whispered.

Once again, he wiped her face gently. Rubbing her eyes, Daniella sat up, appearing somewhat disoriented as she looked around the cabin.

"John, are we still in the air?"

"I certainly hope so," he laughed. "But not for long, so you have to wake up. Stacie is bringing coffee, or would you prefer orange juice?"

"Coffee is fine. So where are we?"

"You'll find out soon enough," he smiled.

He had planned not to reveal their location until the jet parked on the tarmac. However, he was having second thoughts. Having waited on the cabin crew for over an hour before they left Florida, they arrived just as the sun was making its early appearance. The sun's rays brilliantly glistened off the behemoth tall glass-enclosed skyscrapers. It was spectacular and best seen from the air. He did not want her to miss the incredible view of the New York skyline as it captured the rays of the early morning sun.

After giving her a short seductive kiss, he opened the window shade.

"Okay," he smiled.

Taking a quick look below, as the jet banked sharply over the towering structures and the immense city skyline bathed in the early morning rays, Daniella gasped.

"Oh John, New York," she exclaimed, fixated on the site below. "This is incredible. Never before, in my entire life, have I seen anything so spectacular. It looks like one of those posters I saw in the travel agency window. It's breathtaking."

Watching her reaction put a massive smile on his face. She was like a child reflecting the wonder of Christmas morning. It made him love her even more.

"Sweetheart, it is pretty darn amazing. I didn't want you to miss seeing the skyline of New York bathed in sunlight. So what do you think? Are you up to doing the tourist thing for a few days?"

"John, I don't have any clothes. So what am I going to do? I can't stay," she explained with a sad look of disappointment.

"I'm not sure you need any clothes," he winked. "But if you insist, I believe this will take care of it," he grinned, handing her an impressive store card. "Trust me. It's not a problem."

"John, I don't know what to say? I'm speechless."

"Daniella, I love you. Are you ready for a cup of coffee, or would you prefer orange juice? Also, would you like to have breakfast now or wait until we arrive at the hotel?"

"Coffee sounds wonderful, but I'm not hungry."

"You'll never hold out to do all that shopping if you don't eat," he smiled.

"John, where have you been? I certainly don't remember wishing on a star."

"Daniella, I've waited my entire life for someone like you. Trust me. The first night we met at the restaurant, I knew you were different. You've endured such tragedies for someone so young, and it's about time that changed. You deserve a little happiness. This weekend is just a snippet of what our life could be like," he winked.

He stopped short of going further. It was not the time or place to propose that would come later. There was no hurry. However, moving in closer, he kissed her with such passion she felt time stood still. Nothing at that moment mattered except the handsome man who held her in his arms.

As Stacie approached to inquire further about breakfast, she paused, seeing their display of affection. What she witnessed between them during the flight was common too familiar. If the walls in this aircraft could only talk, she smiled. Joining the mile-high club was only the tip of the iceberg. She had seen it all. The influential men, who worked for McDermott Corporation, were, for the most part, sexual deviants. Their money bought everything including, escorts, hookers, assistants. Only their first names ever seem to change. However, she worried for Daniella. She had observed this scenario being played out time after time with John and the other men. She could only hope for Daniella's sake he was serious. She hated to see these young women getting their hearts broken.

However, little did Stacie know this time with John, it was different. He was tired of playing the field. He was playing for keeps. John knew most of the women who had come in and out of his life over the past were only with him for his money. Daniella did not fit that mold. She was different. He knew it the first time he met her. However, he loved her tenacity and ability to fight for what she wanted. Tonight, he felt drawn to her on many levels. This weekend he hoped to prove to her how much he adored her. He was prepared to give her everything. Daniella had no idea the lengths he was willing to go to ensure she lacked for nothing. Love had found Daniella for the second time. Someone she could have never imagined or wished for had walked into her life.

As the jet landed, it was early morning in New York, the city that never sleeps. If she thought the ride into New York had been exhilarating, she had not seen anything yet. McDermott Corporation owned penthouses in almost every country in the world.

"Sweetheart, I'll have the limo take us to the hotel. We can have breakfast and the day is yours. What would you like to do?" he winked wickedly.

"John, if it's alright, I'm not sure that I want to do anything at all. Would it be possible to spend the entire day in bed, not leaving the room? I still feel emotionally and physically drained. What I really want is to shut out the world and just feel the closeness of your body next to mine," she asked demurely.

Wow, had he heard her correctly? She never failed to surprise him. Was it possible she was reading his mind? Most of the women he had been in relationships with in the past would have burned a hole in his credit cards within hours. Yet, she seemed oblivious to the idea. Where had she been all his life?

"Honestly, I couldn't think of a better way to spend the day," he winked. It seems you must have read my mind." How lucky could a guy get, he thought?

As the plane rolled to a stop on the tarmac, a limo waited for their arrival.

"Enjoy your time in New York," Stacie smiled, watching Daniella and John descend the steps of the aircraft.

"Thanks, Stacie, see you on the return. Don't get Stan and the guys in trouble this weekend," John grinned.

"Oh, Mr. McDermott, they'll do that all by themselves. Those guys don't need any help from me," she laughed. "Have a wonderful day."

"Thanks."

Taking Daniella's hand, he led her over to the limo.

"Good morning, sir. Is it downtown to the hotel?" Charles smiled. "Are you traveling with luggage this morning?"

"Good morning, Charles. Yes. Thank you. We are staying downtown at the hotel. Surprisingly, we are without luggage," John added with a smile.

Afterward, Charles closed their door. Soon they were on their way into the heart of the city.

It seemed Daniella was trying to take in as many sights of the city as she possibly could from the car windows.

"Sweetheart, don't worry, you're not going to miss anything. Just tell me when you're ready, and I'll be your tour guide."

"Thanks, John," Daniella replied, laying her head against his shoulder.

Traffic was light at this hour in the morning, and with no road construction insight, it wasn't long before they arrived downtown at the Drake Hotel. Parking next to the curb at the front entrance, Charles immediately opened their door.

"Have a wonderful weekend," Charles grinned.

"Thanks, Charles."

"Wow. This is where you stay, the Drake? I have only seen pictures of this hotel. It's gorgeous," Daniella whispered as they walked into the lobby.

The staff quickly recognized John as he approached the front desk.

"Good morning, sir. Do you have luggage?" the concierge inquired.

"Not today."

"You're all set. I hope everything is to your liking. Have a wonderful stay."

"Thanks. Oh, please hold all calls. Also, I'd prefer no one knows I'm in town today."

"Yes, sir, Mr. McDermott, I understand."

He put his arm around Daniella's slender waist and escorted her over to the elevator.

"Good morning. Welcome back," the young elevator attendant stated, immediately pushing the button to the 21 st floor, the penthouse apartment.

"Thanks, Gary. How's your morning?" John inquired.

"Not bad, sir, thanks for asking?"

Daniella was intrigued by the inner workings of the magnificent hotel and the fact everyone knew John. It was only moments before they reached the top floor.

"Here you are, sir," Gary announced.

Entering the beautiful, ornate foyer, John took Daniella's hand, leading her to the penthouse apartment door. Unlocking the door, Daniella gasped.

"John, you didn't mention the fact you had a penthouse apartment?"

"Well, maybe it was the fact you never asked," he grinned.

"John, your apartment is amazing," she smiled. Then, slowly looking around the living room, she attempted to focus on every detail of its stunning décor.

Tall floor-to-ceiling windows immersed the room with an abundance of sunlight. A large European tapestry depicting a Tuscany village hung above a sizeable baroque credenza and matching dark leather sofa's faced each other in the center of the room. An oversized dark oak antique coffee table sat between the two sofas. It was unexpected yet beautifully crafted. As a result, the room felt sophisticated, giving an ambiance of old-world charm.

"Thanks. You like it?" John winked.

"Like it? It's incredible. Immediately going over to the window, Daniella paused, fixated on the views of the surrounding high-rise buildings.

Walking over, he took her hand.

"Sweetheart, what was it you said about staying in bed all day and shutting out the world. You were serious, right?" he teased.

"Completely," she smiled demurely.

"Okay. I think we have some robes in the bathroom. I'll be right back."

Walking out, he held two luxurious Egyptian cotton bathrobes.

"I think we should change. You'll be more comfortable. I'll show you to the bedroom and adjoining bathroom. You can change while I order breakfast."

Taking her hand, he pulled her playfully over to the bedroom. Opening the double doors, it revealed an opulent main suite.

"The bathroom is to the left. I believe you'll find everything you need, including a jacuzzi bath and a steam shower."

"Geez, John, do other people live this lavishly?" she questioned.

"Sweetheart, I'm not sure. However, I do," he smiled with a wink.

As their eyes met, they both laughed like young kids at play.

"Listen, you change or do whatever. I'm going to order breakfast. I'm starved."

"Okay. I'll be right out," Daniella answered.

As she slowly made her way throughout the room, she felt compelled to touch everything. The room was exquisite. Elegant blue damask wallpaper covered every inch of the walls. An ornate chandelier hung directly above a sitting area off to one end of the room. The room, even though large in scale, seemed cozy and comfortable. A dark mahogany king-size bed sat against the back wall facing two large windows. The bed was covered impeccably in a light blue duvet that matched the damask wallpaper and drapes. Noticing another door, Daniella suspected it was the main closet. Curiosity consuming her, she had to check it out. Opening the door, it was John's closet. Cedar lined the inner walls. However, it smelled overwhelming of his cologne. Taking a quick look through the racks of men's shirts, she pulled one from its hanger. It was a white dress shirt, yet it felt incredibly soft. Taking the initiative, she put it on after removing her clothing. Hopefully, he wouldn't mind. Finally, she put the luxurious white robe over his shirt and walked back out to the living room.

"Wow," John grinned. "I must say you look stunning."

Walking over, he pulled her close. Removing the clip from her hair immediately loosened her long blonde curls, allowing her long hair to fall below her shoulders.

"Much better," he complimented, gently running his hands through the silky lengths of her hair. Then, just as he was about to kiss her, there was a knock at the door.

"Great. Breakfast has arrived," John remarked. His attention instantly shifted from her to answer the door.

The young man whose duty was to provide room service pushed a cart laden with food inside the room. After giving him a generous tip, John saw him to the door. Taking a moment, he ensured the do not disturb sign was visible.

"Okay, Sweetheart, let's eat. We haven't eaten since we left yesterday. Aren't you starved?" he asked, pulling her over to a small round table near the kitchen. "On second thought, let's eat in the living room," he suggested changing his mind. "It will be more comfortable."

John immediately began removing the silver tops from the dishes. They revealed scrambled eggs, hash browns, bacon, toast, and cups of fresh fruit.

"Geez, do you think you have enough food?" Daniella questioned with a laugh.

He took a plate and put a bit of everything on it for her. Then he popped the cork on a bottle of Moet & Chandon Dom Perignon Brut, pouring them each a glass.

"Here's to our first time in New York," he toasted. "I love you."

"Thanks," Daniella answered, leaning over to give him a quick kiss.

After enjoying a relaxing breakfast, John caught Daniella rubbing her eyes. It was evident she was falling asleep. Scooping her up in his arms, he carried her into the bedroom.

Turning back the duvet, he sat her down on the edge of the bed. Then, untying her bathrobe, he laughed.

"Sweetheart, it seems you've found my closet," he winked.

"John, I hope you don't mind, but I had nothing to wear. So I took the liberty of putting on your shirt," she explained. "It feels incredibly soft."

"Daniella, you look stunning. Please, keep it with my compliments," he teased.

"However, I don't think it's necessary," he smiled wickedly, slowly undoing the tiny buttons down the front of the shirt.

Putting her under the warm covers, he removed his clothes and slipped into bed beside her. Now, her only demand was, at last, coming true. She didn't wish to see New York. She didn't wish to shop. She only wished to feel the closeness of his body against hers.

"So, Sweetheart, is this what you wanted?" he whispered, lovingly caressing her body.

"Well, since you asked," she smiled.

For the rest of the day and remaining time in New York, it was spent as only two lovers would, *shutting out the world.*

Chapter Seven

Arriving back in Destiny Cove after a magical weekend in New York with John, she felt as if she was under a weird interrogation. Entering the kitchen to get a much-needed cup of coffee, it started.

"Oh, child. What in the name of heavens made you go off and do such a thing with a man like that? Have you lost your good senses? What kind of example as a mother is that for Gracie and Jillian? I was shocked," Ava raged.

"Ava, first thing, I am not a child. Furthermore, I am a grown woman, completely capable of making my own decisions without any advice from you or anyone. I am sorry you were shocked and didn't approve."

"What were you thinking?" Ava continued.

"Well, maybe for the first time in my life, I wasn't thinking. I mean, it just felt right. The trip wasn't planned. It was spontaneous and spur-of-the-moment. John realized how sad and depressed I was over the fact his corporation demolished the Sea Oates. So it was his way of trying to make things better."

"And he had to take you all the way to New York City to make things better?" Ava questioned with a scowl.

"Listen, Ava. John is different than anyone I've ever met. Besides, I've fallen in love with him.

"Oh, child, you don't know what you're saying."

"Ava, I truly can't explain it to you. I loved Dimitri. However, now that I've met John, I've been given a second chance at happiness. Do you even know what that means?"

"Daniella, that man lives in a completely different world than you."

"Ava, you're right he does. You've finally said something I agree with. Trust me, I got a glimpse of his world this weekend, but none of that matters. I fell in love with him, not his money. Ava, I love you. You've been like a mother to me, and I appreciate your advice, but you need to let me live my life the way I choose. Now, no more talk about this weekend or John."

"Well, I just don't want to see you get hurt."

"Then, let me worry about that. What did the girls do this weekend?" Daniella asked, changing the subject.

"Gracie slept at Lexie's house, and Jillian has lived on the beach. I swear that girl spends more time in the water than she does on land. She is playing volleyball this morning with her girlfriends. It seems they ran into some boys from Harvard over the weekend. You know Jillian. She has such a gregarious personality. I worry about that one. She reminds me a lot of you."

"Did she happen to mention their names?"

"If she did, I can't remember?"

"Well, John has a son who's attending Harvard. I believe he told me last week that his son, Matt, and a couple of his buddies were coming down for a few days. However, he didn't mention it this weekend."

"Great, that's just what Destiny Cove needs another McDermott."

"Ava, you promised. No more talk about John or his son. Keep your crazy thoughts to yourself."

At that moment the phone rang. "Do you want me to get that for you?" Ava questioned, walking towards the counter.

"No. Maybe it's John. I want to ask if Matt is here," Daniella mentioned sprinting over to answer it.

"Goodmorning, Sweetheart. I wanted to check your plans for today. If you're free for a few hours, I'll be down at the Sea Oates project. I have something for you."

"Okay. What time?"

"How does 2:00 p.m. sound?"

"That works. By the way, is Matt down with his buddies?"

"Yes. They came in over the weekend while we were in New York?"

"I thought so. Jillian and her girlfriends ran into them on the beach this weekend. Destiny Cove is such a small place. Ava said they were down at the beach playing volleyball."

"Great. I'm sure they're having fun. He'll be here until next Friday. So maybe we can all have dinner one evening this week. I'll check my schedule. See you at 2:00 p.m. Love you."

"Okay. I'll be there. Love you too."

"Ava, that was John. It appears Jillian may have met Matt and his friends. John said they were here."

"Well, great. Just what I thought a few seconds ago, another McDermott," Ava bitterly complained.

"Ava, please, no more rude remarks. What are you making for dinner?"

"Well, I was just looking through the pantry. How does lasagna sound?"

"It sounds delicious. I'm meeting John at the construction site at 2:00 p.m. I'm not sure when I'll get back. But, Ava, I just had an amazing thought. Why don't you make extra, and I'll invite John and Matt over?"

"Daniella, you can't be serious?"

"Yes. Ava, I think it's time you let go of your hostilities towards him."

"Well," she paused, seriously pondering Daniella's words. Maybe she was being too hard on her. "Oh, alright, I guess that's the least I can do after getting you upset earlier. Why don't you tell them dinner will be at 6:00 p.m. It gives me time to put one of my chocolate cakes in the oven."

"Thanks, Ava. I'll call John and remind him to ask Matt. Oh, if

Jillian comes in, you might want to let her know that I've invited John and Matt to dinner this evening."

"Okay. Do you think Matt's friends will come as well?"

"I'm not sure. Maybe you should make two, just in case. You know boys and their appetites."

"No problem. I've got you covered. I suppose I should get started on dinner."

"Thanks again, Ava. I love you."

At 2:00 p.m., Daniella met John at the site. She had not gone back since the McDermott Corporation had demolished everything. It seemed strange that all that remained of her former home was the gorgeous views of the sparkling turquoise waters. Nothing had been left which indicated she'd ever lived there except her memories. Now, all that remained on the lot was machinery and the early beginnings of the new tower. Watching her drive up, John walked over and greeted her with a quick kiss.

"Hey, Sweetheart, I'm glad you came. Let me walk you down to the trailer. I want you to see my vision for the new Sea Oates. I've completed the architectural drawings. I think you're going to love what you see, but first, we'll walk over to the vacant lot. It might be the last time you can stand on the exact spot of the former Sea Oates before we start our construction. I know you didn't feel like watching the day we demolished it, but I thought you might want to come down and have a moment before we move forward with construction," John smiled, taking her hand.

Daniella felt as if she was having an out-of-body experience as she stood on the very ground where most of her life up to this point had taken place. Noticing she was becoming rather emotional, John suggested they continue to the trailer, which was used as a temporary on-site office for the McDermott Corporation and crew. Taking her hand, he gave her a quick kiss.

"I have something for you. It's down at the trailer. Let's go," John thoughtfully suggested.

It was cluttered as they entered the tiny cramped trailer. Two desks sat near tall filing cabinets, architectural drawings, notepads, hard hats, and a water cooler filled the small overcrowded space.

"Geez, John, how do you get any work done in here?" Daniella asked, surveying the small, cramped trailer.

"Oh, trust me, it's not a problem," he mentioned pulling over one of the desk chairs for her. "Sit down. I'll get my drawings."

Rolling out his design, she was awestruck.

"Wow, you're good," she smiled. "It's unbelievable."

"I'm glad you approve. I would never have wanted to build a new hotel on this parcel of land unless you were happy with the design," he stated with a quick kiss. "It's going to have eighteen floors, with the top floor strictly being reserved for penthouse apartments. Each unit will have a balcony and contain high-end components in their décor, such as the kitchens and baths. The hotel's main entrance will offer a few shops, a restaurant, lounge, and coffee shop. What do you think?"

"It's gorgeous. You're brilliant," Daniella complimented, staring at the drawings of the tall glass-enclosed high-rise structure. It highlighted an outdoor Olympic-sized pool surrounded by lavish tropical greenery and Queen Palms. The pool was easily accessible amid a massive stone patio and a maze of lighted walkways. "So, what's the time frame for having the project completed?"

"We've targeted the completion date to be next April. I've constructed hotels all over the world for over thirty years, or I should say my company, McDermott Corporation," he smiled. "I'm anxious to move ahead with this project."

Walking to the back of the trailer, he picked up a colorful etched sign.

"Sweetheart, I told the crew to hang on to this. It was the sign you had on the wall above the reception desk in the lobby. I felt you might want to keep it. It's such a gorgeous depiction of the Sea Oates," John explained.

"Oh, John, that was so kind of you. Thank you, I don't know how it got overlooked when we moved. I appreciate your thoughtfulness," Daniella remarked, kissing him. "Are you hungry? I'm sure Ava has dinner ready. Will Matt be joining us?"

"Yes, as a matter of fact, he's probably on his way over," John answered, looking down at his watch. "I gave him your address earlier. So let me lock up, and we'll be on our way. Lasagna sound delicious. I am sure Ava is a great cook."

"Did you know she worked as a chef in one of the hotels you constructed in Atlanta?"

"Wow. What a small world. Then I'm sure she's a great cook." Locking up the trailer, John took Daniella's hand and led her back up to the parking lot.

"Sweetheart, I'll follow you. See you in a few minutes."

Driving up, Daniella noticed an unfamiliar car parked in the drive. Surely this was Matt's. The fact he was driving a shiny new black BMW convertible must have made all the girls on the beach take notice. Daniella decided to wait for John to arrive. It seemed he was only a few minutes behind.

"Geez, the traffic over the bridge never seems to get easier," John remarked, getting out of his car.

"Yes. You're right. It can be congested, especially on weekends. Let's go in. I believe I can smell Ava's lasagna.

Taking John's hand, Daniella led him inside.

"Why don't you sit down on the sofa, and I'll pour us a glass of wine. Then, let me find our kids." Walking into the kitchen, Ava was busy folding napkins. "Are you ready to serve dinner, and have you seen the girls and Matt?"

"Yes. Everything has been taken care of, and I'm ready to serve dinner. Jillian and Matt are outside on the back patio playing with Truffles. I'll let them know you and John have arrived. Gracie is eating at Lexie's house," Ava paused as she looked up. "Lexie only has another week before she leaves, and Gracie was invited to have dinner with them," Ava mentioned.

"Great. I'll let everyone know dinner is ready," Daniella smiled, walking back into the living room.

"Oh John, the bathroom is right around that corner if you'd like to wash up before dinner. I'll take our wine glasses into the dining room."

Walking into the dining room, Daniella caught her first glimpse of Matt. He resembled his father in every way. His handsome, chiseled features and jet black hair were noticeably traits of his father.

"Mom, I'd like you to meet Matt McDermott," Jillian announced, walking in from the patio.

"Matt, it's nice to meet you. I've heard a lot of great things about you from your father."

"Thanks. It's nice to meet you as well," Matt replied with a gorgeous smile.

"Hey, Son, looks like you arrived before me this evening."

"Hey, Dad. Jillian and I were at the beach earlier. So we decided to come over after the volleyball game."

"Where are the boys, Brad and Dexter?" John inquired.

"Oh, they decided to stay in town this evening. They met up with a few of the locals and wanted to try out the Oyster Bar down at the pier," Matt answered.

"Everyone, please have a seat. It looks like Ava has outdone herself this evening. It looks wonderful and smells delicious."

As everyone sat around the long dark oak Italian dining table, the chandelier hanging from the beautiful trey ceiling infused the room with soft ambient lighting. Ava had painstakingly set the table's décor to reflect the Italian serving dishes. Each place setting was a work of art. Conversation flowed easily among the four of them as Daniella enjoyed listening to Matt describe his time at Harvard. It seemed all too soon dinner was over, but not before Ava served her famous chocolate cake.

"Mom, Matt, and I are going to drive into town and meet up with Brad and Dexter. Matt will bring me home afterward."

"Okay, honey, you two go and enjoy yourselves. John, let's take our wine and enjoy the evening outside on the patio."

"Great. I'll follow you," John smiled, pulling Daniella's chair back from the table.

Ava watched from the kitchen window as Daniella took John's hand, pulling him outside. She knew beyond a doubt that Daniella had fallen in love with John. "Heaven help that child," Ava whispered prayerfully.

The full moon cast a radiant reflection on the sandy shore and gave an iridescent shimmer to the water's surface. The evening seemed enchanting as everything appeared lit by the natural light of the full moon.

"Sweetheart, why don't we take a walk down to the beach. We must take advantage of this gorgeous moon," John suggested reaching over to grasp her hand.

"Sounds wonderful," Daniella answered, removing her heels.

A warm breeze gently blew through Daniella's hair as they walked down the lighted boardwalk. Then, finally, her feet touched the cool soft sands of the beach. Putting her arm around John, she looked up, noticing an abundance of twinkling stars.

"Wow, I must say this is romantic," Daniella mentioned pulling John into the edge of the warm phosphorous saltwater. The waves appeared translucent as they gently rolled ashore.

"Sweetheart, I didn't plan on getting wet. Let's just walk down the beach," he suggested attempting to pull Daniella away from the glistening water.

"If you're sure you don't want to go for a swim," she smiled, taking his arm. Finally, becoming more attentive to this gorgeous man, she paused, captivated by the intensity of his blue eyes. "So John, what are your plans after the new Sea Oates Hotel and condominiums are finished?" she asked, unprepared to hear his answer.

"I have two more projects coming online. One is a high-rise tower in Hong Kong, and the other is a hotel in Amerstadam," he answered, noting her reaction.

Watching as her playful demeanor changed instantly, he knew it wasn't exactly what she had wanted to hear. However, she'd asked the question, and he would never be anything other than honest with her. But, unfortunately, it seemed silence had invaded their lively, fun walk along the shore. Burying her head into his chest, she desperately tried to keep her tears in check.

"Sweetheart, I love you, let's just stay in the moment," John answered. With the back of his hand, he wiped tears from her moist face. Then, pulling her close, he kissed her passionately. He knew she was fishing for answers. Answers that he was not willing to give at this time. A forever commitment was hard for him to imagine. However, there was no one other than her in his life, and he hadn't exactly ruled out the possibility.

"Daniella, I promised you a trip. I have a few days before construction gets underway. We're waiting on permits, and it would be a perfect time. What do you think?"

"I couldn't think of anything I would love more." Kissing him once again, she grabbed his hand, playfully pulling him further down the beach. She would never stop loving John. He was everything she could have ever wished for and more much. Suddenly, she pulled away from him, sprinting faster down the beach under the light of the full moon. Stopping, she turned around to watch as he caught up with her. She loved this man running towards her. She would never let him go.

"John, isn't this evening gorgeous?" Daniella mentioned with a smile.

Once again, he saw the playful young girl that had so intrigued him at their very first meeting. Of course, he was falling in love. But, maybe, he was only fooling himself by trying to keep his emotions to himself. He had played the field for so long, and never once had he met anyone like her.

"Roll up your pants. The water is warm," Daniella laughed, pulling him into the water behind her.

Suddenly, a wave caught Daniella off balance. Grabbing hold of John, without thought, they both toppled into the water. Caught up in the unexpected excitement of the moment, he held her in his arms, kissing her passionately as waves gently washed over them. Time simply ceased to exist as John pulled her close to his chest, shielding her from the incoming waves.

"Now what?" he asked, staring into Daniella's sparkling eyes.

As their eyes met, they laughed hysterically. Taking Daniella's hand, John pulled her up from the iridescent water.

"Well, I guess we get back to the house and find some towels."

Running back down the beach towards the house, she teasingly begged him to catch up with her taunting him to play along.

At first, he just watched the spirited young girl running down the beach. Then he let himself go, as only a child would, and chased after her. Finally, catching her, he pulled her to his chest once again, kissing her passionately.

Finally, making it back to the patio, they were both soaked and covered in sand.

"Wait out here. I'll go in and get some towels."

Unexpectedly bumping into Ava, Daniella gasped.

"Oh child, what have you gone and done now?" Ava could only imagine that Daniella and John were acting more like children than Jillian and Matt.

"Geez, Ava, it was an accident. We fell in the water, and we need some towels." Looking down at her wet clothes, Daniella laughed.

"Stay put. You're wet and covered in sand. I'll grab some towels," Ava demanded. "You can't come inside looking like that."

Returning with warm towels, Daniella and John began to dry themselves off while remaining on the patio.

"Hand me John's clothes. I'll wash and dry them," Ava insisted.

"Okay, John, Ava wants your clothes," Daniella instructed, giving him a whimsical look.

"Babe, just tie the towel around your waist and get out of those wet clothes. Afterward, come inside. I'll show you to the shower."

Having no other choice, he did exactly as she asked. Soon he was standing under the hot water of the shower.

"John, I'm putting a bathrobe on the vanity. I hope it fits. It's Ava's," Daniella laughed.

Watching as he walked out of the bathroom wearing Ava's bathrobe," Daniella whistled, handing him a glass of chardonnay. Later sitting on the sofa while John's clothes were drying, they enjoyed another glass of wine.

"Geez, Sweetheart, maybe I should keep an extra set of clothes here for your friskier days," he winked.

After his clothes had finished the dry cycle, he quickly dressed. Finally, it was time to call it an evening. Daniella walked out with him to his car.

Daniella kissed him goodnight and silently longed for him to stay, which unbeknown to him meant forever.

"Thanks for dinner and a wonderful evening," he winked, kissing her goodbye. "Sweetheart, one more thing before I leave, could you get away as early as the day after tomorrow? I want to take you somewhere special, but I also need to be back within a week. Would that possibly work for you?"

"Yes. I'll make it work. Don't worry," Daniella smiled, giving him another quick kiss. "I love you."

As John drove out of the drive, she blew a kiss in his direction. She had now met Matt, his son, and was even more sure of wanting to spend the rest of her life with this amazing man.

Chapter Eight

It seemed the next two days flew by extremely fast. Daniella was busy getting things at home squared away for the following week. She was looking forward to spending time with John. Everything was finally arranged, and she was once again free.

Hearing the doorbell, Daniella dashed over to let John in.

"Daniella, can you get the door?" Ava yelled from the kitchen.

"Yes. It's John. Will you let the girls know that I will call them? See you in a few days."

Ava feared Daniella had utterly lost her mind. She was perplexed to know that Daniella was again leaving with John after shortly returning from her weekend in New York. Daniella was not a jet setter who frequently flew around the world. Even though she had money from the sale of the Sea Oates, the new lifestyle she seemed to be living wasn't conducive to a young family. How would she ever be able to make Daniella stop and think about her behavior? It appeared the old saying, 'How ya gonna keep 'em down on the farm after they've seen Paree,' ran through Ava's mind. John owned a massive conglomerate, McDermott Corporation, and was a billionaire.

On the other hand, Daniella was a widow raising two young daughters. They were from two different worlds, and she didn't feel they belonged together. Ava had not considered the power of the word *love*. It crossed all barriers and knew no boundaries. Watching as the chauffeur picked up Daniella's luggage, Ava would soon learn how much this one small word influenced Daniella and John's decisions.

"Okay, I think I have everything. But, you know it would have been a lot easier if you'd informed me where we were going?" Daniella mentioned as the chauffeur picked up her luggage. John took her by the hand and walked her out to the waiting limo.

"Sweetheart, you do have your passport, right?" He had to make sure.

"Of course. It's in my purse."

"Looks like a great day for flying. Are you excited?" John asked, assisting her inside the limo.

"Well, I still feel a bit hesitant about flying," Daniella frowned.

"You just stick with me, and you'll soon become a pro," he winked.

It didn't take long to reach the private jet waiting for their arrival at the local airport.

"Goodmorning, sir, welcome aboard," Stacie smiled, greeting them as they boarded the plane. "Nice to have you traveling with us again," she acknowledged seeing Daniella.

"Thanks, Stacie. Would you please bring two glasses of champagne?"

"Not a problem. I'd be happy to get that for you." Stacie returned his smile as she secured the door for take-off.

Gently grasping Daniella's hand, John led her to a window seat in the middle of the aircraft. "Okay, sweetheart, I'll buckle you into your seat."

Immediately, Stacie returned with two glasses of sparkling champagne.

"Okay, let's toast to our second trip," John suggested as he lifted his glass.

"But shouldn't we toast to the destination?" Daniella asked with a curious smile.

"Oh, we'll toast to that later, once we arrive," he winked.

"Would you care for anything more before we're airborne?" Stacie asked, refilling their glasses.

"No thanks. However, we would like to have dinner in about an hour."

"Great. I can offer you a choice of either rosemary chicken or grilled salmon. I'll be back later to get your decisions."

Stacie was shocked to see Daniella accompanying John once again. Maybe after all these years, he was finally serious and ready to settle down with one person. She could only be hopeful for Daniella.

As the plane began moving towards the runway, Daniella grabbed John's hand, squeezing it tightly. It appeared her fear of flying never left.

"Sweetheart, let me rid you of your fears," John winked wickedly, reaching over to pull her into his arms. Then, passionately began kissing her as the aircraft smoothly ascended, reaching its cruising altitude. Melting into his arms, the intensity of his kiss erased any lingering fears.

"So," he teased, waiting for her response.

"What?" Daniella blushed.

"The kiss," he smiled. "As before on your first flight, did it work?"

"John, you are by far the silliest man I know, but, of course," she smiled demurely.

"Great. Now relax and enjoy the flight."

It seemed his kiss had once again worked its magic. He wasn't about to let an opportunity like that escape him.

Once the plane had leveled, John reached into the overhead bin to get his briefcase.

"Well, I had planned to keep our destination a secret for a bit longer, but perhaps you might want to take a look at these brochures."

Taking a quick glance, she almost screamed. However, the realization they were in an aircraft subdued her reactions. She needed to control her emotions.

"John, Santorini, Greece," she beamed. "How did you know?"

"Sweetheart, you're easy to read. I remember your saying how you always wanted to visit Dimitri's birthplace. I must be insane taking you somewhere that might dredge up painful memories. However, it is a beautiful country, and I think it's time we make some new memories. Are you up for it?"

"Oh, John, it's not like I don't already love you. On the contrary, I love you even more if that's possible. I've always wanted to go to Greece. But, like you said that day we were standing in front of the travel agency, posters can never replace visiting those countries. I should pinch myself. This can't possibly be real."

"Not the dreaded pinch test," John laughed. "Daniella, I assure you it's for real. In fact, I have a yacht waiting for us when we land in Athens. We're going to tour the Greek islands in style and luxury."

"John, are you serious?"

"I think so," he laughed. "Everything has already been taken care of for the entire week. I was only missing one thing to make it perfect, you," he winked. "So I hope you packed a bikini and suntan lotion."

"John, sometimes I can't believe you're real. Where did you come from?" she asked lovingly, rubbing his face with the back of her hand. "Honestly, I never imagined I would find love again after losing Demitri. Thank God your corporation was chosen to revitalize our small town."

"Daniella, listen, I'm not trying or would ever try to compete with Dimitri. I'm sure he loved you. I just happen to be lucky enough in life to afford a few luxuries. What is money if you can't make those you love happy? I would do anything for you. Even take you to Greece," he smiled, pulling her over to him. He kissed her once again with such passion that it invaded her whole body with warmth, sending tingles throughout her petite frame. She felt as if she would faint had she not been sitting. It made her forget time and space—the fact she was afraid of flying or at 36,000 feet never entered her mind.

"Would you like dinner, or would you rather sleep?"

"Well, to be honest, I'm not hungry. Do you think there's a blanket on the plane?"

"Sweetheart, there's always blankets. Now you're the one being silly. I'll get one and a pillow. How does that sound?"

"Wonderful. I just feel tired. I think the champagne has me relaxed."

Reaching once again into the overhead bin, John grabbed a blanket and pillow. Wrapping her snuggly in the blanket, he put the pillow under her head. Staring down at the love of his life, she would never know, but he felt he was the lucky one to have found her. Trying to get comfortable, she pulled the pillow from beneath her head, placing it against John's shoulder. Cuddling against the warmth of his body, she fell asleep. Now that she was sleeping, he opened his briefcase. He would get a little work done while she was resting. He needed to crunch some numbers regarding expenditures and overruns on the Sea Oates project. Motioning for Stacie, he asked for a glass of bourbon, nothing like a strong drink to ease the pain of disbursements. Finally, after a short while, he began to feel tired. Putting away his paperwork, he turned off the overhead light, grabbed another blanket, and snuggled against the beautiful woman who slept so peacefully beside him. Stacie noticing they were both asleep, never bothered to inquire about dinner. She would wait until later.

It seemed he had been asleep for over an hour when Daniella woke with an urgent request.

Unsure of the direction of the bathroom, as she had not required its use on their previous short trip to New York, she woke John.

"John, which direction is the bathroom, the front or back of the aircraft?"

"Oh, that," he laughed. "It's in the back of the plane. I don't possibly see how you can miss it." Her naivety regarding such things made him love her all the more. "Do you want me to show you?" he laughed.

"No. I just wanted to make sure. I'll be right back."

Standing to stretch his legs, he walked up to the front of the aircraft while waiting for her to return.

"Stacie, I believe we are ready for dinner. We'd both like the baked salmon."

"Great. Give me a few minutes, and I'll have it ready."

The rest of the flight was enjoyable as they dined on baked salmon with wild rice and passed the time deep in conversation. It appeared Daniella was somewhat getting used to traveling by private plane. After stopping in Frankfurt, Germany, to refuel, they were finally on the last leg of their trip. Fortunately, It seemed as if time had flown by fast as

Stacie approached their seats to announce their impending arrival at the airport in Athens.

"Mr. McDermott, we're just a few minutes out from the airport. Would either of you care for a warm towel or coffee before we arrive?"

"Yes. Please bring two towels, and afterward two coffees. Please add a touch of Bailey's to mine," John instructed.

"Sweetheart, open your window shade. I don't want you to miss the spectacular views of the Aegean Sea and the Parthenon as we approach Athens. I think you'll discover the vibrant colors of the Aegean Sea resemble the waters of the Gulf of Mexico. Also, would you like to spend our first night in Athens or on the yacht once we arrive? It's your choice?"

"That's a hard decision. But if you're asking, maybe staying in Athens overnight would be best. I'm exhausted, and the time difference will be a struggle. I feel as if I've lost a day already."

"Okay. You've got it. I know just the place," John winked.

As the jet banked sharply on its approach into the airport, Daniella gasped, viewing the sights below. The panorama was breathtaking.

"John, this is incredible. The water seems a variant mixture of blues, azure, and sapphire. It's gorgeous. You're right. The Aegean Sea does reflect the colors of the Gulf of Mexico."

Pointing out the Parthenon, John felt like a tourist guide. He loved watching the expressions on her face as he emphasized points of interest. She seemed utterly absorbed at the moment, like a young school girl on her first field trip.

Once the jet touched the runway, it was only a short time before the aircraft parked on the tarmac. Watching out the window as the limo arrived, John was anxious to show her Athens. He had been here many times and knew the city well. The Alexander Hotel was one of his favorite hotels. However, each time he checked in, as an architect, he'd always in his mind go over details of things he would have done differently. He felt all architects must feel the same when entering other hotels or buildings they had not designed or constructed. However, he knew the Alexander would certainly not disappoint Daniella.

Once inside the limo, they were on their way downtown. It felt like history came alive as they drove through busy streets lined with ancient stone buildings and open-air cafes. Arriving at the Alexander, Daniella was impressed. Its architectural features seemed to blend in with its surroundings. Tall stone columns held the arched portico cascading in lush purple blooms of Wisteria, which resembled tags of grapes. Following John inside through the double wrought iron doors, Daniella was more than impressed with the overwhelming grandeur of the Alexander.

"Good evening, Mr. McDermott, welcome back," the concierge smiled. "I believe you will find the suite and its accommodations to your standards this evening. If not, please let me know. Chilled champagne and fruit have been sent up per your instructions, also your luggage. Enjoy your stay."

"Thanks, George." John smiled.

Taking John's hand, Daniella followed him down a long corridor.

"Wow, Sweetheart, does everyone know you? I'm quite impressed."

"I think I mentioned the fact McDermott Corporation has suites all over the globe. My project crews and I stay here frequently when we're developing properties in this part of the world. I think you'll love this hotel, even though I didn't personally have anything to do with the remodel," he grinned.

Unlocking the door, Daniella was awe-struck with its décor, which replicated the culture of Athens. The suite had aged tiled floors, and sitting at the room's perimeter were large stone pots filled with tall ornamental Palms. In the foyer, ornate wrought iron sconces gave a soft glow to the living quarters. Looking further around the room, dark oak furniture with unique inlay designs sat against white textured walls. Oversized glass doors opened to the balcony revealing a sparkling blue pool that was lit to enhance the brightly colored mosaic tiles that lined its circumference. It was sheer opulence.

"John, this is impressive."

"I'm happy you're impressed," he winked. "Unfortunately, as I said, my company did not do the renovations, but I have to admit, the design was well executed. "Let's check out the balcony and the pool."

Walking straightway outside to the balcony, she had to get a closer look. The backdrop for the pool and terrace were the brilliant shimmering lights that reflected the city of Athens after dark, and a perfect view of the Parthenon lit in the distance.

"Would you like to go for a swim? It might relax you after the long flight. Change into your swimsuit, and I'll get the champagne."

"Well, maybe, that's an intriguing offer," Daniella smiled.

"Sweetheart, the luggage was taken to the primary suite. It's the first door on the right once you enter the hallway."

Entering the suite, she was not disappointed. Its décor mirrored the living area. Gold silk curtains draped the tall door at the back of the room, which opened outside onto the balcony and pool. A huge baroque four-poster bed sat against the white textured walls in the middle of the room. Walking over, she felt compelled to touch the white gauze curtains that draped the four-posters of the bed. Taking in the overwhelming luxury of the space, she almost forgot her reason for walking in. However, glancing at the suitcases sitting on the luggage rack, she remembered. Hurriedly, she changed into her black two-piece halter bikini. Deciding to pull her long blond curls upward in the back using a gold comb to secure it, she was ready to meet John outside by the pool. However, before Daniella left the bedroom, she felt somewhat exposed and decided to tie a white lace sarong around her waist.

Walking out to the patio, she found John already in the pool, enjoying a glass of champagne.

"Sweetheart, that's sexy," he winked seductively.

Getting out of the pool, he walked up to meet her. Giving her a quick, passionate kiss, he untied the lace wrap letting it fall.

"I don't think you need that." We are going for a swim, right?" he teased.

Handing her a glass of champagne, he took her hand, helping her into the warm water.

"Let's just sit here for the moment and enjoy our drinks," he suggested leading her down to the next step.

"John, this is breathtaking, but I'm beginning to feel a little guilty about running off and leaving the girls again."

She felt herself becoming somewhat emotional. Finding it hard to hold her feelings inside, she unleashed her worries and concerns.

"John, I love you. Honestly, I do. Probably more than you know," she continued trying to contain her emotions. "But your world is entirely foreign to me. What may seem normal to you, I sometimes find hard to believe. I appreciate the fact that you wanted to take me on this unforgettable trip as a way of thanking me for not holding up the sale of the Sea Oates. It was truly a sweet gesture. Just look around, this place is amazing, but Ava says our relationship will never work. She believes we come from two different worlds, and merging the two would be impossible. You're used to traveling the world at a moment's notice. I'm not. This is all new to me, and sometimes it feels weird. All I know for sure is that I've fallen in love with you." Trying not to look at him, she wiped her eyes with the back of her hand, hoping to keep a myriad of tears from flowing down her cheeks.

"Sweetheart, honestly, I wouldn't even be here right now, in this pool, in Athens, if it weren't for you. Look at me. I love you," he winked, gently wiping her moist face with his hand. Furthermore, when did our relationship become a three-some? I don't give a damn what Ava thinks. The last time I checked, it was just the two of us. I think you're just tired from the flight. It was long and exhausting. I've ordered dinner. Why don't we eat and call it a night? I love you. Nothing else matters. You trust me, right?"

"Yes. Explicitly."

"That's my girl, no more crying. Babe, for heaven's sake, you're in Athens tonight. Let's go inside. I'll have them put a rush on dinner."

Grabbing two towels, he wrapped her warmly in one towel and tied the other around his waist. Then, scooping her up in his arms, he carried her inside.

"Put this on, and I'll meet you in the living room," he suggested handing her a soft, luxurious robe.

When she walked out, the room was glowing with lit candles. Hearing a knock at the door, John answered immediately.

"Room service," the young man answered, pushing a cart into the room. After generously tipping the room service attendant, he was on his way.

"Whatever you've ordered smells delicious."

"I hope you like it. I ordered while you were changing clothes earlier. It's a few of my favorite things. Lobster, Mediterranean style, with no claws, grape leaves stuffed with rice and onions, zucchini seasoned with oil and lemon, and my favorite sweet bread. The bread has a glaze of honey and contains nuts and slivers of lemon peel."

"Oh, these foods are very familiar to me. Dimitri loved them," Daniella remarked as the tops were removed from the dishes exposing the delicacies inside.

"Sorry. I forgot about Dimitri. I'm sure he loved these as much as I do," John said perceptively, pouring her a glass of wine.

Leisurely eating by candlelight and consuming two glasses of red wine seemed to ease her worries and concerns. However, she was tiring quickly. John smiled as he caught Daniella rubbing her eyes.

"You look exhausted. Let's go to bed."

Picking her up, he lovingly carried her into the bedroom. Putting her under the warm covers, it appeared she had fallen asleep. Quickly kissing her goodnight, he smiled. He was captivated by her and her honesty. Daniella was totally different than anyone he had ever cared about before. She didn't fit the mold of the young girls he had dated. He was a billionaire playboy who usually stayed out late his first night in Athens. He would have hit all his regular haunts and drank until the wee hours of the morning. But, instead, it was still early, and he was in bed with a beautiful woman who was out for the night. Just watching her breath, little did she know the effect she was having on him. Snuggling next to her warm body, he was surprisingly content for the evening.

As the morning sun peeped in through the curtains, it bathed the room in a soft radiance. Waking up first, John rolled over and began kissing Daniella awake. It was their second day in Greece, and he couldn't wait to get the day started. However, it seemed sleeping beauty had other ideas. She returned his kisses with passion, and it was easy to see they were not going anywhere for the moment. Holding her in his arms, nothing else mattered. Even the Greek islands could wait. Loving Daniella was easy. It felt natural, as if they'd been together for a lifetime.

Finally, looking over at the clock, he panicked.

"Sweetheart, it's almost 11:00 a.m. We have a yacht waiting for our arrival, and we're over an hour late. I need to make a few phone calls. How fast can you get your things together and get dressed?"

"Well, I didn't exactly unpack last night, only my swimsuit. So it shouldn't take that long."

"Great. I'll call room service and order coffee and pastries. Then, we can eat on our way out. The limo will be here in about thirty minutes."

After making all the necessary phone calls, getting their luggage together, and enjoying a quick cup of coffee, they were finally ready to leave.

The limo wound its way through tiny, narrow, hairpin turns leading to the harbor. Arriving at the docks, Daniella couldn't fathom the number of huge yachts moored at the marina.

"Geez, is everyone in Athens rich? Look at the size of those yachts," Daniella stated, amazed by the sheer number of vessels moored in the inlet.

"Not everyone, but I can't think of a better place on earth to have a decent size yacht. After all, there's no better way to explore the Greek islands than from the privacy of one of these stunning boats."

The chauffeur carried their luggage down the weather-beaten wooden dock, stopping next to a luxurious yacht.

"She's called the Athena, and she's over two hundred feet in length. What do you think of her?"

"Oh, my gosh, John, the yacht is incredible. It looks like a floating palace."

"Well, I'm glad you like her, considering the fact she'll be accommodating us for the next week. She's equivalent to a five-star hotel and has four levels. We'll even have a private movie theater. But, I can't imagine taking the time to watch a movie when you're onboard such luxury in the Mediterranean Sea surrounded by the Greek islands. Oh, one last thing, she's all ours. I asked for a reduced crew of nine to be available. Are you ready to go aboard?" John winked.

"Are you kidding?" Daniella felt like Cinderella going to the ball. Once again, the degree of luxury was overwhelming. "Babe, this is truly unbelievable," she smiled, taking John's hand.

The crew and the Captain were standing in dress attire, waiting to greet them as they boarded the vessel.

"Welcome aboard, Mr. McDermott. I'm Christos, the Captain of the Athena. First, allow me to introduce my crew, Giorgos, my first mate, engineer and deckhands, Kostas, Adian, and Alex, our beautiful young stewardess, Antheia, Elissa, and Khloe. Last but not least, our chefs, world-renowned Nikolaos and Aris.

Daniella smiled as she greeted everyone. However, her mind was a dizzy blur wondering how she would ever remember their names.

"Elissa will give you a guided tour of the Athena and take you to your private stateroom. I hope everything meets with your satisfaction. If not, please let one of my staff know immediately. We'll be underway in the next few minutes. Santorini is our first stop, and you'll be tendered ashore once we drop anchor. Again, welcome aboard," Christos smiled. "Enjoy your stay."

Daniella grasped John's hand as they followed Elissa on a tour of the yacht and finally below to their private quarters. Entering the stateroom, it was elegant. A curved wall of windows completely encircled the front end of the stateroom. It allowed the magnificent views of the Mediterranean and adjoining islands to be enjoyed in comfort and privacy. A heart made of rose petals decorated the top of the white duvet that covered the bed.

"Okay, if there's nothing further, I'll leave you. Please let one of our staff know what time you would prefer to have dinner. Enjoy your time aboard the Athena," Elissa smiled, closing the door behind.

Once she had left, John pulled Daniella down onto the bed.

"So, Sweetheart, what do you think?" he winked.

"John, you never cease to amaze me. Once again, I find it all hard to fathom. You live a life of indulgence."

"Daniella, sometimes I think you forget. This would be nothing, absolutely meaningless without you." Pulling back her long blonde hair, he tenderly kissed the nape of her neck."

"Babe, sometimes I think you forget. I'd still love you as much if we were in a cheap motel," she smiled.

"Oh, that's cute, a motel," he laughed. "Come on. Get real for a second. You know you're impressed and wouldn't truly rather be in a motel," he winked, brushing away the rose petals as he playfully pulled her down to the bed. "We have the rest of the day to swim and soak up the sun," he smiled playfully. "But, first, I need to remind you how much I love you," he teased, brushing aside the remaining petals as he turned back the duvet.

"John, pinch me. It all seems unreal," she laughed.

"Sweetheart, you and your reality checks. I think I can take that one step further," he winked, playfully kissing her.

Later, after exploring the yacht, they decided to relax in the hot tub on the starboard deck, enjoying a glass of wine.

"I think you're going to fall in love with Santorini. I asked Captain Christos to drop anchor offshore for the evening. We'll get an early start in the morning. How does that sound?"

"Wonderful. I've only seen photos of Santorini in books. It looked unbelievable. Dimitri always said he was going to take me one day, but I guess that day never came," Daniella explained with a look of sadness.

"Well, I'm sorry you never got the chance, but I'm excited to be the one to show you the astonishing island of Santorini and its postcard views. Sweetheart, please don't let sadness creep into our time together. You told me how much you wanted to see Dimitri's native country. Maybe, this is his way of showing you. Stranger things have happened. Here's a toast to Dimitri and Greece," John said, raising his glass.

After enjoying an incredible dinner under the stars and relaxing with several glasses of Moet & Chandon Dom Perignon Brut, it seemed Daniella was getting a little tipsy.

"John, I'm not sure I can stand up. The champagne was phenomenal, but I probably shouldn't have had a third glass," she laughed.

Noticing her predicament, John smiled.

"Not a problem. I'll carry you."

Scooping her into his arms, she appeared angelic as her blonde hair shimmered in the moonlight. Daniella was stunning in her black sequined halter dress. Catching a hint of her perfume, it was hypnotic. But, unfortunately, she was out the minute he picked her up. Not even the cool breeze wafting in from the ocean revitalized her. Taking her below to their stateroom, he removed her heels, and gently trying not to wake her, he slipped her under the warm covers of the duvet. It was evident she was out for the night. Easing into bed next to her, they were on their way to Santorini.

Early the following day, John woke first from the sheer excitement of the day ahead. Pulling open all the shades, it revealed a breathtaking view of the whitewashed village of Santorini. Set against the sapphire blue waters of the Aegean Sea and the caldera, it was paradise at its best. They were moored just off the shore of Fira, the picturesque capital. Santorini was the most popular tourist destination in Greece. For a brief moment, his thoughts turned to Dimitri and how unfortunate it was that he never had the opportunity to bring Daniella. However, looking over at the beautiful woman who slept so peacefully in his bed, he found himself whispering 'thank you' to someone he never knew. Then, quietly, he ordered breakfast to be brought down to their room. He wanted her to awaken to the smell of coffee, breakfast, and the incredible view.

Hearing a quiet knock at the door indicated the arrival of breakfast. The aroma of freshly brewed coffee filled the room. Hopefully, Daniella would awaken refreshed and ready to start the day. Nonetheless, he asked for aspirin, juice, and toast just in case. Not wanting to waste a minute more, he woke sleeping beauty.

"Sweetheart, time to get up," he softly whispered. Pulling back her long blond hair, he once again whispered endearing words encouraging her to wake up. Deciding to pour her a cup of coffee, he was sure this would do the trick. Finally, she slowly opened her eyes as the aroma of coffee began to do its magic. Taking a look around, she sat up, rubbing her eyes.

"John, are we here?" she asked sleepily.

"Well, take a look, and you tell me," he teased.

"Wow. It looks like a painting." Daniella gasped in awe.

"Sweetheart, come over and take a look. I've ordered breakfast."

"Oh, John, this is breathtaking. It's beautiful."

The cobalt waters sparkled like diamonds as it reflected the rays of the early morning sun. It provided a magnificent backdrop for the whitewashed village adorned with blue-tiled roofs that sat high on the caldera's rim.

"Let's eat, and afterward, we'll get dressed. Pack your swimsuit," John suggested.

Hurriedly eating breakfast, they were like two kids waiting to be let out to play. Daniella decided to wear a long white strapless dress over her swimsuit with sandals. However, John felt more comfortable in a pair of tan shorts, a blue polo shirt, and sandals. They were finally ready to be tendered over for an unforgettable day of shopping, dining, and afterward relaxing on the beach.

Arriving, they decided to take the railway up to the top. Daniella revolted at the idea of riding donkeys or attempting the numerous steps. Reaching their destination, they strolled along the narrow cobblestone streets of Fira. In contrast to the whitewashed village, the views of the cobalt waters below were spectacular. However, they were at a loss as to what they should do first. Santorini offered boutique shops, trendy restaurants, and lively bars. After passing nearby shops, Daniella was determined to purchase lace items. John sought out incredible viewpoints along the jagged cliffs and encouraged Daniella to model as he took photo after photo. Finally deciding to stop at one of the wineries, they sampled Santorini's exceptional wines. The volcanic soils and unique process in which the Assyrtiko grapes are grown made stopping at the local wineries an absolute must.

Finally, after spending a few hours on the beach, they found a perfect place to eat. It was a vibrant whitewashed open-air café, sitting so close to the rim of the caldera that you felt like you were suspended in mid-air above the cliff. The distant vistas revealed unforgettable scenery as the sunset cast brilliant hues of pink and orange over the contrasting vivid cobalt waters of the Aegean Sea. It was breathtaking and provided the perfect ambiance. They dined on some of the local cuisines, including Santorini cherry tomatoes and tomato-keftedes, deep-fried patties of Santorini tomatoes, and onions, along with braised lamb and stuffed grape leaves. Topping off their delectable meal with shots of ouzo, John thought it would be the perfect strong drink that would provide Daniella with the nerves of steel required to ride the donkeys back down the steep, winding, narrow streets. However, he again underestimated her low tolerance for such a strong drink. He had to arrange transportation back to the yacht. Nevertheless, it was the ending to a perfect day, one that would leave Daniella forever reliving their experience.

Back onboard the Athena, John managed with one of the deckhands to get Daniella below to the stateroom. The aroma of freshly brewed coffee once again worked its magic to revive her.

"John, thanks for such a fantastic day. It was unbelievable. Sorry, I wasn't brave enough for a ride on the donkeys. It was a bit terrifying to watch. Maybe next time."

"We'll save that for our next visit. Tomorrow, I will show you the island of Mykonos. Isn't that where Dimitri was born?"

"Yes. You remembered."

Walking over, Daniella took his hand and pulled him towards the bed.

"Now, who's the frisky one," he winked.

"Let me show you how much I love you," she teased mischievously.

Scooping her into his arms, he carried her towards the bed.

"Sweetheart, I couldn't possibly think of a better way to end a perfect day."

The past twenty-four hours had been near perfection. John was looking forward to showing Daniella the beautiful island of Mykonos. However, fate would soon change their plans.

Chapter Nine

In the early hours of the morning, a soft knock woke John. Thinking whatever the reason, it better be a darn good one to wake him from a peaceful sleep. He felt agitated, grabbing his robe.

"Mr. McDermott, we've just received a communication stating you have an emergency back in the states," Khloe informed him.

"What kind of emergency?" he asked, still half asleep.

"I don't have all the details, but Captain Christos would like to see you immediately. He asked that you come alone to the lounge. He'll explain the nature of the emergency. Oh, he asked if Daniella was asleep, not to wake her. He prefers to explain the recent communication with you."

"Tell him I'll be right there." Closing the door, John quietly dressed, not wanting to disturb Daniella.

Quickly, he made his way up to the lounge.

Noting Captain Christos's worried expression as he walked in seemed reason enough to be alarmed.

"Mr. McDermott, I truly hate to be the bearer of bad news. However, do you know someone by the name of Ava Albright who resides in Destiny Cove, Florida?"

Thinking for a moment, surely he wasn't referring to Ava, Daniella's chef. However, she was the only person in Destiny Cove whom he knew by that name.

"Yes."

"Ava Albright sent an urgent communication via David Stone from your office in Destiny Cove. It appears your son and his friends, along with Daniella's two daughters, are missing?"

"What do you mean by missing?"

"She relayed a message that stated the kids went sailing yesterday and never came back. Ava Albright seems to think they are possibly in trouble. The Coast Guard is already looking for signs of them or their boat. How can I assist you? We have a helipad. I can have a helicopter here within minutes to get you back to Athens."

"Yes. Immediately. But first, I need to make a ship-to-shore connection with my office in Destiny Cove. So I'm not possibly going to wake Mrs. Demos with this news until I officially confirm it."

"I'll make those arrangements straight away. Stand by, and we'll get your call through. Then, if needed, we'll have you picked up by helicopter, leaving as soon as possible."

Unbelievably, it was confirmed after talking with David Stone, his partner on the Sea Oates project. It appeared the kids had not returned from a day of sailing and were possibly in serious trouble offshore.

"Please make arrangements for us to be picked up as soon as possible. Then, I will go below and inform Mrs. Demos of the situation."

Walking back to the stateroom, he didn't cherish the thoughts of waking Daniella to such dreadful news. Without knowing more, he knew she was going to panic. What were the odds that both Jillian and Gracie had gone out with the boys? Matt was a very responsible person. How could he have let anything like this happen? Hopefully, they were all alright, and they had come ashore somewhere other than Destiny Cove. However, that seemed a remote chance.

Walking over to the side of the bed, he held his breath, knowing what was to come.

"Sweetheart, I need you to wake up," he whispered. Then, after repeating himself, with no response from Daniella, he decided to run into the bathroom and warm a towel. Walking out with the towel, he went over to the bed. Gently he pulled her long blonde hair back and softly began wiping her face.

"Daniella, I need you to wake up," he whispered once more.

"Oh, is it morning? Did I oversleep," she asked, barely opening her eyes.

"Sweetheart, I don't even know how to begin. I just received an urgent communication from David Stone. He's the lead project manager in Destiny Cove. It seems Ava contacted him regarding some dreadful news which involves the kids."

Looking perplexed, Daniella was attempting to wake up and at the same time comprehend what John had just said.

"John, what are you saying?" she curiously demanded, sitting up in bed.

"Daniella, it seems the kids went sailing yesterday and didn't return. The Coast Guard is searching for them right now."

"What kids?" she asked in unbelief, not wanting to accept the truth.

"Daniella, Matt took his friends sailing yesterday. I'm so sorry to tell you the girls, Jillian, and Gracie, were with them. No one has heard from them. We're leaving immediately," he explained, putting his arms around her.

"No. I don't believe you. I can't believe you," Daniella screamed. "I lost Dimitri in those waters. I won't lose my girls. Do you hear me?" she yelled furiously, unable to process the tragic news.

"Daniella, I know this is hard. Matt is smart, and he's an excellent yachtsman. I believe they are fine, but we're leaving right now. Sweetheart, I'm so sorry," John whispered reassuringly. As he held her tight in his arms, he knew this was the worst news possible.

"Captain Christos has arranged for us to be picked up by helicopter. It will take us back to Athens, where the jet is on standby. Let me help you get your things together. We're leaving as soon as our transportation arrives."

Boarding the helicopter, it seemed Daniella was in a daze. She refused to accept the tragic news. It was her way of insulating herself against the heartbreaking possibilities. John felt it was probably for the best. They were thousands of miles away, and the thought of her crying the entire flight back to Florida made him feel ill. There was nothing he could do for the next several hours but console her. He had his worries about Matt and the girls.

Finally boarding the private plane, they were on their way back to Destiny Cove.

"Good evening Mr. McDermott. The crew and I were devastated to hear the news. Please, try not to worry. What can I bring you before we're airborne?" Stacie inquired, greeting John and Daniella.

"Thank you. A glass of bourbon and merlot," John suggested, quickly helping Daniella into her seat.

"No, make that two glasses of bourbon," Daniella interjected.

"I'll be right back with those. We should be in the air soon. Stan says the weather looks good tonight. So it should be a smooth flight. Please let me know if you require anything further."

"Thanks, Stacie."

It was only minutes before Stacie returned with their drinks.

"Sweetheart, I know this is not easy. I can't even imagine how you must be feeling, especially after losing Dimitri in those waters," he sympathized, taking her hand. "The thoughts of losing Matt are beyond comprehension. He's my only son."

Immediately downing the bourbon, John asked for another round before the aircraft readied for departure.

"Maybe another drink will help with your nerves," John mentioned getting two blankets from the overhead bend to make them comfortable.

Instantly downing the second drink, Daniella straightaway demanded a third.

"Sweetheart, considering your tolerance for strong drinks, do you think that's a wise decision?"

"John, I don't need your advice. I want another drink. You have no idea what I'm going through right now."

"Alright," John reluctantly agreed, motioning Stacie for another round.

Maybe it was for the best. Perhaps she was right. Unfortunately, they were going to be in the air for hours. He couldn't think of a better way to cope than sleeping the entire flight. It seemed to be working, as Daniella had not even once mentioned her fear of flying as the jet climbed sharply to its cruising altitude.

Watching out the window as the city lights of Athens began to fade in the distance, it was going to be a long, somber flight. It seemed the bourbon was starting to work its magic as Daniella snuggled against his chest. Softly pulling her long blonde hair away from her face, and covering her with the blanket, John for once fully realized the pain of losing someone he loved. Matt had always been the grounding force from which his whole world revolved. He decided against informing Matt's mother, Gail, his former wife, until he knew more. No need to upset her until he had all the facts. The flight back to the states had been quiet. Daniella slept. The day before in Santorini had been fun but exhausting. Perhaps the exhaustion, along with the bourbon, had worked in keeping her asleep and away from her thoughts.

On the other hand, he'd not been able to sleep. Thoughts of losing Matt swirled inside his head. He was the type of son any father would be proud to have. He was accomplished and only had one year remaining until he graduated from Harvard. Wiping tears from his eyes, John was glad Daniella was asleep. He didn't want her to know the turmoil he was enduring. He needed to be strong enough for both of them. Finally, it seemed the dreaded flight was almost over.

"Mr. McDermott, we're only one hundred miles out from the airport. Would you like warm towels and hot coffee," Stacie asked. "Perhaps you would like a snack or something to eat before we land," she added. "We may encounter a little turbulence on our approach into the airport this evening. The storm that caught the kids unexpectantly offshore is still lingering in the area."

"Yes, on the towels and coffee, but I think we'll eat later. Thanks."

"Okay. I'll be right back with those," Stacie smiled.

Deciding to wait until he had the warm towels, he would let Daniella sleep a few minutes longer.

"Here are the towels," Stacie said, handing them to John. "I'll be right back with the coffee."

"Sweetheart, we're just a short way from the airport. You're almost home. You need to wake up," he said, lovingly wiping her face.

"John, I can't do this, I can't," she cried. Rivers of tears cascaded down her face.

"What happened to my confident girl? Sweetheart, you were so stoic as we boarded the flight last night," he reminded her, wiping the tears from her face. "You can do this. We can do this. I'm not leaving you. We'll have the limo take us to your house. I'll make some phone calls, and we'll take it from there. This may have all been a huge mistake. We don't know anything definite. You trust me, right?" he smiled, wiping her face.

"John, I love you. Yes. I trust you," she replied with the hint of a smile.

"That's my girl. I love you too," he winked, handing her a cup of coffee.

As the plane rolled to a stop on the tarmac, it was late in the evening. The weather outside was formidable. It was raining torrents as thunder and lightning rumbled overhead. The limo drove as close to the steps of the aircraft as possible to avoid the heavy deluge.

"Mr. McDermott, the crew, and I will be praying. Please try not to worry. If there's anything we can do, don't hesitate to call," Stacie said before he descended the steps of the aircraft. "I'm sure everything is going to be fine."

"Thanks."

John poured them each another glass of bourbon as they entered the limo for the ride out to the new house.

"Just a little something to keep you calm," John said with a quick kiss.

As the limo approached the house, several cars were in the drive. Most of which Daniella didn't recognize. Walking inside, it was a beehive of activity. Henry was there with several men from the Sheriff's Department. Ava ran over immediately, seeing them walk in.

"Oh, Daniella, I'm so sorry I had to interrupt your trip," Ava cried, wrapping her arms around Daniella. "It's unbelievable."

"Ava, we don't know anything for sure yet. You stop getting her upset. Right now, do you hear me?" Henry demanded.

"Good evening, I'm Brad Griffin with the Sheriff's Department. "The Coast Guard is searching every possible inch of the Gulf of Mexico where they were last known to be, but unfortunately, the weather isn't cooperating."

"What happened? I need to know everything," John demanded.

"Why don't we go over to the sofa and sit down."

"Ava, bring out some coffee," Henry suggested.

Taking Daniella's hand, John led her over to the sofa.

"Ava Albright, your housekeeper, contacted our office yesterday morning. She inquired about filing a missing person report for your daughters, Jillian, and Gracie, along with your son, Matt, and two of his friends. She informed our office the kids had gone sailing the previous day and never returned. We, in turn, contacted the Coast Guard to help with the search. However, the sudden storm and its velocity have tremendously hampered their search and recovery efforts. The search has been temporarily halted until morning. Gale force winds and extremely high waves are reported in the area where we believe the kids might have been. We located the marina where the boat was rented and its owner. He made it quite clear that even though your son was an extremely knowledgeable yachtsman, that particular sailboat, the Sea Spray, would have had a difficult time enduring such rough seas."

"Wasn't Matt given a weather report the morning he rented the boat? My son would never have taken a boat out in those conditions."

"Yes. However, there was no way anyone could have predicted the sudden onslaught of this weather system. The boat was fully equipped with up-to-date communications and emergency weather systems. So we have no way to know why they were caught off guard. Matt stated he planned to take the kids out to Crab Island. There's an old abandoned lighthouse, making it one of the most popular spots for the kids in our area. The best we can conclude is they probably anchored and swam the short distance to the shore. If no one stayed with the boat, which kids often don't without thinking, any incoming warnings regarding the weather would have fallen on deaf ears. Probably by the time they realized a change in the weather, it caught them off guard with a sudden fierceness as they sailed back to Destiny Cove. This is only our best guess, as to what might have happened, without actually hearing from one of them. The Coast Guard helicopters will continue their search and rescue at daylight. Trust me, we are doing everything possible to find them," Brad explained.

"Ava, thank you for making the call. Please bring out coffee for everyone."

"Child, don't worry. They're in God's hands, and he isn't going to let anything happen to those sweet girls or your son and his friends. I'm sure of it," Ava sympathetically assured them.

No amount of kindness or words of encouragement would ever keep her from worrying. So even though she appreciated Ava's reassurance, it meant nothing to her.

"Yeah, Ava's right. You don't worry," Henry interjected. "I'm sure Mr. McDermott's son, Matt, is an experienced sailor. He'll bring them home safe and sound. You just wait and see."

"Well, if there's nothing further I can do here, I've got to get back to the station. Unfortunately, we're short on personnel this evening because of the storm. But, I will be in contact with you. Here's my card. As soon as we receive any news, I'll call you immediately. Oh, one other thing, I need the names and addresses of the two boys with your son. Someone from our department will be contacting their parents this evening."

"I can do that if you'd like," John suggested. "I can make those calls."

"Well, if you'd like to make contact with them, that's fine. However, since this is an official investigation, someone from our department will also be contacting them from the Sheriff's Office later tonight."

Quickly writing down the names of the boys' parents and their addresses," John immediately handed it to Brad as he was leaving.

"Thanks. Someone from our office we'll be in touch with you. Try not to worry."

"Thanks. I want to be kept up to date the moment you have any news. You can reach me here tonight. Daniella, do you mind? I think it would be best if we stayed together. I don't want to leave under these circumstances," John asked.

"I wouldn't have it any other way. I don't want to be alone. Ava, what's the strongest drink you have in the kitchen," Daniella inquired.

"Well, my trusty old bottle of Jack Daniels."

"Bring it out with some glasses," Daniella suggested.

"John, what are we going to do? It's so hard to sit here knowing the kids might be fighting for their lives in this storm. I feel like I need to be doing something, anything to help get my kids back," she cried as tears flowed down her face.

"Sweetheart, I know you are worried. I feel the same way, but honestly, there's nothing we can do at this moment except pray. I have faith everything is going to turn out okay," John reassured her, reaching for a box of Kleenex.

"Yeah, Daniella, John is right. So, you don't worry," Henry remarked, getting up to help Ava return the tray of empty coffee cups to the kitchen.

The night seemed to drag by slowly as everyone stayed awake in the living room, unable to sleep. It seemed Daniella somehow managed to drift off intermittently in an unrestful sleep. John put his arms around her, holding her, and wiping away tears, as she occasionally woke with bouts of crying and loud moans. It was killing him to watch the love of his life have to endure such pain and misery. Yet, considering that his own son's life was in peril, he was barely keeping his emotions in check.

Finally, the first rays of the morning sun were visible through the curtains. Hopefully, the dawn of a new day would bring good news. News that would tell them the kids had somehow managed against all odds to survive miraculously. Hearing the phone ring, John jumped up from the sofa with anticipation running over to answer it. Again, praying hopefully, it was good news.

"Good morning, this is Sheriff Bradly Griffin. I was at your home last night. I'd like to speak with Mr. McDermott."

"This is John McDermott. Is there any news?"

"Yes. That's the reason for my call. The Coast Guard resumed their search at first light this morning. It's truly a miracle, but it seems some of the kids were found clinging to a life raft about fifty miles south of the lighthouse. They are being flown to Methodist Hospital in Destiny Cove. They should be arriving soon."

"Do you have any further details? How many kids? What were their names?"

"I'm sorry. I don't have all the information. We just intercepted the call coming in from the Coast Guard over our dispatch. I'll meet you at the hospital."

"Thanks. We'll be right there."

Hanging up the phone, John knew even though the news seemed fantastic at the moment, knowing that some of the kids might not have made it gave him an uneasy feeling. Waking Daniella, they rushed to the hospital. It would only be a short drive.

Walking in, news reporters crowded the lobby.

"Mr. McDermott over here," Sheriff Griffin shouted, seeing him walk in. "Follow me. We need a quiet place to talk. Please, both of you have a seat," he mentioned closing the door. "I'm sorry. I'm afraid the news isn't as good as we'd hoped. This never gets any easier for me. It's the hardest part of my job. However, I wanted to be the one to tell you before you went upstairs."

"Oh my God, John," Daniella screamed, burying her head into his chest.

"Mrs. Demos, your girls are safe. They were among the group picked up this morning. You'll be able to see them shortly," Sheriff Griffin stated somberly, looking over at John. "Mr. McDermott, I'm so sorry to inform you that your son, Matt, didn't make it. I'm truly sorry. You have my deepest sympathies."

"What makes you say that? How can you possibly know? If some of the kids are still missing, perhaps there is a chance he's still out there," John answered in unbelief. "You are still searching the area, right?"

"John, your son, Matt, is the only one not accounted for at this time. It appears the Sea Spray sustained tremendous damage due to the continued onslaught of waves that broke the mast and later capsized it. One of the young girls, I believe your older daughter, Jillian, said that

Matt went below to get Gracie while the other two boys grabbed the life raft. It seems Gracie panicked and wouldn't leave what she thought was the safety of the cabin. Matt went below to get her, pushing her topside. However, the boys said Matt became trapped inside as another wave washed debris into the cabin blocking his exit. After shoving Gracie out of the cabin and topside, the next wave washed over the boat, capsizing it taking it under with Matt trapped inside. Mr. McDermott, your son, is a hero. Unfortunately, his bravery took his life, saving the young girl. The boys were able to rescue Gracie and get the girls inside the safety of the life raft. You have my sincere sympathy. Is there anything I can do? I'm truly sorry."

"Oh, John, I'm so sorry," Daniella cried.

Sitting in silence, John buried his head in his hands. His loss was inconceivable. He had lost his only son. Saving the life of Gracie was an act of courage that exemplified his son's very existence. He knew that Matt would never have hesitated to save someone, even if it meant putting his life in danger. Consumed with grief, John chose to remain silent. He was determined to keep his emotions private. Then, after a moment, he stoically looked up at Daniella.

"Let's go up and see the girls," he suggested, gently taking her hand.

After ensuring the girls were alright, John called his ex-wife, Gail.

The following week, John flew back to Atlanta along with Daniella, Jillian, Gracie, and his friends from the current project to attend the memorial service for his son. He wanted the services kept private. His parents were both deceased. Except for his ex-wife, Gail, Matt's mother, his other remaining relative, his uncle lived outside the country. It only left Gail to attend the services with Daniella and the girls. His life had forever changed. Never one to show his emotions, the tragedy had scarred him deeply. He was about to do something he had done on only a few rare occasions without thinking of how it might affect Daniella. He loved Daniella, and now more than ever, he wanted to propose to the love of his life. However, before starting a new chapter in his life, he first needed closure. He needed direction for his life, and he knew just the person.

Chapter Ten

A few days after returning from the memorial for his son, John walked into the trailer, which had become his transitional office at the Sea Oates project. He handed his secretary, Sandy, an envelope. Deciding against talking to Daniella in person, John knew she would only beg him not to go or choose to go with him. Even though he loved her more than life, neither of those were an option. He had to do this one thing for himself and alone.

"Would you please make sure Daniella Demos receives this today? It's important."

"Yes. Not a problem. I'll take care of it," Sandy answered nonchalantly, laying it on her desk. However, not knowing the importance of its contents and being extremely busy, she unintentionally shuffled it aside. She later inadvertently tossed it into the trash at the end of the day. As a result, the note would never find its way to Daniella.

"Sweetheart, I love you more than life. I don't expect you to understand my reasons for leaving. Just know this is something I need to do and that I carry you with me in my heart. I want to spend the rest of my life with you, but I need to find closure first. Losing Matt has given me such heartache. I feel I can't move forward with my life until I make peace with the past. So I'm asking you once again to trust me. See you soon." Love John

The following day Daniella walked into the kitchen, finding Ava whipping up another one of her famous chocolate cakes.

"Ava, by any chance did John call?"

"Nope, can't say that he has. Are you expecting a call from him?"

"Well, I just find it odd that I haven't heard from him?"

"Oh, I'm sure he's busy. Building high-rise condominiums must require a horrendous amount of work. Plus, he just lost his only son. So, he probably doesn't feel much like being sociable," Ava commented as she wiped her hands on her apron.

"Well, then I should stop by his office. He probably just needs a break. Why don't you cut a slice of your cake when it gets done. I'll take it down to his office."

"Okay, that sounds good. Give me another hour, and I'll have it ready."

"Thanks, Ava, you're a lifesaver," Daniella said, pouring herself a cup of coffee.

Later that afternoon, Daniella drove down to the construction site. Taking the piece of chocolate cake with her, she walked down to the trailer.

"Hey Sandy, is John here? I know it's almost time to close for the day, but I brought him a slice of Ava's famous chocolate cake."

Sandy was in her early twenties. She had worked for McDermott Corporation, specifically John, for a brief time. She had long, vibrant red hair that fell past her shoulders. It complimented her freckles and green eyes. Walking over to one of the filing cabinets, she was noticeably tall and slim.

"No. He left earlier this morning." Remembering the envelope, she searched her desk. However, it was nowhere to be found. Panicking, she decided not to mention it. If it turned up later, she would call Daniella. But, for the moment, she wouldn't bring it up.

"Did he happen to say where he was going or when he might be back?"

"Not really. However, I overheard one of the guys saying he was going to the airport. Sorry, I can't be of more help," she remarked, covering the fact she had lost the envelope.

"Well, just in case they were wrong, and he comes in, will you please tell him I came by."

"Yes, certainly," Sandy answered, feeling somewhat inept that she had not kept the envelope in a safer place.

"Well, I suppose you might as well enjoy the piece of cake. You do like chocolate cake?" Daniella teased, sitting the cake on her desk.

"Of course, who doesn't? Thank you." Now she felt terrible about losing the envelope. Hopefully, it wasn't as important as John had implied.

Daniella contemplated why John would go to the airport on the drive back. Perhaps it was a spur-of-the-moment business trip. However, even that didn't seem logical to leave without calling. It wasn't until the following morning and later that day that Daniella began to sense something was wrong.

Daniella's curiosity was killing her once again as she walked into the kitchen. It was the one place she could always find Ava.

"Ava, have I missed any phone calls today?"

"Child, for heaven's sake, it seems like every time you walk in here lately, you're asking about phone calls. Have you not heard from him?" Ava inquired.

A million thoughts were running through Ava's mind regarding John McDermott. She was still not a fan, and she had warned Daniella about him from the very beginning. Now it appeared she might have been right all along. They were from two different worlds. How could Daniella not have seen that, she wondered? Things had escalated too fast between them. She knew it. However, she would keep her thoughts to herself, at least for now. Daniella had been through enough lately, and she didn't want to be the cause of more worry.

"Daniella, if he calls, I'll be sure to let you know. So what are your plans for the evening?"

"Well, that's just it, I don't have any plans. I was hoping to hear from John," she frowned.

"Why don't you and the girls take in a movie? I'm sure Gracie and Jillian would love that," Ava suggested.

"Oh, thanks, Ava, but I'm not in the mood. I think I'll go for a short run on the beach. I shouldn't be gone long," Daniella remarked, grabbing her sweater.

"Okay, suit yourself. Oh, I forgot, I promised Henry I would meet him down at the docks later this evening. The Wave Runner is supposed to be coming in tonight loaded with a huge catch of fresh mullet."

"Great. See you later."

Nepal

Unbeknown to Daniella, John arrived in Pokhara, the second-largest city in Nepal.

"Mr. McDermott, we're only an hour out from the airport. Would you like the usual, a warm towel, and hot coffee? Also, you have a connecting flight to Kathmandu. Would you care for something to eat before we land in Pokhara?" Stacie questioned. "I'm sure you remember there are no large airports in Kathmandu," she laughed. "This is as far as we can take you."

"Yes. I remember. This isn't my first trip. I came over when my father passed and before Gail and I were divorced. I'll wait on eating, but please bring the towel and coffee."

"If I might ask, who is it that you came to visit in this part of the world?" Stacie asked rather curiously.

"Jim McDermott, my father's younger brother. He came over several years ago on a spiritual quest and fell in love with the people and the country. So he decided to stay, having never married, and has since worked in a monastery in Kathmandu."

"Where is your friend, Daniella? She's so gorgeous. She didn't come with you?"

"Not this trip. I need time to sort through some things," John smiled.

"Geez. I talk too much. I better get the coffee and towel before we land. Oh, one last thing, I miss Matt. I'm sorry for your loss. I'll never forget all the trips and fun times we had together. He made my job a joy," Stacie commiserated.

"Thanks, Stacie, that's nice to hear. He's a large part of the reason I came."

"I'll be right back with the coffee and towel."

Arriving in Pokhara, John was on his way to Kathmandu, the largest municipality of Nepal. It sat at 4,600 feet and was considered the gateway to the Himalayas. Pokhara's remote location in the early 1970s meant John had to transfer to a much smaller aircraft, a vintage twin-engine Cessna. However, peeling paint, dents, and rust didn't hinder John from throwing his bags on board the questionable plane for the duration of the short ride.

Upon John's arrival, no one was expecting him, and he had no way to contact his uncle. Still, he'd been informed Jim had remained in Kathmandu. Unfortunately, Jim was eccentric and considered the family's black sheep. He felt more at home in Kathmandu than in any place on earth. However, John knew different. He knew that his uncle wasn't as weird as his family believed. Having been born into a wealthy family, no one had ever understood why Jim McDermott didn't want to become a partner in the family law firm.

However, John understood him more than anyone, knowing that he never desired to follow his dad into the family business. His interest had always been in architecture and engineering. John knew what other family members had misunderstood about his uncle was a deep spirituality. Jim had a mysterious way of looking into someone's soul and seeing the real person. The problem with the other family members was that he reminded them they weren't perfect. They considered him a hippie and misfit. It was easy to understand why his uncle had never returned from Kathmandu, especially after connecting with the monks who lived at the Kopan Monastery. Jim felt more comfortable on Freak Street in Kathmandu than at home in New York. However, John had always gone to him for advice, and this time would be no different.

Grabbing his one bag, John had arranged for someone to drive him the twenty minutes to the monastery. Upon his arrival, he inquired about his uncle. Everyone at Kopan knew and loved Jim. However, he was told that he had since relocated to a small house in Kathmandu. After being given the address, John was anxious to get back to the city. Luckily enough, his driver had remained parked, deep in conversation with a friend. Running over, he gave the address to the driver, hoping he could find Jim.

After what seemed like an eternity, John reached the tiny dilapidated house. Its crumbling outward appearance at first glance made it appear unsafe. Walking up to the entrance, he was nervous. Lightly knocking on the small primitive door, it opened.

"Wow, John McDermott. What a surprise. What brings you to the other side of the world?" Jim teased. Jim was all that remained of the McDermotts except himself, now that Matt was gone. He was in good health for a man of sixty, physically fit, tall and lean. His jet black hair and deep blue eyes clearly reflected the McDermott genes. His rugged, handsome features were still very noticeable even after the hard years living in Kathmandu. "Come in, let me take a good look at you. Geez, I think the last time I saw you was six years ago, just before you and Gail were divorced. How's that handsome son of yours?" Jim inquired, stopping to give him a huge hug.

It seemed Jim had already picked up on his reason for coming. He'd not expected to answer questions about Matt so suddenly.

"Well, that's my reason for coming to Kathmandu. I just lost Matt."

"Oh, my God, John, not Matt. He was so young, and he had his whole life ahead of him. Please, come in and sit down. Give me your bag. What happened?" Jim gasped. Words failed him as he rubbed his furrowed brow.

"Matt rented a sailboat to take a few of his friends sailing. But, sadly, they were caught in a vicious storm. Do you mind if I don't go into further details right now? I'm just so glad to be here, to see you. I felt I had to come. You've always been the one person in the family

I could count on when I needed someone to talk to and for guidance in my life."

"John, ever since your father died, I've felt as if you were my son. We'll talk later about Matt. I'm just thankful you came all this way. I had no way to know. Why don't I make us a pot of coffee? I hope you like it strong. That's the way we drink it over here," Jim smiled, walking over to the small cramped space that had been allocated to serve as a kitchen. It was simplistic, containing a one-burner stove, a minuscule, archaic icebox, and two open shelves.

"Thank you. Coffee sounds good, and the stronger, the better." John got up to stretch his legs, following Jim to the coffee pot.

"How's the hotel business these days?"

"Well, I'm in the Florida Panhandle building condominiums. I was approached by the mayor and city council members of Destiny Cove while I was working in Atlanta. It seems the Panhandle has become a tourist mecca these days, and the small adjoining towns have been caught off guard without adequate properties for people to either rent or purchase. So it's a gold mine for building condos at this time."

"Wow. Who didn't see that one coming?" Jim mentioned pouring them each a cup of coffee. "Let's go back into the living room. Please, overlook my accommodations. It's meager at best. After working at the monastery, I guess it's easy to see that housing or belongings are not the focus of my life these days."

"Jim, you've never had to explain your reasoning for moving halfway around the world to Kathmandu or your lifestyle to me, and you certainly don't have to start now. I get it. After losing Matt, becoming wealthy has lost some of its appeal. Trust me. Money doesn't insulate you against heartache," John frowned.

"That may be, but I don't think it's the money. I think it's more like what people do with their money. It's not the money that's evil," Jim explained. "We have very little of it over here, yet we live comfortably. Not lavishly, but we get by. It's amazing how easy and simplified life becomes when your focus changes from the material aspect of life. But, of course, my lifestyle isn't for everyone. John, I'm sad as well as shocked that we lost Matt. I can't imagine your grief. I loved that kid. He was studying at Harvard, right?"

"Yes. I've taken two weeks' leave from my current project. I felt like I was going insane, and I needed to be alone. I didn't want to burden those closest to me. Losing Dad hurt, but nothing like losing Matt. I was so proud of that boy. I'll always be proud of him."

"You just mentioned you didn't want to hurt those closest to you. Is there someone special in your life?"

"You always could read me like a book. But, yes, I suppose you could say I have someone special in my life, her name is Daniella Demos. I purchased the hotel she owned. It was facing substantial repairs. Plus, I needed the waterfront lot. She's different than any of the other women I've dated," John explained, taking a sip of coffee.

"How so? What makes her different?"

"Well, for starters, I took her to New York on a spur-of-the-moment getaway. You know I'm famous for spontaneity. We had no luggage and no extra clothing. I offered her one of my more expensive store cards to purchase whatever she felt she needed, and she completely turned me down. Now what girl would ever turn down a chance to burn through one of my credit cards?" John questioned. "Especially in New York."

"Yes. John, you're right. I've met a few of the girls you've dated before, and they definitely would've had no trouble burning through one store card and not shy about asking for others. They would have gone through your cards like candy," Jim laughed. "So what else makes her different?"

"Well, I guess you could say there's the fact that my being a billionaire seems completely irrelevant to her. The three days we were in New York, she didn't want to visit any local tourist attractions, and it was her first time being in the city. Can you believe she craved alone time, just the two of us? She referred to it as shutting out the world. What kind of woman does that?"

"A woman that's in love, that's who. So I guess my next question to you would be this. Do you love her?"

"I'm madly in love with her. Can you even imagine at my age, after a divorce, dating hundreds of socialites, jet-setters, women who wanted nothing more than my money, that I would have found her? She's the only reason I'm still breathing after losing Matt."

"The way I see it, you've been blessed. Some of us spend our entire life and never meet that special someone. I'm a pretty good judge of character and have an uncanny ability to see into the heart of another person. From what you've told me, I don't know what you're waiting for?"

"I'm relieved you feel that way. I've always sought and respected your advice. That's why I came. I desperately need your help dealing with the loss of Matt," John explained somberly.

"Not a problem, tomorrow I want you to tell me about Matt. Tonight it's late, and I think we should both get some rest," Jim suggested handing John a threadbare mat that was rolled up and a musky pillow. "As I said before, you know my existence is meager. So, I suppose as always when you come over, you're fated to a way of life that's far from that of a billionaire," Jim smiled, giving John another hug. "I love you, and I'm so glad you came. I'll see you in the morning."

"You do know it's not the five-star accommodations that bring me to Kathmandu. It's spending time with you," John smiled.

As John fell asleep on his first night in Kathmandu, it seemed the stress and worries of the day escaped him. But, amazingly, the hardness of the floor brought him the best night of rest he'd had since losing Matt.

Waking early the next morning to the smell of coffee, John couldn't have felt more relaxed. It seemed the remoteness of Kathmandu and its people, especially Jim, brought him into a realm of enlightenment. Today, he would face the most challenging reason for his visit.

However, many hours earlier, Daniella had awakened on the other side of the world to another day of questions about John's sudden disappearance. A day in which Ava, without thought or hesitation, would unleash her opinions regarding John McDermott.

Destiny Cove....the previous day

"Geez, Ava, I love the smell of bacon in the morning. Did you make pancakes?" Daniella asked, pouring herself a cup of coffee.

"Yes. I thought the girls would enjoy pancakes and bacon this morning. So what are your plans for today?"

"Nothing special. I thought I would drive back over to the construction site to see if anyone has heard from John."

"Daniella, sit down. I need to talk to you about that man. I mean, John McDermott. Listen, you know that I love you, but it's just like I figured all along, you're going to get hurt by him. Child, you don't have anything in common with him. He's a billionaire. You're a widow with two young girls. Can't you see what's happening? How plain does he have to make it for you to understand? He's already moved on. I'm sure of it. You've allowed yourself to be used by him. How could you? You took off to New York, forgot about your girls, and stayed the entire weekend with that egotistical man. I don't remember seeing a ring on your finger. That's what I call a mighty loose woman. But, Daniella, you're not one of those women. You've always been a respectable young woman who adores her children and puts them first. I bet Dimitri is turning over in his grave," Ava ranted continuously.

"Child, he tried to take advantage of you with that damn low ball offer on the Sea Oates. He practically tried to steal it from you, and then he came to his senses and upped his offer. Daniella, powerful men like John McDermott are not a match for you. He was going to wind up with your property one way or the other. Trust me, developers like him have unsavory ways of getting what they want when they want. Daniella, have you heard anything I'm saying? I'm just speechless. That man makes me so angry," Ava raged.

"Well, it doesn't seem like you're speechless now. Ava, I love you. However, you are not my mother, and I think you need to keep your vicious, rude remarks to yourself. You don't know him the way I do, and I don't expect you to understand. But, I do expect you to respect my decisions. As far as my girls, I'm a great mother. Just ask them, I dare you," Daniella continued. "Listen, I didn't walk in here this morning to get into a fight with you. I appreciate everything you do for me, Jillian, and Gracie. I've just come through a difficult time. I almost lost my girls. The worst part is that John did lose Matt. I don't know how he's dealing with it. When I lost Dimitri, I was devastated. At least, I had Jillian and Gracie to keep me going. John has no one except me, and now the worst part is that I don't even know where he is or what's going on with him. Losing a child is the worst thing that could ever happen to a parent. I don't rightly know what to say as far as my morals. I guess what comes to mind is, 'those without sin cast the first stone.' Ava, you have no idea what it feels like to fall in love after all these years. I would marry him tomorrow if he asked. I'm that sure of my feelings for him. You should be happy for John and me. So what if he's a billionaire. I'm not in love with him for his money," she paused. "I'm pouring myself another cup of coffee and going for a walk on the beach. Oh, one last thing. Don't you dare involve my girls with your crazy notions about John. Trust me. If you do, they'll let me know. If they ask, tell them I went for an early morning jog on the beach," Daniella furiously vented as she slammed the door.

She had to get out of the house. Ava was driving her mad with her repeated preconceived notions. She didn't know John or the fact he was loving, generous, and compassionate. Ava knew nothing of the man she had so easily fallen in love with. However, as Daniella ran along the beach trying to release some of the anger she held inside against Ava, she was becoming concerned. Why did he leave and not tell her? It didn't make sense. Pulling her hair away from her eyes, she stopped for a moment. Had she done anything that might have upset him? However, not one thing came to mind. As she paused to gaze at the shimmering vibrant colors of the turquoise water, thoughts of their day on the island of Santorini flooded her mind. Where was he? She had to go back to his office and see if anyone had heard anything. She was beginning to go crazy, but she could never let Ava suspect her true feelings. It was time to go back to the construction site. Running back to the house, she would change clothes and devise a logical excuse for dropping by his office.

Walking into the kitchen from the patio, it seemed everyone had already finished with breakfast. The kitchen was clean, and no one was there. Great, she would just leave a note to let the girls know she had gone into town. Hurrying into her bedroom, she changed into a bright flowery sundress and grabbed a pair of sandals from her closet. There was still no sign of the girls or Ava as she made her way through the living room and out the front door. Just as well, she didn't relish running into Ava at the moment.

Grabbing her keys, it didn't take long to drive over to the project site. As she arrived, it was a beehive of activity. Large cranes were now on-site, waiting for the start of construction on the first two floors. It seemed to be a massive undertaking. Surely, John would have needed to be there. Why was he missing? She was about to start asking questions, but first, she needed a reason to be there. After a few minutes of thought, it was simple. She was making too much of this. She had every right to be there. Everyone knew that she and John were together at this point. She would simply say that she tried to reach him regarding a time change for Gracie's soccer game.

Walking into the trailer, it seemed every eye was on her.

"Hey, Sandy, has anyone heard from John today?"

"No. Can I help you with something?"

"Well, I came by to let John know that Gracie's soccer game was going to start an hour later this evening. If he comes in, would you please let him know?"

"Certainly. I'll make a note of it. If he comes in, I'll let him know you came by."

Sandy was now more than ever beginning to feel guilty about losing the envelope. She could sense the worry in Daniella, and she almost thought of letting her know that John had left the envelope, but this would admit her guilt and the fact she had lost it. This fact alone could jeopardize her job as his secretary, and she wasn't ready to risk it. Undoubtedly, the envelope held nothing important. It was trivial at best, she assumed.

"Daniella, have a great morning. It was nice to see you again. Don't worry. I'll let him know if he comes in. Oh, be careful. There's a lot of heavy construction equipment out there. The back lot has turned into a zoo of machinery," Sandy smiled.

Geez, where did John get her? Surely, there were more girls in the secretarial gene pool to choose from other than Sandy. Daniella quickly felt she could be more proficient and keep a cleaner desk. Walking out the door, she bumped into one of the men who worked for John.

"Hey Craig, you wouldn't happen to know where John disappeared to, would you?" Daniella smiled.

Craig was John's assistant foreman on the project. Even though he knew the whereabouts of John at this very moment, he'd been sworn to secrecy. Craig had been with McDermott Corporation for years. He was not about to go against the wishes of his best friend. Now in his mid-forties, he'd never married. However, his tall physique and rugged good looks from spending too much time in the sun seemed befitting for a man his age. It complemented his salt and pepper hair.

"No. Why is he lost?" Craig chuckled. "Sorry, one of my tasteless jokes. Doll, I haven't seen or heard from him in the past two days. However, if I run into him, I'll let him know you were asking for him."

Hopefully, his crude attempt at humor would lighten her spirits. He only had to look at her to see how distraught she was. Personally, he thought John should have told her. Hopefully, he would soon return and mend the hurt he saw in her eyes.

"Thanks, Craig. It was nice to see you."

Driving back home, Daniella was feeling lonely. Surely, not a single vile word that Ava spewed out of her mouth this morning could be true. What was happening? Why were these strange doubts seeping into her head? Nobody knew John better than she did, but not hearing from him wasn't making things easy. After their weekend in New York and especially the trip to Greece, she was confident his feelings towards her were real. If not, he was a darn good actor, and Ava wouldn't have to take care of him. She would kill him herself or make a reasonable attempt.

Driving into the house's driveway, memories of John flooded her mind. His charm and charisma were intoxicating. Their first impromptu trip to New York had been unforgettable and left her breathless. Yet, she had to remain strong. Hopefully, it was just a weird test of their relationship, and she didn't intend to fail.

Walking in, she could smell Ava's famous meatloaf in the oven. Maybe she'd been too hard on her. She knew that even though they had exchanged some rather heated words, the bottom line was that she adored Ava. She had been for a long time the mother figure in her life. Even though she'd not exactly made her aware of the fact, maybe it was time. Even though they seemed cruel, the words coming out of Ava's mouth earlier this morning could easily have been spoken by her mother if she were alive. Sometimes you hurt those closest to you by saying mean, vile things. She knew that Ava loved her and was only looking out for her best interest. It would be hard ever replacing her. She doted on the girls. It was time to put the morning behind them. It seemed Ava had already taken the first step by cooking her favorite dish. The aroma coming from the oven was mouthwatering.

"Hey, Ava, I love you," Daniella smiled, putting her arms tightly around her broad waist. "I'm sorry. It was just words. Thank you for the meatloaf. It smells heavenly," she paused, taking in the delectable scent. "Ava, so that you know, you've always been the mother figure in my life. I wouldn't want it any other way. I love you."

"Oh, child, I love you too. I'm sorry. I've got to learn to watch that tongue of mine. Sometimes, it gets me in trouble," Ava answered with tears in her eyes. "I don't know what would become of me if I didn't have you and the girls."

"Well, you don't worry about that. It will never happen. You're not going anywhere. Where would I find a cook like you?" Daniella teased. "I love you. I think I'm going to take a short nap before dinner."

Walking away, Daniella stopped for a moment. "Any calls?"

"No, child. Not a single one."

Kathmandu

"I've cooked oatmeal this morning. Hope you like it," Jim grinned, walking out from the kitchen. "There's more sugar in the bowl next to the stove if you like it sweeter. Sorry, I'm short on grocery items. However, I have most of the basics, and being as it's just me most of the time, it doesn't take much to get by. But tonight, we'll go down to my favorite little café off Freak Street. How does that sound?" Jim suggested stirring his oatmeal.

"That sounds wonderful. It's on me," John added. "Make a list of things you need, and I'll get them. You might as well enjoy yourself while I'm here. You can go back to doing your thing after I leave," John lovingly teased.

"There's much you could learn from our way of life."

"I'm sure. There's no doubt about that. However, there are a few creature comforts I don't think I could give up," John answered, taking a sip of coffee.

"John, I hope it's not too early in the morning, but I want to know more regarding Matt's accident on the boat. What happened? I laid awake half the night just thinking about Matt. I loved that boy. He was so bright and handsome, just like me."

"Well, that's debatable. What do you want to know?"

"Everything, if you don't mind? I know it just happened, and I'm not trying to sadden you at the beginning of this beautiful day. I just need to know," Jim questioned, pouring them another cup of coffee.

"Well, as I said yesterday, it happened when they decided to go sailing. You do remember Matt was an excellent yachtsman?"

"Yes. How could I ever forget? Dad always let him steer the boat and help out when we sailed. He loved the water."

"Well, Matt rented a sailboat, the Sea Spray, from a local marina in Destiny Cove. He invited Daniella's two daughters, Jillian and Gracie, along with his college buddies, Brad and Dexter. The boys were all proficient yachtsmen. So, there were five on the Sea Spray, a beautiful vessel. She was almost thirty-nine feet. I later talked with the owner, and he showed me several photos of the boat. The day was gorgeous from all of the accounts I've heard. Apparently, Matt sailed out to Crab Island. There's an abandoned lighthouse on the island. It's a popular spot for the young people who live in Destiny Cove. However, they were the only ones on the island this particular day. The sheriff said they probably dropped anchor close to the shore and swam over to the island. I'm not sure how deep the water is in that area. I guess no one was on board the boat to hear alerts for sudden inclement weather systems in their vicinity. I guess the kids were having so much fun, and they hadn't noticed how ugly the weather conditions were getting until it was too late. Finally, realizing they needed to start back, they were caught in the middle of a pretty vicious storm. The local sheriff said the waves were enormous. The first wave broke the mast, and the next overturned the boat. However, the worst of it was that Gracie, the younger girl, got scared and panicked. She thought she was safer inside the boat. So she went below just before the boat capsized. Brad and Dexter grabbed the life raft and put Jillian inside. Matt went below to get Gracie." Becoming too emotional to continue, John paused to wipe his eyes. "Give me just a moment. This is so hard to relive," he paused, wiping his eyes with the back of his hand. "Well, you know Matt. You know the brave son I raised. I'm sure he thought nothing of the dangers to himself by going back inside the cabin to rescue Gracie. Then, it seems another huge wave hit them just as Matt lifted Gracie from below. She was pushed upward to safety just before the force of the wave pushed Matt deeper inside the cabin. Debris blocked his exit sealing his fate. Unfortunately, there was no way he could get out before the boat capsized. The next wave took the boat under suddenly with my precious boy trapped inside," John explained, pausing once more to wipe his moist face. "Oh, Jim, that's why I came all this way. I needed to talk with you. You're the only one in our entire family who understands me. I need you to help me understand how I'm supposed to keep living without Matt. It's the hardest thing I've ever had to endure, and it's killing me. I honestly feel like giving up on life," John continued. "I thought when I lost Dad, it was hard, but this is truly much harder."

Walking over, Jim put his arm around John.

"John, I'm so sorry. Matt was such a brilliant young man, and as I mentioned before, he had his whole life ahead of him. It's so hard to believe he's been taken from us. I feel the hurt and pain in your voice. If I had only known, I would have been at the memorial," Jim replied sympathetically, trying to absorb the horrible news. I'm so glad you came over to see me. I loved Matt. Everyone loved Matt. John, there is one thing I want you to know, you raised an incredible son, and nothing could have ever stopped him from saving Gracie," Jim explained as he walked over to light a candle. "You came halfway around the world to hear my thoughts. We believe our spiritual realms incorporate more than death. Death to us is just transcending to a higher plane. John, Matt is not gone, only the fact you can't see or touch him. He's right here with us now in this room. I know you believe in God. We do, too, just in a different form. I'm not trying to change your beliefs. I just want you to know that life has a greater purpose. The Bible says, 'that no greater love has he than one who lays down his life for another.' I know everyone in our family always considered me strange. Maybe, I deserved that title," Jim reflected, scratching his head. "I'm not sure. I just know since I've been in Kathmandu, studied, and lived with the monks, I've truly learned the real meaning of happiness and contentment for the first time in my life. People so easily get caught up in the trappings of life. By that, I mean material things. Look around, what do you see? Not much, right. It's freeing not to burden yourself, your soul with things. Things that you never take out of this life but seem so overly important. I can't say enough how glad I am that you chose me to help you bear this burden. I feel honored to be your uncle, even though I feel like you're my son. Please take these next few days or weeks and let me show you Kathmandu again and reintroduce you to the monks at Kopan. There is so much to be learned here. I love you, and I want you to be able to return home with no worries. I also want you to know the young woman you described to me yesterday, I believe you called her Daniella. She is going to be an important part of your life. I see you together for a lifetime. John, her spirit is much like what we've discussed. You commented that she said the fact you're a billionaire was irrelevant to her. John, you are blessed to have found her. It is rare to find anyone who doesn't value material things. I've had to come halfway around the world to learn the truth of that statement. Regrettably, I don't claim to have all the answers to your questions. However, I do know that having someone new in your life at this time is not coincidental. She will be your strength if you let her.

I feel comforted to know that she will be waiting for you. I'm here in Kathmandu. I haven't lived in the states for many years. Let her give you comfort and love. That's why she has come into your life at this time. Have I helped at all this morning?" Jim questioned.

"Immensely, that's why I came all this way and, of course, to visit with you. We haven't been together in years, too long. Now, let me buy you a few material things. By that, I mean groceries. You do eat, right," John laughed.

"Great. Your smile has returned. Kathmandu will be good for you too, just like it was for me. Just wait, you'll see. Okay, I'll give you a small list of food items if that makes you happy." Looking through his paltry cabinet, Jim was right. He could definitely use some groceries.

John stayed in Kathmandu for seven days. He not only met the monks who lived at the Kopan Monastery, but he also worked alongside Jim each day, laying bricks and mixing cement to house over a hundred children in a new orphanage. It was cathartic. Sore muscles and aching, tired feet soon replaced the hurt and anger he held inside. His trip to Nepal and the priceless time he'd spent with Jim had been indisputably the best way to cope with Matt's loss. He was finally at peace with the sudden loss of his son and ready to move on with his life.

Cutting short his trip, he was anxious to get back. Jim had been right on so many things, one of which was Daniella. He'd never been more certain of anything in his entire life. He had found his soul mate, and he couldn't wait to get back and start their life together.

Saying goodbye to Jim wasn't easy. He owed him such a debt of gratitude. There was no way he could ever repay him. However, as they said their goodbyes at the door, he'd thought of the perfect way.

"Jim, you've taught me many things. You're right. Money isn't evil. It's what you do with it," John smiled, handing him a check for a million dollars. "Thanks for everything. Oh, I'm sure you'll know exactly how to use it. Perhaps, you can finish the orphanage," he suggested. "Maybe, you could invest in a little real estate around here. I think your dwelling could use a little work," John smiled.

John was at last on his way back to Daniella.

Ascending the steps to his private jet in Pokhara, he was going home.

"Welcome aboard, Mr. McDermott. How was your stay?" Stacie smiled.

"Perfect."

Destiny Cove

After seven days of not hearing from John, Daniella felt hopelessly lost. She had finally started to entertain thoughts that Ava was possibly right. Sleepless nights had made her completely miserable. She felt as if she was going insane. Without John, nothing seemed to work. Not only was she miserable, but she was also making the girls and Ava unhappy. Most days found her relentlessly jogging on the beach. It was the only distraction that appeared to work. It seemed her life had spiraled downward so quickly that turning to alcohol was beginning to look like a great alternative. How could one's life go from globetrotting around the world with someone you adored to complete devastation. She had gone almost every day to the project site to inquire about John. It seemed no one knew anything, or if they did, they were undoubtedly keeping quiet. She vowed not to show up again. She wouldn't give his secretary the impression she was desperate, even though she would have been right to think so.

"Ava, I'm going down to the beach. I feel like a brisk run is just what I need to get the day going. If the girls ask, please let them know that I shouldn't be gone long. Then, quickly pulling her hair into a ponytail, she ran out the door.

"Okay, child, whatever helps. I'll let them know," Ava mentioned putting a pan of biscuits in the oven.

Daniella had only been gone for a short while when Ava heard the doorbell. Quickly wiping her hands on her blue polka dot apron, she hurried into the living room to answer the door.

"Oh, my God, if it isn't the devil himself," Ava gasped.

"Thanks, Ava. It's nice to see you too," John smiled. "Is Daniella home?"

"Do you have any idea what you've done to that poor girl? She went for a jog down on the beach. She's been jogging so much since you've been gone that I'm sure there's a deep groove along that shore. She's lost so much weight from all this crazy running twice a day that not even my good cooking can stay on her bones, and it ain't exactly like she needs to lose any weight. That child is skin and bones. I suspect you'll find her down on the beach. Oh, hell, come on in. You can go out through the kitchen," Ava fumed. "One more thing, with all your money, did you forget how to use a telephone? One call, just one call would sure have made my life a lot easier, not to mention hers," Ava continued yelling as she followed John into the kitchen.

"Thanks, Ava. I appreciate the warm welcome," John grimaced, hurrying through the kitchen and towards the back door.

He was within moments of finally seeing Daniella. Running down the beach, it didn't take him long to catch up to her.

"Daniella, Daniella, slow down. Wait up," John yelled.

Suddenly, surprised at hearing his voice, Daniella stopped dead in her tracks. Then, turning around, she smiled.

"John, where did you come from, or I should ask where have you been?" she questioned, removing her sunglasses as she stared up at him.

"Didn't you get my note? The one I left in the envelope with Sandy down at the office. I told her to make sure you received it."

"No. Sandy never mentioned an envelope, and, believe me, she had several opportunities to let me know. I was at your office almost every day inquiring about you."

"Sweetheart, I'm so sorry. Can we go somewhere and talk?" he questioned, taking her hand.

"Oh, Sweetheart, is it? John, how do you expect me to feel when you disappear like that, and I never receive one single phone call?"

"I expect you to feel like this," he winked. Then, pulling Daniella into his arms, he kissed her with such intensity even the seagulls flying overhead blushed.

Helplessly, she fell into his embrace, feeling her legs go weak. It appeared his passionate kiss had dissipated the hostilities and resentment she felt.

"Geez, Babe, did you miss me?" he smiled, holding her in his arms.

"John, that's not fair. I'm supposed to be mad at you, and then you kiss me like that."

"Daniella, I never meant to leave you without at least writing a note. But, it seems, for whatever reason, you never got it. I went to Kathmandu." Reaching for her hand, they slowly began walking back towards the house.

"Kathmandu, seriously, John, that's not funny."

"No. I really went to Kathmandu. My Uncle Jim has been living there for over fifteen years. I've always been close to him. Daniella, you have to know that losing Matt turned my world upside down. Honestly, I didn't feel like living anymore. Seriously, it had nothing to do with you. I've made other trips to Kathmandu in the past, for instance, when I lost my dad. I'm not sure how much you know about Nepal, their culture, or their monasteries, but it's a very spiritual environment. Jim has adopted their way of life, and he's always given me guidance in the past when my life started to unravel. I went to Kathmandu just before I divorced Gail. I had to know that I was making the right decision. Sweetheart, I need you to understand," he explained, kissing Daniella on the cheek.

"Did you get the answers you were looking for?"

"Yes, as a matter of fact, I did. One day when we have more time, I'll tell you everything. Getting back to the moment, Ava sure gave me a nice greeting when she opened the door. She implied that I was the devil. Can you believe it? She actually referred to me as the devil," John reiterated with a scowl.

Hearing that, Daniella burst into laughter. She found it genuinely hilarious. It was only seconds before they were both laughing hysterically out of control.

"Wow. I needed that. You know Ava's all bark and no bite, right?"

"Well, if you had heard the viciousness in her rant, I don't know how anyone could be so sure. I think she hates me," John smirked.

"Please, stop," Daniella laughed. "Ava doesn't hate you. She simply has never gotten to know you. She says a lot of things, but I'm not sure she means any of it. Just words," Daniella explained.

"She told me you were jogging like a fanatic every day, and she was sure you'd probably left a rut along the shore. Really, Babe?" John winked. "So that's how you relieved stress," he teased.

"Well," Daniella paused, looking down at her athletic wear. "I guess that's where you found me, isn't it?" she smiled demurely, somewhat embarrassed by the fact.

"Okay. I'm back. I can think of a better way to reduce stress," he winked, stopping once again to kiss her madly.

"John, we're on a public beach. Control yourself," Daniella smiled.

"I love you. I'm not bothered by other people. Life is too short, and I plan to live fully in the moment. Life isn't a dress rehearsal."

"Wow. You seem different. Maybe Kathmandu did enlighten you. I love you too."

"Why don't you change, and I'll take you out to dinner."

"Sounds good. Maybe I have lost a little weight."

Walking back inside the house, John feared Ava like most people fear pit bulls. However, Daniella assured him she was harmless.

Before arriving at the Whale's Tail for dinner, John had one stop to make.

"Daniella, I need to stop by the office for a moment. Hope you don't mind."

"No. But you're not getting away from me. I'm keeping my eye on you. No sneaking off again."

"Don't worry. I thought we already covered that, remember?" John smiled, giving her another quick kiss on her cheek.

Walking inside the trailer, he went over to Sandy's desk. Instantly, she looked up, surprised to see him.

"Hello John, I didn't know you were back." she paused.

"Sandy, clean out your desk. You're fired," John stated without hesitation. "I've arranged for your replacement. She starts tomorrow."

"John, I'm sorry. It must have gotten shuffled under some paperwork on my desk and accidentally thrown out," she reluctantly recanted.

"That's not why I'm firing you. It's the fact Daniella came by the office almost every day enquiring about me and not once did you ever bother to tell her about the envelope. Inexcusable, I want you out immediately."

"Sorry. I just needed to take care of a little business," John winked, looking over at Daniella. "Let's go," he added.

"Oh, John, I never meant for you to fire her," Daniella mentioned as they walked over to the car.

"Sweetheart, I don't put up with incompetence on my staff. She's a smart girl. I'm sure she knew it was coming. Now let's eat," he smiled, opening her car door.

Over dinner at the Whale's Tail, John explained his seven days in Kathmandu in further detail. Daniella appeared totally fascinated, and she especially loved the fact that Jim had said such endearing things about her. Hopefully, one day, she would get to meet him.

After dining on delicious seafood, which included lobster, and crab cakes, it seemed their evening was coming to an end.

"Daniella, I hate to take you home so early, but I've got a hectic schedule tomorrow. First, I need to meet with Craig and ensure everything was kept on schedule while I was gone. Second, I need this project completed ahead of time if possible. Third, I've got a huge project coming online in Hong Kong in the spring, and time is of the essence," John explained as he opened her car door. "Why don't I pick you up tomorrow after work. We'll get something to eat."

On the drive home, she was reticent. Once again, she felt anxious and emotional reminded that he would be leaving for Hong Kong in the spring. She had just gone through the worst seven days of her life, excluding the loss of Dmitri, and she wasn't prepared to live without him. There was no doubt that she loved him. She simply feared being without him. Staring out the car window, Daniella avoided looking at him. Feeling her eyes moisten, she bit her lip to keep from becoming an emotional wreck.

Entering the driveway, she was glad to be home. John opened her car door, helping her out of the car.

"Daniella, it's so good to be back. I missed you so much," he whispered, pulling her into his arms. Then, gently brushing her long blonde hair behind her ear, he kissed the nape of her neck. "I love you, Sweetheart. I'll see you tomorrow afternoon."

"Thanks for dinner. I love you too," Daniella answered, unlocking her door.

Later, getting into bed, sleep would not come easy. Her mind kept repeating the fact he would be leaving for Hong Kong in the spring. Finally, completely exhausted, sleep began to invade her petite body. She would see him tomorrow.

Chapter Eleven

The next afternoon, Daniella heard the doorbell as she walked out of the kitchen. Running into the living room, she hurried over to answer it. She was anxious to see John.

"You look stunning," he winked, giving her a quick kiss. "Are you ready to go?"

"Yes," she smiled, closing the door.

He took her hand and led her out to the car, opening her door.

"Sweetheart, I hope you don't mind if I mix a little business with pleasure this evening. I need to check on one of our projects before it gets dark. I am still trying to play catch up at work. It seems like the seven days I spent in Kathmandu put me further behind than I had expected.

"Sure, that's fine." What else could she do without knowing what it entailed?

It appeared they were driving towards the edge of town. Finally, turning into the small airport that serviced Destiny Cove, Daniella became apprehensive.

"I guess from the look on your face, I should explain why we're here," he grinned. "I have a helicopter waiting for us. It just happens to be the quickest mode of transportation for us this evening. I have to fly down the coast and check the status of one of our latest high-rise projects. We have just enough daylight, and it will not take that long. Do you mind taking a short ride with me this evening?"

"Okay. But I'm not sure about the helicopter. I've never flown in one, and I must admit I'm a little nervous.

"Will it make you feel any safer if I tell you I'll be the one at the controls?"

"John, you fly helicopters? How often do you fly?"

"A lot," he smiled. "Don't you see my corporate logo on the side? As an architect, it makes my life much easier. I can get to my projects a lot faster. It saves time."

Parking the car, he came around to open her door. Grasping her hand, he led her across the tarmac towards the helicopter. A gentle warm breeze swept across the asphalt as they walked over to the waiting aircraft. Opening the door, he helped her inside, reaching across to buckle her seat.

"Are you comfortable?"

"Yes. I suppose," Daniella nervously replied.

"Don't worry. You're safe with me," he teased.

After buckling his seatbelt, he reached over, grasping her hand for a brief moment before taking the controls and contacting the tower.

"Don't worry. It's only a short flight down to Crystal Beach, but I have to ensure my workers have been on top of their game. I can't afford to get behind on this project."

Noticing her uneasiness, he smiled.

"Sweetheart, just sit back and enjoy the ride," he winked. "Don't worry. You're in great hands," he added, handing her a headset.

With that being said, the helicopter soon lifted into the air. Immediately, it banked sharply to the left in the direction of the beach.

Getting over her initial jolt of nerves, she bravely looked down. The view was incredible. John pointed out a school of dolphins. The emerald water sparkled like diamonds as it reflected the rays of the afternoon sun. Following the pristine white shoreline, it only took about fifteen minutes to catch a visual of the twin high-rise towers. It was apparent they were still under construction. John safely landed the helicopter on a helipad located on top of one of the towers.

"See, it wasn't that bad," he smiled, removing his headset. "Are you okay?"

"I guess," Daniella smiled as he unbuckled her seatbelt and removed her headset.

"I'm going to come around and help you out. Just stay put," John instructed. She was wearing heels, and he wasn't taking any chances with the fact she might fall. John walked around to open her door, gently lifting her down.

"It may feel a little breezy, so hold on to my hand. We're walking over to the elevator."

The wind immediately swept her long blonde hair across her face. She was eloquently dressed, with heels and accessories. Grabbing two hard hats, they entered the elevator. After putting on the yellow protective hat, John put the other one on Daniella and quickly fastened it under her chin. For the first time, she felt a bit angry with him. How could he bring her onto a construction site dressed in heels? As the elevator descended, he glanced at her, trying not to laugh.

"I'm sorry," he grinned. "I'm sure you must feel inappropriately dressed. My plans changed suddenly this afternoon after receiving a call from one of my supervisors on this project. I should have called to let you know. Instead, I simply thought you might enjoy the ride."

"Well, to be honest, you should have called. Look at you, you're wearing jeans, and I'm in heels," she frowned.

"Does it help if I mention how cute you look wearing the hard hat," he winked.

"Maybe," she laughed. However, she felt like a fish out of water.

After viewing the ongoing construction on several floors and spending almost an hour at the site, John was finally confident the project would come in on time.

"Okay, I think we're almost done. Let's get back up top. I think I owe you dinner."

The flight back was mesmerizing. The beauty of the sun setting over the sapphire blue water was incredible. Vivid hues of bright orange and pink streaked across the sky. The tranquil waters of the Gulf of Mexico sparkled and shimmered as it reflected the rays of the sun. It reminded Daniella of Santorini.

"The sunset is gorgeous. Does it remind you of somewhere?" Daniella asked.

"Yes. Santorini," John smiled. "Look who's finally relaxed. I thought you would enjoy the ride."

However, after flying past the airport, Daniella was confused and totally unaware of his plans. His car was there, and yet he had flown past.

"Hey, you missed the airport," she yelled.

"You're right," he winked. "You've got sharp eyes," he laughed.

Flying further down the coast, he finally landed on a helipad sitting next to an elaborate beach house. It was on a remote stretch of the beach and glowed brilliantly from within, not to be missed. It was two levels completely encased with glass on the ocean side to reveal the beautiful sparkling emerald waters of the Gulf.

"John, this place is gorgeous. Who owns it?"

"It belongs to one of the guys who work for my corporation. He is overseas on another project, so I got the keys from Craig. It's all ours. What do you think?"

"It's spectacular."

Landing the helicopter safely on the helipad, John was excited to have Daniella alone finally.

Removing his headset, he walked around and unbuckled Daniella's seat belt. Then, taking her hand, he helped her down. Next, he led her over to a wooden walkway that led to the house.

"Geez, this is stunning," Daniella remarked, walking inside the foyer.

Its décor was eloquently modern. The sun brilliantly streamed in through an oversized sliding panel of glass, casting its reflection across the white marble floors. A grand piano set off to one side of the living room, and a circular, white leather sectional grounded the room enclosing a large glass coffee table. The nautical artwork hanging on the walls was lit to enhance its beauty and used stylishly to emphasize the house's theme.

Taking off her shoes, the coolness of the marble floors felt refreshing as she walked into the living room to take a closer look.

"Your employees live like this?" she gasped.

"Not all of them, I certainly don't tell them how to live their lives," he laughed, walking into the kitchen.

"I'll get us a glass of wine. By the way, I am cooking tonight. I hope you don't mind."

"You cook? This is a first. I thought you always ate out or ordered room service?"

"No. Sometimes, unbelievably as it might sound, even I like to cook. How do grilled steaks sound?"

"Great, but ask me after I've tasted one," she laughed.

Walking into the living room, John placed two glasses of wine on the coffee table. Next, he slid back the immense glass doors. It exposed the living room to the beautiful outdoors and allowed a fresh warm breeze to waft inside. Then, handing Daniella a glass of wine, he suggested they take their drinks outside. The property contained a sparkling Olympic-size pool and hot tub, which was incorporated into the tiled patio.

"I think we should go for a swim. What do you think?" John suggested taking a sip of wine. "I had one of the guys drive out earlier. He turned on the pool lights and set the temperature for the hot tub. Also, I asked him to bring everything I would need to grill steaks along with an ample supply of champagne."

"John, you always think of everything? But, I have no extra clothes."

"Sweetheart, when did that ever stop us? Remember our three days in New York, we brought no clothes, but I must say you rocked that dress shirt," he smiled with a wink. "Drink your wine. I'll be right back."

It appeared they were going swimming, as he returned a few minutes later with two luxurious white bathrobes and towels.

"Okay, Babe," he teased, removing his shoes. Afterward, stripping down to his underwear, he was like a kid at play.

"John, I'm in a new dress."

"Well, I think we can fix that," he grinned. Slowly unzipping her dress, he kissed the nape of her neck. Leaving only her underwear, he stood back amazed at how beautiful she looked. Now, you have a swimsuit," he laughed.

"John, I don't think a bra and panties qualify as a swimsuit.

"Well, I don't know about that. Trust me. I've seen swimwear that didn't cover as much," John winked playfully, pulling Daniella into the warm water.

"Wow, doesn't this feel great," he smiled. "I forgot the wine," he laughed. "I'll be right back." Stepping out of the pool, he made a mad dash back inside to the kitchen.

Returning with the wine and glasses, he placed their drinks near the edge of the pool as he stepped back inside the warm water. Then, taking Daniella in his arms, he carried her further into the middle of the pool, kissing her rather mischievously as he removed her remaining undergarments.

"Now, isn't this better?" he smiled wickedly, slipping off his briefs. "Daniella, you've got to let go of your inhibitions. It's just you and me. I don't see anyone else, do you?" he teased. "Haven't you ever been skinny dipping?"

"No, and it certainly seems you have no self-confidence problems," she laughed.

"Sweetheart, remember what I said about living in the moment. Losing Matt has made me a different man. But more than that, I've fallen in love with you."

Pulling her close, he held her securely. Then, playfully, he whirled their bodies around in the water, kissing her passionately. Daniella had never loved him more. He was right. Life was about living in the moment.

Swimming back over to the edge of the pool, he collected their wine glasses. After finishing their drinks, he briefly contemplated his next move. It felt natural to make love to the beautiful girl whose warm body clung so tightly to his. The evening went by in a dizzy romantic blur as the darkness of the night sky revealed millions of twinkling stars.

"John, I don't think I've ever been in a more idyllic setting. You can hear the waves washing ashore," she paused. Staring at the brilliance of the night sky, she was awe-struck. "Wow, look at all the stars. It's like being under a canopy of sparkling diamonds." Feeling her eyes moisten, she wiped her face.

"Geez, sweetheart, beautiful things make you cry," he teased, wiping her eyes. "I think I need to get the grill going. I think I'm losing you too early to the wine," he laughed. "Stay here. I'll get the towels."

After drying off, John and Daniella put on the luxurious white bathrobes. Following him into the kitchen, Daniella watched as John prepared the steaks for the grill. Pulling her wet hair into a ponytail, she decided to help.

"Would you like help with the salad?" she asked, opening the fridge.

"Sure. I think you'll find everything inside."

As Daniella prepared the salad, John skewered an assortment of vegetables to put on the grill next to the steaks. Afterward, he popped the cork on another bottle of wine.

"Would you like to eat outside?" he asked, taking the steaks to the grill.

"Yes. Of course. I couldn't imagine eating inside. The ambiance is perfect. I'll bring out the dinnerware," Daniella answered, searching through cabinets and drawers for silverware. I'll be right out."

After arranging everything on the hot grill, it didn't take John long to cook the steaks and the vegetables. Finally, the table was set. John refilled their wine glasses, deciding to make a toast to their unbelievable evening.

"Here's to a beautiful night under the stars with my gorgeous girl."

At last, they were ready to eat. Sitting next to each other, wearing only white bathrobes, they enjoyed each other's company along with the wine. The evening was perfect.

"Is this the life or what?" John smiled, taking his first bite.

"It's incredible, and the steaks are fabulous. Thank you. It's amazing."

Conversation over dinner became more amusing as Daniella continued to enjoy several glasses of wine. It was apparent she was getting tired and giddy. Finally, it was time to take his gorgeous, sleepy blonde to bed. John hurriedly closed the grill and cleaned the table, ensuring everything was back inside. At this point, Daniella had fallen asleep. He would have to carry her upstairs.

Scooping the love of his life into his arms, he carried her inside and up the impressive marble staircase to the main suite. Removing her robe, he slipped her under the warm duvet. She was out for the night. Running back downstairs, he secured the house alarm and finished the cleanup detail in the kitchen. One glass of bourbon, and he was ready for bed. Almost forgetting, he remembered to throw their wet clothes into the dryer. Ascending the stairs, he stopped for a moment. Looking around, he reflected on their remarkable evening. He smiled. Perhaps, it was time to make a lifetime commitment to the beautiful blonde who rested so peacefully upstairs. Quietly entering the bedroom, he disrobed and slipped into bed. Snuggling against her warm body, he gently kissed her goodnight.

Waking up to the brilliance of the morning sun as it immersed their room, it appeared they had both overslept. Looking over at his watch, it was almost 10:00 a.m. John needed to be at the construction site before 1:00 p.m. He had appointments scheduled with several vendors that couldn't be rescheduled.

"Daniella, I'm sorry to wake you, but it's 10:00 a.m.," he whispered, kissing her awake. "I have appointments this afternoon."

Slowly, she opened her eyes. Turning to face him, she smiled.

"Do we have to go? Can't we just stay in bed all day?" she asked sleepily.

"Sorry. It's a workday for me. How about a raincheck? Maybe we can fly to New York this weekend or San Francisco, you decide. Right now, I need to get downstairs and check on our clothes. I almost forgot to throw them in the dryer last night. I'll make us a cup of coffee and some toast. We have to hurry."

Watching her roll over and close her eyes, he laughed. John knew the feeling, but this wasn't the morning for sleeping late. Maybe the smell of coffee would bring her out of her stupor. Running downstairs, he made coffee and grabbed their clothes from the dryer.

Slowly getting out of bed, she was finally awake. Putting on her robe, she quickly began to make the bed. As she walked over to straighten his side, she paused for a moment, reflecting on their magical evening. Picking up his pillow, she briefly inhaled his scent. "It would be wonderful if their arrangement were permanent?" she thought.

Smelling the robust aroma of coffee, John walked in holding two cups of the hot brew and their clothes.

"I was afraid you might have gone back to sleep."

"I wish. I heard you. I know you have appointments this afternoon."

"Drink this," he smiled, handing her a cup. Here are your clothes."

Sitting on the edge of the bed, they slowly sipped their coffee.

"John, last night was amazing. I wished this house belonged to us," she admitted, slowly looking around.

Realizing the implications of her statement, he felt the same. However, he wasn't quite ready to go there. Instead, he wanted to plan the perfect proposal. Something that she wouldn't expect yet would never forget.

"I think I remember a helicopter sitting on the helipad. Your chariot awaits," John teased. I need to get back to the airport and pick up my car. Are you ready?"

"As ready as can be," she smiled, quickly getting dressed.

Walking downstairs, John reset the alarm.

Taking her hand, he hurriedly pulled her down the weathered walkway towards the helipad. They were soon in the air and on their way back to Destiny Cove. During the duration of the short flight, John lovingly glanced at Daniella. She appeared relaxed and fixated on the scenery below. Arriving back at the local airport, he secured the helicopter and ushered her to his car.

It was only a short drive to Daniella's new home. As he entered her driveway, it was unbelievable how fast the past twenty-four hours had gone. Walking her to the front door, he softly kissed her goodbye. It was time to focus on work. However, on his drive to the construction site, his attention turned elsewhere for the moment. It was time to strategize a proposal. Maybe this weekend would be the perfect opportunity. Perhaps, an unexpected flight to Oahu would be the picture-perfect location. He smiled, knowing that she would soon be a permanent addition to his life even though he lost Matt.

Chapter Twelve

As usual, the following day, Daniella dressed in her typical athletic wear. After pulling her long blonde hair into a ponytail, she planned to continue her early morning jogging sessions along the beach. It was her way of clearing her head and bringing things into focus. The evening with John at the beach house had confirmed more than ever her desire to marry him, and she couldn't see a future, which did not include him. Little did she know his efforts behind the scene to make it official?

Walking out from her bedroom, Daniella detected an irresistible aroma of fried bacon, biscuits hot from the oven, and coffee. Ava was busily preparing breakfast which always included grits and eggs. She smiled, thinking the smell alone was enough to make you gain weight. Daniella decided to enjoy a cup of coffee and chat with Ava before she began her usual morning routine of jogging along the pristine beaches.

"Good morning Ava. You sure know how to make a house smell heavenly. The aromas of your cooking make this house feel like a home, even if it is new. I am so glad I have you. I don't know what I'd do with you," Daniella smiled, pouring herself a cup of coffee.

"Child, you'd probably starve. However, I think Jillian would be an excellent cook. So how was your evening with John?"

"Ava, did you know John can fly helicopters?" Daniella mentioned taking a sip of coffee.

"Can't say that I did, but nothing surprises me about that man," Ava paused, adding more bacon to the hot skillet.

"He flew us out to a beach house owned by one of his employees. It was a mansion by any description of the word. It had white marble floors—even a grand piano and the coolest artwork I have ever seen. However, the neatest thing was the massive glass sliding doors. It felt like the entire living room was sitting outside when you opened them. It allowed the ocean breeze to infiltrate the house, at least on the bottom level. The patio was enormous and surrounded an Olympic-size pool and hot tub," Daniella remarked, sneaking over to grab a piece of fried bacon from the stove. "The place was amazing, and John even cooked dinner for us. I cannot say that he is up to your standards as a cook, but it was certainly delicious. I meant to call you. However, we spent too much time in the pool. Afterward, I helped in the kitchen making our salad. Oh, Ava, it replicated everything I have ever wanted, including John," Daniella excitedly explained.

"Daniella, there you go again, getting stars in your eyes. He is a billionaire. Your first husband simply fished for a living, yet you always seemed happy with Dimitri. Child, don't go confusing happiness with money," Ava sternly warned.

"Oh, Ava, there you go again, finding fault with him. I assure you that is not what attracts me to John. I can't explain it. I think it feels more as if we are best friends. I love his personality, and he's funny in a loving way. I think we complement each other. Geez, I have sat here talking about John, and my coffee has gotten cold. I think I will go for a jog. Make sure to save me some bacon," she teased.

"Child, you don't worry about the bacon. I think it is the least of your worries. Instead, you scare me falling head over heels in love with this man. Like I've said a hundred times, I think you need to slow down."

"Ava, stop right now," Daniella indicated, raising her hand in a loving gesture. "Remember, we called a truce. You promised no more derogatory remarks about John," Daniella reminded her with a smile.

"Okay. Go on with your running or whatever you do on that beach.

Personally, I think you have lost your mind. Your jogging every morning just proves it," Ava insisted, pouring herself another cup of coffee.

"Oh, Ava, I love you and your weird ideas regarding money and happiness. I won't be long," Daniella smiled, closing the kitchen door.

Daniella had only been gone about forty-five minutes when she returned. Walking into the kitchen, she got the scare of her life. Ava was sitting at the kitchen table, gasping for breath and holding her hands tightly over her chest. It appeared she was having difficulty breathing, and she looked white as a ghost.

"Ava, what's wrong?"

"Oh, I'm just having a few chest pains. It's probably just indigestion."

"Ava, you're whiter than a sheet. I'm getting you aspirin and calling for an ambulance," Daniella panicked, quickly reaching for the aspirin bottle and a glass of water.

"No, child, I'll be fine. Just give me a few minutes. It's nothing, I'm sure. Don't worry," Ava, wheezed gasping for breath.

"Ava, take this," Daniella demanded. "Only drink a tiny amount of water, just enough to dissolve the aspirin.

Immediately, Daniella called for an ambulance. Afterward, she screamed for Jillian since Gracie had already left for school.

"Jillian, I need you. Something is wrong with Ava. I just called for an ambulance," Daniella yelled.

Walking in, Jillian was confused.

"Mom, for heaven's sake, what's wrong?" Then she saw Ava slump over in her chair. "Oh, my God, what's happening?" Jillian screamed.

"I'm not sure."

Checking her pulse, it was faint, barely discernible. "My guess would be a heart attack, but I'm not a doctor. The ambulance should be here soon. I will accompany Ava to the hospital if they let me. When it arrives, Jillian, this is important. Here is John's telephone number can you call him and see if he can meet us at the hospital. I am sure they will take her downtown to Methodist Hospital. You can drive to the hospital if you want after making the call. But there's not anything you can do. Either way, I will stay in touch."

Hearing a siren, Daniella knew the ambulance was nearby. She ran into the living room and opened the door just as the ambulance drove into the driveway. Daniella immediately explained that Ava seemed fine earlier as the paramedics rushed in. Then she related that she had gone jogging for about forty-five minutes and returned to find Ava in a ghastly condition. As the paramedics began checking her vital signs, Daniella could tell by the sound of their voices the prognosis did not bode well for Ava. Watching as they began inserting an intubation tube to keep her airways open, Daniella felt overcome with panic.

"We will be transporting her to Methodist Hospital. It's the nearest," the medic stated, strapping Ava to a gurney.

"I want to come with her," Daniella demanded. "I'm her only family."

"Okay. We are ready to go. Stand by until we have her inside, and then you can ride down with us. However, she is unresponsive. She won't even know you are there."

"It doesn't matter. I'm not leaving her."

Watching from the living room, Jillian was devastated as Ava was carried out on a gurney and put inside the ambulance.

"Jillian, I am riding in the ambulance with Ava. Call John, and if you know how to get in touch with Henry, we should let him know. Tell Henry they are taking her to Methodist Hospital."

"Mom, don't worry. You just make sure the doctors take good care of her."

After the ambulance had left the drive, Jillian called John's office. Dialing the number, his new secretary answered.

"Good morning, McDermott Corporation. This is Carrie. How can I help you?"

"Hello, this is Jillian Demos. I'm trying to get in touch with John McDermott. We have a family emergency."

"I'm sorry. He's out of the office right now. Would you like to leave a message?"

"It's urgent. I need to speak with him now."

"I can try to reach him on his radio right now. Do you want to remain on the phone while I try to contact him?"

"Yes. Thank you. Would you please inform John that Ava Albright had a heart attack this morning? The ambulance is taking her to Methodist Hospital. My mom, Daniella Demos, wants to know if he can come to the hospital. Immediately."

It only took a moment before Carrie had John on the radio and relayed the message.

"He's on his way. Is there anything else I can do?"

"No. Thank you."

"I hope she's going to be alright."

"Thank you."

Not having Henry's phone number, Jillian thought the best way to get in touch with him would be to drive down to the docks where Henry was known to hang out.

Back at the hospital, the ambulance had arrived. The paramedics wheeled Ava into the emergency room.

"Are you Ms. Albright's family?" the nurse inquired.

"Yes. She has no living relatives, but she lives with me, and I'm sure I would be considered her next of kin," Daniella explained.

"I need you to fill out these forms for Ms. Albright. The doctor will be out soon. So, please, take these papers and just wait over there," she instructed, pointing to a row of chairs in an adjacent room.

"Thanks," Daniella answered, taking the clipboard. She had hardly gotten her pen out of her purse when she heard someone making inquiries about Ava. Turning around, it was John.

"Oh, my God, Daniella, what's going on?"

"I am not sure, but I suspect it's probably a heart attack. I went jogging this morning, and when I returned, Ava was sitting at the kitchen table looking whiter than a ghost. She was having trouble breathing. So I gave her an aspirin and called an ambulance. But before the medics arrived, she slumped over in her chair and wasn't responsive. Thankfully, she still had a faint pulse and was breathing.

"Sweetheart, I'm sorry," John answered, putting his arm around her. Try not to worry. Hopefully, everything will be fine. As soon as the doctor gives us a diagnosis, and if she's stable, I can have her transported to Atlanta or any hospital that specializes in her condition.

If he determines she's not well enough to transfer, I'll make a few phone calls and have a specialist flown into Methodist. Money isn't an object, do you understand. I'll make sure she's in the best hands possible," he offered sympathetically.

Daniella had hardly finished the paperwork when the doctor came out.

"Are you Daniella Demos?"

"Yes."

"I'm Dr. Kline. I'm afraid it doesn't look good. Ms. Alrbight has suffered a massive heart attack. After my initial tests, I'm afraid there's more than one blockage. We have to get her into surgery immediately. Our thoracic specialist is on his way to the hospital right now. The diagnosis is grim at her age and weight. However, there's always hope. We have a chapel on the next floor. I'll keep you updated on her progress. Also, there's a waiting room upstairs. One of our nurses will be available if you have further questions. I'm truly sorry to give you such devastating news."

"Dr. Kline, I'm John McDermott, a friend of the family. Is there a chance we could have her transferred to a larger hospital?"

"I'm sorry, that would not be an option. Mrs. Albright isn't stable and wouldn't survive the trip. Her only chance is to get her into surgery as soon as possible."

"You mentioned a thoracic specialist coming in to operate. What are his credentials? How many times has he performed this procedure?"

"Mr. McDermott, I understand your concern. Dr. Winesburg is highly qualified. His credentials are impeccable. He graduated from one of the finest medical schools in this part of the country. Regarding the number of times he's performed this procedure, trust me, he's the best we have at Methodist. Listen, I know you're both concerned, but she's in good hands. I'll keep you updated. I am sorry, I need to go. One of our nurses is available if you have more concerns."

"Daniella, do you feel comfortable with his answers. I agree she's probably too sick to transfer to another hospital right now. But, my offer still stands. If you feel we need a better-qualified doctor, I'll not stop until we locate the best. Hopefully, she'll make it through the surgery. Sweetheart, do you understand?"

"Yes. Thanks, John. What would I do without you?" she smiled as tears streamed down her face.

Wiping her moist face, he put his arm around her.

"Why don't we go up to the chapel?"

"Daniella, what happened to Ava?" Henry yelled.

"Hey, Henry."

"Jillian drove down to the docks. I was working on one of the fishing boats that came in this morning. What's going on?"

"Oh, Henry, Ava had a heart attack. They've just taken her into surgery, and the doctor isn't holding out much hope. Dr. Kline thinks she might have more than one blocked artery."

"Oh, hell no, not Ava. We can't lose her. So when did it happen?"

"This morning after I returned from my usual run on the beach. I had just walked in when I discovered Ava sitting at the kitchen table. She was in bad shape, so I immediately gave her an aspirin and called for an ambulance. Unfortunately, Ava became unresponsive not long before it arrived. It all happened so fast. She was fine when I left. We were drinking coffee earlier," Daniella explained. "Henry, John, and I are going up to the chapel. Would you like to join us?"

"No. I haven't been in a church in years. I don't reckon there's no need to start now. You go ahead. I'm going outside to smoke a cigarette. Is there a waiting room around here?"

"Yes. It's up on the next floor. Henry, Dr. Kline said it could take a while. Are you sure you want to wait?"

"Yes, ma'am. I ain't leaving until I know my girl has come through this. She's going to make it. You'll see. Ava is strong. You two go on up to the chapel. I'll join you later in the waiting room after I finish my cigarette."

"Okay, Henry, suit yourself. I'll meet you in the waiting room."

"Mom, I'm so glad I found you," Jillian exclaimed, running up behind her. "How's Ava?" she asked, trying to catch her breath.

"She's just been taken to surgery. It was a heart attack. We won't know anything for a while. John and I are going up to the chapel. Do you want to go?"

"Yes," Jillian answered, looking over at John. "Hey, Mr. McDermott."

"Sweetheart, just call me John, no need for Mr. McDermott."

"Okay," Jillian smiled. "Hey, Henry, why didn't you just ride over with me to the hospital?"

"I need my car. I'm not sure how long I will stay, but I ain't leaving until Ava comes out of surgery. She's a strong woman. She's going to make it. I know it. I'm going outside to have a cigarette. I'll catch you, folks, upstairs," Henry mentioned walking towards the exit doors.

"Girls, are you ready to go upstairs?" John compassionately inquired.

"Yes. Let's go, Sweetheart," Daniella cried, grasping Jillian's hand.

Finding their way to the chapel, John and the girls quietly walked inside. John put his arm around Daniella as they sat down in the front row next to Jillian. Daniella reached for Jillian's hand and began praying.

"Dear God, I know we haven't talked in a while. I need a miracle for Ava. She means the world to my girls and me, but I'm sure you already know. God, she's a humble woman, a good person. She's taken such great care of us, and she's become a part of our family. I don't know what will happen to us if you take her. God, you took Matt. Please, spare Ava. If it's not your will, take her peacefully. Please, don't let her suffer. Please give us strength and comfort."

Tears flowed down Daniella's face as she kept her head bowed, not wanting to look up. Then, finally, cold, stark reality hit her that Ava might never come home again. It was unbearable. Watching her mom become emotional, Jillian covered her face with her hands, crying softly. Trying to give comfort, John stretched out his arms, attempting to hold them both. He now had the responsibility of comforting Daniella and Jillian. He needed tissues, lots of tissues.

"I'll be right back. I'm going to find some Kleenex."

Unbelievably, he didn't have far to go. A box of Kleenex was at the end of the front row across from where they were sitting. It gave him goosebumps as he didn't remember seeing it when he walked in. Walking over, he took the box and pulled several tissues out for Daniella and

Jillian. It seemed as though someone was watching over her from above. Hopefully, Daniella's prayer would be answered, and Ava would recover.

Handing Daniella and Jillian each a tissue, they were still emotional.

"Sweetheart, please don't cry. I know how hard it is for you both. I just lost my son not even a month ago," he reminded her thoughtfully, taking another tissue to wipe her moist face. "Remember the other night. I told you we should always live in the moment. This is another reminder for us to live each day as if it might be our last," he softly whispered. "Girls, I think we should go over to the waiting room. I'm sure Henry's back from his smoke break. Do you both feel like walking over?" he asked, pulling a few more tissues from the box to take with him in case they were needed.

"Oh, John, I can't lose Ava. What would I do? She's been with me since Dimitri died. She's always been there to take care of the girls and me. I can't do this alone. I can't," she repeated as tears streamed down her face.

"Daniella, you and the girls will never be alone. I promise. You trust me, right?" he smiled.

"Geez, John," she smiled, looking up at him with huge streaks of black mascara smeared down her cheeks. "That's the sweetest thing ever. That has always been your comeback phrase for as long as I've known you. I needed to hear you say that. It gives me comfort. I do trust you. Explicitly."

"Sweetheart, you look like a Harlequin Doll," he smiled. "Have you got a mirror in your purse? Your mascara has run down your face. Heck, give me one of those tissues," he asked, trying his best to remove the black smears from her cheeks. It was the funniest thing he'd ever seen. Just like finding the Kleenex, to experience anything remotely amusing at this time seemed like it happened to stop her tears. Wow, he wasn't a very religious man. Still, sitting in the chapel, it appeared extraordinary manifestations were occurring as if they were receiving guidance from someone. Looking up, John whispered, "Thank you, Son."

"Girls, we need to go." Reaching down, he grasped their hands. Finding the waiting room, it appeared Henry had been there for a while.

"Is there any news?" Henry asked, seeing them walk in.

"Nothing so far. We just came from the chapel. Has anyone come in the waiting room?" John asked.

"No, not since I've been here."

"Well, Ava has only been in surgery for about an hour. So we probably have a long wait ahead. Would anyone like something to eat?" John inquired. "I can go down to the cafeteria and get sandwiches and coffee."

"That sounds good. I could use a cup of coffee," Daniella requested.

"Great. Jillian, would you like to go with me to the cafeteria?"

"Sure, why not. Mom, what do you want?"

"Just coffee."

"Henry, are you hungry? Would you like a sandwich?" Jillian smiled.

"No thanks. Just coffee."

"Okay. Two coffees. We'll be right back," John mentioned as he walked towards the door with Jillian.

Walking over to the elevator, Jillian was happy that John had thoughtfully invited her to accompany him to the cafeteria. Entering the elevator, she felt proud to be with him. She took the opportunity to make him aware of her feelings.

"John, I want you to know that I appreciate all the love and kindness you've shown to my mother. It's like she's come alive again. She's in love with you. You do know, right?" Jillian smiled. She was taking a significant risk by informing him of her mother's feelings towards him, but she needed to see his reaction. It would be a great indication of how he truly felt.

Looking over at Jillian, John smiled. "I love your mom more than you know. She never has to worry about anything ever. I promise you and Gracie that I'll always be there for her, but not only her, both of you as well. Can you promise to keep a secret?" he grinned.

"Yes," Jillian smiled.

"You promise not to tell her?" he repeated.

"Yes. You have my promise. What is it?" Jillian inquired.

"I'm going to propose to your mom. I had planned to take her on a surprise getaway to Hawaii this weekend. However, because of Ava's surgery and the seriousness of her condition, I have to postpone our trip for a while, depending upon Ava's outcome. Jillian, I have loved your mom from the first day I met her. After losing Matt, I would cherish the idea of raising two daughters. Do you think you could handle the idea of having me as your Stepfather? Plus, I can't think of a better way to spend the rest of my life than hopefully being surrounded by three beautiful women," John grinned. "It finally gives me a reason to be excited about life again. So what do you think?"

"Oh, John, yes, a thousand times yes," Jillian beamed as her eyes glistened with moisture from happy tears. "Sorry, we're known to be somewhat emotional," she smiled, wiping her eyes with the back of her hand. "You have no idea what this is going to mean to mom, especially after today. I guess you're going to be starting over with three girls. Are you ready for that?"

"Sweetheart, more than you know. However, I am afraid the manufacture of Kleenex is going to make a fortune off me," he laughed. "Come over here. Can I hug you?"

"You better," Jillian laughed, throwing herself into his arms.

"A promise is a promise, not a word of this gets out to your mother. Okay?" he insisted. "Oh, one final thought. Do you think you could watch Gracie for the weekend that I take your mom to Hawaii? I want to surprise her."

"Yes. I'll watch Gracie, and I promise not to say a word."

"I think we better get down to the cafeteria. She's going to worry that something happened."

Walking into the cafeteria, they were both wearing huge smiles on a day that wouldn't ordinarily be pleasant. After purchasing a soda and three coffees, they were finally on their way back up to the waiting room.

Walking in, Daniella was sitting in a chair against the back wall. She looked very distraught, wearing black athletic pants and a sleeveless tank. Henry was pacing the room like a caged tiger.

"Sweetheart, here's your coffee. Henry, here's your cup of coffee. Have you heard any news from the doctor?"

"Not a word. It's sure taking a long time," Henry complained.

"Well, I imagine it's a pretty complicated surgery," John reminded him taking a sip of the hot beverage.

Walking to the back of the room, John took a seat next to Daniella. She appeared extremely worried. If he could only tell her about his plans, he was sure it would make a huge difference. She wouldn't have to worry about being left alone with the girls if Ava didn't make it. However, he needed to keep everything under wraps, or it would spoil the reason for surprising her with a trip to Oahu. Putting his arm around her, he kissed her on the temple.

"Daniella, don't worry. Everything is going to be alright. You look cold. Do you need my jacket?" he asked, standing to remove it.

"Thanks. That would be wonderful," she smiled.

Putting his jacket around her to keep her warm, he whispered in her ear.

"I love you. You have nothing to worry about," John reminded Daniella once again.

Taking his jacket, she pulled it tight around her shoulders. Briefly, she inhaled a faint hint of his cologne. It gave her a sense of security. Then, without thought or hesitation, she couldn't resist inhaling his cologne on the jacket once more. She loved the smell of his fragrance. It was calming. He had no idea how much she needed him at this very moment. Today reminded her of the pain she felt when John's team had demolished the Sea Oates. When she came under duress, her way of dealing with a difficult situation was simply to run away. Just like the night she had run away with John to New York, it had provided her an escape, a release from her anguish.

"Sweetheart, you have a thing for jackets," John teased, noticing her quick sniff. He knew what was going through her mind. The pressure was beginning to get to her. His heart ached for her. He knew the recent pain of losing someone you loved. Yet, he felt helpless as he whispered a prayer.

"God, please bring peace to the love of my life. She's heartbroken, and I fear she can't take much more of the waiting. It's so hard to watch her sitting here in agony. She's so worried about Ava, being left alone with two children, and the direction of her life. Please give her comfort."

Once again, it looked as if he asked, and someone listened. Dr. Kline walked into the waiting room and over to Daniella. He held his breath, not knowing the outcome. However, Daniella immediately stood to meet him. Hopefully, it was good news.

"Mrs. Demos, I am truly sorry to inform you Ms. Albright didn't make it through surgery. Giving news of this kind to families or friends is the most difficult part of my job. Is there anything I can do for you?" Dr. Kline inquired.

"Oh, my God, John, Ava didn't make it," Daniella screamed repeatedly. "She didn't make it. Ava's gone," she cried hysterically.

Jillian came running over to hold her mother.

"Mom, please, don't take this so hard. We're going to get through this. I promise," Jillian cried. "I love you."

"Sweetheart, I'm right here," John reminded her as his eyes moistened. "Daniella, you don't have to scream. I'm standing next to you," he answered just in time to catch her as she collapsed. Then, safely positioning Daniella in a chair, John bent down beside her to ensure she didn't fall.

"I'm sorry that I had to give her such devastating news. It appears she's fainted," Dr. Kline stated after checking vital signs. "I'll have one of the nurses come in with smelling salts and a warm towel. Just make sure she's comfortable. Then, if needed, I can prescribe something to help her cope with the next few days," Dr. Kline recommended hurriedly walking out of the room. Almost instantaneously, a nurse came in pushing a wheelchair.

"I'm Brenda. Dr. Kline sent me to check on Mrs. Demos. Are you a member of the family?" the nurse asked, moving Daniella into the wheelchair.

"Yes. I'm John McDermott."

The nurse checked her blood pressure and vital signs and wiped Daniella's face several times with a warm compress. Within seconds, Daniella responded.

"John, what happened?"

"Sweetheart, you fainted. Do you remember Dr. Kline coming in to talk with you?"

"Yes. Ava didn't make it through surgery, did she?" Daniella cried uncontrollably, visibly shaking.

"No. Sweetheart, I'm so sorry."

"Her vital signs are good. However, her blood pressure is a little elevated, but that's most likely due to stress. So Dr. Kline went ahead and prescribed Mrs. Demos a mild sedative to take home. I'm going to give her a small dose to ensure that she stays calm," the nurse explained, giving Daniella a tiny pill. "She's going to feel very relaxed and will probably fall asleep. I'm going to need you to drive your car to the entrance of the emergency room. I'll push her outside and meet you there in a few minutes. Do you have any questions?"

"Thank you for the medication. I'm sure the next few days are going to be extremely hard on Mrs. Demos," John explained.

"Jillian, stay with your mom for a moment. Henry doesn't look very well. He hasn't moved from his chair. I think all the commotion of hearing Daniella's screams has traumatized him. He may be in shock. I need to check on him."

Finally, noticing John walking towards him, Henry stood up. He was visibly shaken.

"John, I know Ava didn't make it. I overheard what the doctor said."

"Henry, you're right. I'm sorry. Ava didn't make it through the surgery. Listen, why don't you follow us over to Daniella's house. We can deal with this in private. The way a family should. I think that would be best for everyone."

"Alright. I don't want to be alone right now," Henry pleaded with tears in his eyes. "Is Daniella okay?"

"She fainted, but she's going to be fine. The nurse gave her something to help her relax. We're all going downstairs. The nurse will push Daniella's wheelchair outside to the emergency room entrance. I have to get my car. Wait here until we're ready to leave. I need to check on Daniella and Jillian."

"Jillian, sweetheart, how are you holding up? Do you think you can drive your car back to the house?"

"I'm not sure. I don't feel very well," Jillian remarked, appearing somewhat dazed and disoriented as she wiped her forehead. She was in no condition to drive, and neither was Henry. The trauma of the past few minutes was taking a toll on everyone.

"Henry, I might need your help with Jillian," John spoke loudly. "I am afraid she might faint like Daniella. Listen, I think you both should ride back with Daniella and me. I don't think either of you should get behind the wheel of a car. Everyone is dealing with a lot of emotions right now. I'll come back later and retrieve the cars. Right now, let's just get the girls to the house," John suggested.

"Good idea," Henry answered.

The nurse pushed Daniella's wheelchair over to the elevator as John took Jillian's arm to keep her steady on her feet.

It was a somber moment as John, Jillian, and Henry walked out of the hospital to the parking lot. The morning had been unbelievably devastating. Within only a few hours, their lives had once again been rocked by tragedy.

Helping Jillian into the back seat of the car, Henry got in next to her. Taking the short drive over to the emergency room entrance, John could see the nurse waiting outside with Daniella. After getting her situated inside the car, they were finally on their way home.

It was only a short drive back to the house. Arriving, John drove his car as close to the front door as possible. It appeared Jillian was able to walk inside without assistance.

"Henry, can you open the front door?" John asked as he walked around and opened Daniella's car door. Then, lovingly, he picked her up in his arms and carried her inside to the bedroom.

"Jillian, do you feel up to getting your mom a glass of water?"

"Yes. I'll bring it right in."

"Henry, just make yourself comfortable. I'm going to sit with Daniella for a few minutes. I don't want to leave her by herself right now."

As Jillian walked into the kitchen, the smell of fried bacon still lingered in the air bringing tears to her eyes. Walking over to the sink, she stopped. Gracie was still at school. With all the chaotic happenings at the hospital, no one had thought about her. Taking the glass of water, she walked back to her mom's bedroom.

"Oh, John, no one has picked up Gracie from school," Jillian reminded him.

"You're right. If you can stay with your mom, I'll get Gracie. Is she at the high school?"

"Yes."

"I'll leave right now. Don't leave your mom. It shouldn't take long. I'll be right back."

The phone rang as John walked out to the living room.

"Demo's residence," John answered.

"John, this is Craig. How's Daniella's housekeeper? I believe her name was Ava."

"Craig, it's not good. She didn't make it through open-heart surgery. Unfortunately, the heart attack was pretty significant. I'm glad you called. How are things down at the site?"

"John, everything is fine. Don't worry about work. We've already started framing the third floor. Listen, I'm sure you have your hands full. You take care of Daniella and the girls. I've got this covered. Why don't we just stay in touch by phone over the next few days? Please, let me know about Ava's services. I'd like to be there for you and Daniella. If there's anything I can do, please call. I know you're out of range as far as your radio. If anything important comes up that needs your attention, I'll contact you at this number."

"Thanks, Craig. We'll be in touch."

Running out the door, he was on his way to the high school to collect Gracie. It didn't take long to reach the high school. Destiny Cove was a small community. His Maserati drew a lot of attention from the kids as he parked. Locating the front office, he walked inside, approaching the desk.

"I'm John McDermott. I need to pick up Gracie Demos from school. I'm a close friend of the family. Unfortunately, a family member passed away this morning, and Mrs. Demos cannot pick up her daughter. Would you please let Gracie Demos know that I'm here to take her home?"

"Yes. Please wait here? I'll have one of our students run down and get her. You look familiar. Now, I remember. I saw you on the front page of our newspaper. You're that developer who came down here to destroy our beautiful beaches with your high-rise condominiums," she frowned with disgust.

"Please. I'm in a hurry," John politely insisted with a smirk. He knew there was no need to get into an argument with one of the locals this morning. It wasn't the time or the place.

"She'll be right out."

Finally, Gracie walked into the school office with her backpack.

"Mr. McDermott, what are you doing here?"

"Sweetheart, no need to call me, Mr. McDermott. How about John?" he smiled. "Why don't we walk outside, and I'll tell you in the car."

Opening her car door, Gracie quickly got inside.

"Okay, John, what's going on?" she demanded with a serious demeanor.

"Gracie, I don't even know how to tell you. Unfortunately, we lost Ava this morning. She had a massive heart attack."

"Not Ava. She was in the kitchen cooking breakfast this morning before I left for school. She was fine."

"Gracie, I know. I understand, but sometimes life throws curve balls at us that are unexpected. We've all been at the hospital. She had open-heart surgery. Sweetheart, she didn't make it through surgery this morning. The damage was extensive."

"Oh, no," Gracie cried. "How's Mom?"

"She's at home. The doctor gave her a sedative. She didn't take the news very well."

"Does Jillian know?"

"Yes. Jillian was at the hospital, along with Henry. Everyone is taking the news pretty hard. Are you alright?" he asked, reaching inside the glove box for a tissue.

"I guess. I can't believe she's gone. Ava has lived with us since we lost Dad. I've always felt she was my grandmother. I can't imagine how Mom must be feeling?"

It didn't take long to reach the house. Gracie ran straight inside to her mother's bedside.

"Mom, are you okay? John told me about Ava." Noticing her mom's unresponsive condition, Gracie suddenly cried torrents of tears as she sat on the edge of the bed.

Daniella briefly opened her eyes. It seemed the effects of the drug still had her lightly sedated.

John sat down on the bed next to Gracie, holding her in his arms. Gently, he pulled her long auburn hair away from her moist face. Then, softly, he kissed her on her forehead.

"Sweetheart, your mom is going to be fine. She's just sedated. The doctor gave her something to help her relax. But it's made her sleepy. I'm so sorry about Ava, please don't cry. This morning has been extremely hard on everyone. Gracie, she's probably going to be unresponsive for a short time," John explained. "She's pretty much out of it right now. Why don't you check on Truffles? I'll take care of your mom. You don't have to worry. I'm not leaving you girls."

"Okay," Gracie softly answered, wiping her face. It seemed his instincts as a father was working.

"Gracie, I didn't know you were back," Jillian smiled, walking into the bedroom. "Mom didn't take the news very well. Thank God John has been with her the entire time. Mom was the one who found Ava in the kitchen this morning when she came back from her morning run."

"Geez, Jillian, what are we going to do? Ava took care of everything around here after Dad passed, even mom. We both know Mom was never the same after we lost him. It was almost like she needed someone to care for her. Ava was like our grandmother," Gracie cried as tears gently flowed down her face.

"Gracie, I told Jillian earlier at the hospital you girls don't have to worry about a thing," John remarked. Walking over, he once again put his arm around Gracie, wiping her tears with his hand. "Where is a box of tissues when you need one," he smiled.

Gracie had no implications of John's statement at the time. He wasn't sure if she even knew why he was in Destiny Cove or realized how wealthy he was. Surely, she did not know his net worth. It didn't matter. Neither of the girls would ever lack for anything ever again.

"Girls, why don't we go in the living room and let your mom sleep. I'll order pizza. Poor Henry has been sitting out there alone. He's having a hard time dealing with this too. Why don't we check on Henry and show him a little love and compassion?"

"Yes. Gracie, let Mom sleep. It's probably for the best," Jillian agreed.

Walking into the living room, Henry had his head laid back on the sofa. He looked downtrodden and distraught. The girls went over to sit next to him.

"Hey, Henry, are you okay?" Gracie asked, putting her arm around him.

"Oh, hey, Gracie, where did you come from?" he asked, looking up.

"John just picked me up from school. Are you okay?"

"Yeah, I suppose. It's just been a bad day. I'm going to miss her so much. She was the best cook in this neck of the woods. Your mom didn't take the news very well. I didn't reckon she would. She always depended upon Ava. But, you know what, Ava never let her down. Oh, they might have had words occasionally, but that was just Ava's nature. She never meant any of it," Henry mentioned looking over at John.

"Oh, Henry, it's alright. I don't think it's a secret that Ava never liked me," John smiled. "The worst part is, I'll never get the chance to prove her wrong," he frowned.

"John, she knew you were a good man. She was just worried about losing Daniella. She and the girls were her entire world."

"Yes. I always felt that was Ava's reason for being so irritable at times. She was probably worried. However, I have to tell you the last words she spoke to me were pretty vicious. She actually called me the devil. Can you believe it?" he laughed. "Of course, I was probably deserving of it. I went to Kathmandu without letting Daniella know."

"Henry chuckled. Well, she never was one to hold back on her choice of words. Wow, Kathmandu, ain't that on the other side of the world? What the heck were you doing way over there?"

"Yes, Henry, it's a long way from here. You'd be right on that. After I lost Matt, I went to visit my uncle."

"John, I don't rightly know what to say. That was terrible, those kids getting caught up in that storm and all. I'm sorry about your son," Henry frowned.

"Thanks, Henry. I wonder if Ava kept any liquor in the house."

"Are you kidding? That woman always had a bottle stashed somewhere, usually Cognac or Jack Daniels," Henry answered.

"Well, I think I'll go search for it," John smiled on his way to the kitchen. "I almost forgot. I promised the girls to call for pizza delivery. So let me make that phone call."

"Oh, if you find a bottle, bring out two glasses. I'm going to walk outside and have a cigarette. Where did the girls go?" Henry questioned.

"Probably in their rooms, they've dealt with this better than expected. I'm sure it has to be difficult for them. It was unexpected and something which Daniella and the girls could never have been prepared for. The girls grew up with Ava. It's like they've lost their grandmother, and we all know how Daniella depended on Ava, especially after losing Demitri. But, Henry, I don't want you to worry. I love Daniella and the girls. They will never lack anything. I've got them forever, that is if Daniella will have me," John smiled.

"John, the way I see it, Daniella and the girls are blessed to have you in their lives. They're darn lucky despite losing Ava. I hope it all works out. I need a cigarette," Henry mentioned making his way outside.

Hopefully, finding the bottle of Jack Daniels wouldn't be a futile attempt as there was no way he could ask Daniella. She was still under the influence of the medication. Finally, after a short exhaustive look through every cabinet, he found the bottle of Jack Daniels. It must have been a new bottle. It was almost full. Reaching for two glasses, he walked back into the living room. Opening the bottle, John poured himself a small glass to start, tossing it back in one continuous gulp. Then, he poured another.

"Geez, cowboy, slow down. Pour me a drink," Henry grinned, returning from his smoke break.

"Henry, I've been called a lot of things, but never a cowboy. Where did that come from?" John teased, quickly finishing his second drink.

"Don't you watch old westerns? I love them," Henry explained, sitting down on the sofa. "That's how cowboys drink sitting at the bar in a saloon. It just came to my mind as I walked in, watching you quickly toss back those drinks. Pour me a small one to start."

"Sure, you got it. A short one it is," John remarked, pouring Henry's drink. This seems a bit odd. I had you figured for a drinking man."

"Oh, it's early. One bottle won't even get this old fisherman started," Henry laughed, downing it in one swallow.

"Yes. I think you're right, especially under these circumstances. However, I promised to look after the girls and Daniella this evening. It might not be appropriate to get wasted under these circumstances. So, guess this bottle will have to do. But, honestly, I have to tell you after a day like today, I think wasted is the only way to survive. The doctor was right to give Daniella a sedative. After receiving shocking news like that, you don't need to be coherent."

Hearing the doorbell, it indicated the arrival of pizza.

"I'll answer the door and pay for the pizza," John suggested. "Why don't you let the girls know the pizza has arrived."

"Okay," Henry replied, quickly reaching over for the bottle to pour himself another drink. Then, downing it in one gulp, he stood up to get the girls.

"John, John," Daniella's familiar voice repeatedly rang out from the bedroom.

She was waking up. After taking the pizza into the kitchen, he immediately walked down the hall to her bedroom.

"You're awake. How do you feel?" John asked, sitting down on the bed.

"I'm still tired. Did Gracie come in from school?"

"Sweetheart, she's been home for over an hour. I picked her up from school earlier. She came in to see you, but I don't think you were completely coherent. The girls are in the kitchen eating pizza with Henry. It just arrived. Do you feel like eating?"

"No. I have no appetite."

"Let me get you out of your clothes and into a bathrobe. I think you'll feel more comfortable for the evening," John mentioned closing the door. Then, walking over to her closet, he found her robe. Taking the robe over to the bed, John helped her change. Gently untying the lace ribbon that held her ponytail, it allowed her long blonde curls to fall gently upon her shoulders. Doesn't that feel better?" he asked with a kiss. "I should have done that when I brought you home. Do you feel like sitting in the living room? Henry is still here. I think he just feels completely lost this afternoon."

"Sure. But, I feel a little dizzy."

"Do you want me to carry you?"

"No. Maybe just hold my hand to keep me steady. I don't want to fall."

"Don't worry, Sweetheart, I've got you."

John grasped Daniella's hand and led her down the hallway and into the living room. Then, without much difficulty, he sat her on the couch.

"How does a cup of hot coffee sound?"

"I think I could use some caffeine."

"Stay put, don't move. I'll be right back."

Walking into the kitchen, John didn't sense any foreboding vibes or sensations from the tragic event which happened earlier. On the contrary, the kitchen was much alive with the merriment and laughter of the girls enjoying pizza with Henry. Certainly, Henry wasn't feeling any discomfort.

"Hey girls, your mom is awake in the living room. I've been sent for coffee. Can you believe it? I think she's going to make it, after all," John smiled. "I see the coffee maker. Do you girls know where Ava kept the coffee?"

"Yes. It's in this cabinet," Jillian answered, getting up to retrieve it.

"Thanks, Jillian." The strong aroma of coffee brewing felt rejuvenating.

Later that evening, John and Daniella, along with the girls and Henry, sat in the living room, recalling their memories of Ava. It was cathartic and emotionally therapeutic. Sometimes families consisted of people who did not share the same genes. However, they were uniquely tied together through the circumstances of life as they were this evening. After Henry left, John slept on the sofa. He didn't want the girls to see him sleeping with their mom in the same bed until it was official. Hopefully, they could make the arrangement work. However, he wasn't holding out much hope. It wasn't something either of them relished but rather something they felt they should do. It was a toss-up as to how long they could survive without sharing the same bed. However, leaving Daniella alone in her new house without Ava had never been an option for him. The girls were right. She needed someone to replace Ava's nurturing ways. Even though Daniella and Ava were famous for throwing hateful words at each other, it was just that, merely words.

John took over the duties of arranging a memorial service for Ava. It was private and attended only by Daniella, the girls, himself, Henry, and Craig. Now, it was time to try and return their lives to their normal routines. However, his life wouldn't be completely typical at the moment. He had the ongoing Sea Oates project, which he'd neglected for almost a week.

Most importantly, he was planning his proposal in Hawaii with the help and secrecy of the girls. He couldn't wait to put a ring on Daniella's left hand. Then he could lay out the life he saw for the four of them. A life so unimaginable, maybe it was a good thing the girls hadn't entirely comprehended the exact value of his fortune. Otherwise, he was sure they would both start making a long list of things they wanted. Contemplating their future, he smiled. Having survived the loss of Matt and now Ava, they were all going to be okay. He would make sure of it.

Chapter Thirteen

After the memorial, life without Ava became hectic. Everyone was learning to adapt to their new routine. John spent most days at the construction site. He was determined to see his project come in ahead of schedule. Daniella was attempting to cook for the first time in years. Needless to say, they were enduring a lot of scorched pots and dinners burned beyond recognition. However, most nights, John chose to pick something up on his way in from the site. It ensured the girls had something to eat that was, at least, recognizable.

Henry volunteered to stay with the girls while John and Daniella were in Hawaii. However, Henry had one condition. Ava's personal belongings had to be removed from her room as soon as possible. He'd made it quite clear. Jillian worked feverishly boxing up everything that remained while Henry made daily drop-offs at the local Good Will Store. Life was returning to normal as much as was possible for such a short period. Now, it was time for John to implement his proposal. It seemed the perfect opportunity to approach Daniella. Walking in after a long day at the project site, he found Daniella relaxing on the couch with Truffles.

"Sweetheart, I think we should plan a date night. How about this

Friday?" he asked with a kiss. "You've been confined to this house for far too long."

"Well, a nice dinner does sound appealing and romantic," she answered somewhat reluctantly, getting up from the couch with Truffles. "I haven't been out of the house in days, and I'm sure the girls could make do for one evening. Okay, Mr. McDermott, you've got yourself a date."

Finally, Friday arrived and not a moment too soon. John, along with the girls, and Henry, had managed to keep the proposal under wraps. However, John feared that someone might have loose lips with every passing day.

"Daniella, are you ready to go?" John inquired as he came in from work.

"Yes. Give me a second," Daniella called out from the bedroom.

Walking out in a stunning black dress with matching heels and pearls, Daniella looked radiant. Wearing her long blonde hair swept back with an antique pearl comb, it exposed the slender nape of her neck and matching pearl earrings.

"You're gorgeous," John smiled, giving her a quick kiss. "The limo should be arriving any minute."

Jillian discretely packed a suitcase for Daniella without her having been aware. Then, watching as the limo arrived, Jillian took it out to the car while John distracted Daniella. Afterward, she came inside to motion John the coast was clear.

"Sweetheart, the limo has arrived. Let's go." John was eager to get the evening started. Finally, they would, at last, be on their way to Oahu after enjoying dinner at the Whales Tail.

Daniella quickly kissed Jillian and Gracie goodbye at the door and looked forward to an enjoyable evening with John.

Taking Daniella's hand, John walked her outside to the waiting car.

"We finally have a night out to ourselves. I'm looking forward to dinner," she smiled.

"Yes. I think it's long overdue," he winked, knowing the importance of the evening and their weekend.

Entering the limo, John poured them each a glass of champagne.

"Here's to a remarkable evening," he toasted.

Arriving at the Whales Tail, John escorted her inside.

"Good evening, Mr. McDermott. Your table is ready. Julie will take you back," the maitre' d greeted with a smile.

"The aromas smell delectable. I'm starved," Daniella whispered, walking back to their table.

"I'll bet you are," John grinned. "It appears when Ava passed, she took all of her recipes with her. "You girls never took notes?" he asked teasingly.

"You know cooking isn't one of my favorite things. So I don't spend much time in the kitchen."

"I'll say," John laughed. "Sweetheart, trust me, I didn't fall in love with you for your cooking skills."

"Geez. Thanks, John." Daniella blushed, knowing he was right about her lack of culinary abilities.

The waitress seated them at a candlelit table near the back of the restaurant. It offered stunning views of the beach at night. The waves appeared illuminated with an effervescent glow as they washed ashore under the moonlight.

"This is romantic," Daniella smiled as John pulled out her chair.

After enjoying steak and lobster, they leisurely enjoyed a glass of wine while discussing events from their day. Daniella had no possible idea of the weekend ahead as she finished the last morsel of her steak. However, looking down at his watch, John knew they should be leaving. He had the crew on standby at the airport. He'd planned a departure time of 8:00 p.m., and it was already 7:30 p.m.

"Dinner was awesome, but I think we should be going. I have an early day tomorrow. Do you mind if we leave?" John inquired nonchalantly.

"No. I guess not. Thank you for dinner. It was delicious."

"You're more than welcome. I think it saved us from another disaster in the kitchen this evening," John grinned, motioning for the waitress.

After paying for dinner and leaving a generous tip, John escorted

Daniella outside to the waiting limo. Once inside the car, he poured them each a glass of champagne.

"Here's to a wonderful evening," he toasted, handing her a glass of the sparkling beverage.

"Thanks, sweetheart."

As the limo entered the highway, it was only a short distance to the airport. At first, it seemed Daniella hadn't noticed their detour as she laid her head on John's shoulder. Then taking another sip of her drink, she looked up in surprise.

"John, we're driving in the direction of the airport," she mentioned with the hint of a smile.

"Are we? I hadn't noticed," John grinned.

"Why are we at the airport?" She knew John was up to something, but what?

As the limo drove next to the steps of the jet, Daniella felt giddy. Then, looking over at John, she smiled.

"Okay, what's happening? John, the girls, are expecting us. I can't possibly leave right now," Daniella asked in desperation. "I have no clothes. What about the girls? Have you lost your mind? Remember, Ava is no longer at home to take care of them," she panicked.

"Sweetheart, slow down. You've got too many worries trapped inside your sweet little head," he winked, giving her a quick, passionate kiss.

It seemed the kiss began to work its magic as she fell under his spell. She did trust him, and she knew he would never take her away from the girls without someone at home to take care of them.

"Jillian packed your suitcase, and Henry is staying with the girls. Does that help?" he grinned.

"I suppose that answers a few of my questions?" Daniella relaxed somewhat, knowing the girls were not alone and were made aware of their trip. "However, that doesn't answer the question of our destination?"

"No more questions. Let's just board the plane. I'll explain once we're airborne. I asked for an 8:00 p.m. departure time, and we're running a little late.

"John, you're crazy, but I love you," she laughed, giving him a huge hug before they ascended the steps of the jet. Taking a glance back before she entered the cabin, the night sky was clear, exposing thousands of twinkling stars. It would be the perfect night for a flight. Tingles of excitement raced throughout her body. Once again, she was placing her trust in the man she loved. Of course, she had no idea of his plans. However, knowing John, she was sure she wouldn't be disappointed.

"Good evening, Mr. McDermott, welcome aboard," Stacie greeted with a warm smile. "Daniella, it's nice to have you with us this evening."

"Thanks," Daniella remarked, following John on board to their seats.

"What can I bring you before we're airborne?" Stacie inquired.

"Two glasses of champagne would be wonderful," John answered. "We might as well continue the evening with champagne," John stated, looking over at Daniella.

Later as he leaned over to fasten Daniella's seatbelt, John took the opportunity to plant a soft kiss on her cheeks.

Stacie hurriedly returned with the sparkling beverages.

"Captain Bradford is anxious to get the aircraft in the air. It seems we're late for takeoff," she explained, handing them each a glass of the sparkling beverage.

John suggested another toast.

"Sweetheart here's to a magical weekend. I love you," he winked with another quick kiss.

"Thanks. Don't you think this would be the perfect time to fill me in on the details of our magical weekend," Daniella asked rather demurely.

"The past few weeks have been brutal. I know Ava's passing was extremely hard on you. So I thought a weekend escape would be great for us both. Don't you agree?"

"I can't argue with that. However, you're still not giving me any details."

"I'd like to keep our destination a secret, at least for the duration of the flight. I love seeing the look of surprise on your face. Let's just say, I don't think you'll be disappointed," John winked.

"So, is it someplace warm or cold?" Daniella laughed.

"Drink your champagne. I'm not giving any details. Trust me. Let's just say that I think you'll be pleased."

Feeling the aircraft's motion as it moved slowly towards the runway for takeoff, she snuggled against John, clinging to him tightly. It seemed she never lost her fear of takeoffs and landings regardless of how frequently they traveled. Noticing her level of discomfort, he pulled her close, kissing her passionately as the plane began its steep climb into the dark skies. It appeared his kisses never failed to accomplish their goal as a distraction. Daniella's vice-like grip once again began to loosen. Finally, the aircraft leveled, reaching its cruising altitude.

"Now, that wasn't so bad, was it?" he smiled.

It quickly appeared their kisses had become a ritual as the aircraft lifted from the runway.

"Would you like another drink to keep you relaxed?"

"Maybe one more, but I can't promise I'll stay awake." Then, taking a glimpse out her window, she watched the lights below become a distant blur.

"Sweetheart, not a problem," he smiled, planting a quick kiss on her forehead. "I want you to feel relaxed." Reaching above, he grabbed two pillows and blankets. After finishing her second glass, he tucked her in like a sleeping child. Gently wrapping her in the soft, cozy blanket, he kissed her goodnight.

Deciding to get in a few hours of work, he reached for his briefcase that he'd secretly brought on board. Trying to stay ahead of schedule on the completion date of his ongoing project meant there was always something that needed his attention. Tonight, it was once again the unexpected costs of overruns. It would be the perfect time to calculate expenses while Daniella slept peacefully next to him. Motioning for Stacie, it seemed a glass of bourbon was desperately needed to soothe the horrendous figures he now watched, adding up on his calculator.

"I'll be right back your drink," Stacie smiled.

Returning within moments, she handed him his drink. Then, noticing that Daniella appeared to be asleep, Stacie thought it the best time to offer her condolences regarding Ava Albright's passing.

"Mr. McDermott, Craig told me about Ava. I'm sorry to hear that

Daniella's close friend passed a few weeks ago. I'm sure it must have been extremely hard on her and her daughters."

"Thanks, Stacie. It was a tragic loss. The past few weeks have been an adjustment for the girls. But, they've handled it extremely well, considering the unexpected nature of their loss. Thanks for asking. I think I'll have another bourbon. Staring at these figures, I think it'll be needed," he smiled.

"I'll be right back. Oh, I almost forgot," Stacie whispered. "Captain Bradford wanted me to inform you that the weather looks great tonight."

"Thanks. We'll have breakfast on board before we land. Perhaps pancakes and sausage along with coffee," John added.

"Not a problem. Let me get your drink."

Walking up to the galley, Stacie wasn't exactly surprised to see Daniella accompanying John on another flight. Seeing the two of them together so frequently, maybe John had finally found his soul mate. After all, he'd certainly played the field long enough. The men who worked for McDermott Corporation never lacked for arm candy. Working as a flight attendant on one of his corporate jets, she had seen it all. However, she liked Daniella. She seemed a perfect match.

The rest of the flight seemed uneventful as John finished crunching numbers while Daniella slept. Looking at the gorgeous young woman who slumbered so peacefully, John smiled. Finally, he now had someone he loved to share his world with, and he couldn't wait to arrive in Honolulu and get their weekend started. He more than ever wanted to make it official.

After several hours of fixating on numbers, he looked down at his watch. It was time to wake sleeping beauty. They were only about an hour out from the airport in Honolulu.

"Sweetheart, it's time to wake up. I've asked Stacie to serve us breakfast before we arrive."

Wiping the sleep from her eyes, she looked up.

"Well?" Daniella inquired, rubbing her eyes. "Don't you think it's time to let me in on our destination?"

"Maybe," John replied, opening her window shade.

"John, we're over water," Daniella questioned, taking a quick peek out her window.

"Yes. You're right," he winked. "I'm sorry. I hadn't noticed. I've been staring at figures and corporate expenses for the past few hours. I think you'll figure it out soon enough."

Motioning for Stacie, he closed his briefcase. It was time to take his focus off business. He had a spectacular day planned.

"Stacie, please bring us two warm towels. Afterward, we'd like coffee along with breakfast."

"Sure. Would there be anything else?" Stacie inquired.

"Yes. Two mimosas."

"I'll be right back with the mimosas and towels."

It seemed the warm towels brought Daniella out of her slumber.

Returning with their drinks, Stacie handed John and Daniella a glass of champagne with orange juice.

"I'd like to make a toast," John smiled, raising his glass.

"Here's to a remarkable weekend," he winked. "Hopefully, one that you'll never forget," he smiled.

"Sweetheart, every moment I spend with you is unforgettable," Daniella teased, lifting her glass. Little did she know the significance of the next few days.

"John, Stan wanted me to inform you that we're only about thirty minutes out from the airport. Would you care for anything other than breakfast before we arrive?" Stacie inquired.

"Regarding breakfast, I think we'll just have coffee instead."

"John," Daniella remarked excitedly. "There's an island coming into view."

"Let me take a look. Wow, I guess you're right," John smiled, taking a glance.

"John, I think it's Hawaii. Are we spending the weekend in Honolulu?" Daniella shrieked. Trying to curb her enthusiasm, she covered her mouth with her hand as she sat fixated on the approaching topography.

"Well, I guess the ruse is up. Are you excited?"

"Excited isn't the word, more like ecstatic. Geez, Babe, I had no idea. I've always wanted to visit Hawaii."

"Great. I guess this is your lucky weekend," John winked, giving her a quick kiss.

Returning with coffee, Stacie smiled. "Welcome to Oahu. We should be on the ground soon. Enjoy your stay. Honolulu is one of my favorite places."

"Thanks, Stacie," Daniella mentioned looking up from her window.

About thirty minutes later, she sat back in her seat, squeezing John's hand as the plane touched down on the runway.

Arriving at the Honolulu Airport, the plane taxied across the tarmac to the waiting limo.

"Have a great weekend. See you on your return," Stacie commented as they descended the steps of the private plane.

Taking her hand, John led her over to the waiting car. Once inside, Daniella's curiosity seemed to be getting the best of her as she snuggled into his arms.

"Okay. So where are we staying?" she inquired excitedly.

"Well, since you asked, I have a beach house on the north shore. So we're staying overnight in Oahu."

"Why, of course, you do," Daniella smiled. She hadn't expected him to say anything otherwise.

"I think you're going to love it. Tomorrow, I have something special planned. Now, no more questions," John winked, kissing her on the forehead.

Daniella sat glued to the window as the limo made its way downtown through the slow-moving traffic. She was awestruck by the beauty of Honolulu. Towering skyscrapers set against a background of mountains covered with lush green foliage and beaches that exposed the sapphire blue waters of the Pacific took her breath away.

"Wow. This is incredible."

Watching her infatuation with the city skyline, John handed her a glass of chardonnay.

"I think you'll love the drive out to the house. Once we get out of this traffic, it's less than an hour," he smiled, taking a sip of wine.

"John, the pictures at the travel agency didn't give a hint of the true beauty of the island."

"Yes. Remember what I told you. There's no substitution for seeing a destination up close and personal."

"You're right."

Winding their way along the road that led out to the north shore, Daniella became excited with each passing mile. Looking over at John, she smiled. "How lucky could one girl get," Daniella thought. She loved him more than she ever thought was humanly possible. Yet, looking down at her left hand, there was only one thing missing. Leaning in to kiss him, she never imagined love would find her once again after losing Dimitri. Maybe, just maybe, this would be the weekend he would propose. She could only hope. Little did she know that fate would step in granting her wish.

"We're almost there, just around the next curve," John smiled with a wink.

The limo turned into a long narrow gated driveway. Brightly lit palm trees and lavish shrubs lined both sides of the drive as the limo wound its way down to the beach. Finally, it ended at the entrance covered by an eloquent wooden portico. Glowing tiki torches highlighted the tall carved pillars and large oversized glass doors invited you inside.

"John, the house is amazing."

"Oh, you haven't seen the best part," he mentioned helping her out of the limo.

As the chauffeur set their luggage under the portico, Daniella couldn't wait to get inside. After generously tipping the driver, John unlocked the massive glass doors. Then, taking her hand, he led her inside. The expansive living area encased an enormous wall of glass sliding doors which revealed a picturesque vista. Immediately, she was drawn over to take a closer look.

"Oh my," she gasped.

Sliding back the tall glass panels, John led her outside to the patio. The cobalt waters of the Pacific gently rolled ashore only a few feet from where they stood. It was breathtaking. Taking off her shoes, she walked down to the beach. Following close behind her, he walked over. Putting his arm around her, he held her close.

"So, what do you think?" he asked with a quick kiss.

"John, this is spectacular. Could you possibly get any closer to the ocean?" she teased. Daniella was mesmerized, taking in the ambiance of the relaxing waves as they gently rolled ashore while inhaling the fresh salt air that lightly blew in with the ocean breeze.

"Sweetheart, did you design this home?" she had to ask.

"Down to the minutest details," he laughed. "Why don't we go back inside? I'll show you the rest of the house. I had the chef prepare a gourmet meal of prime rib with roasted potatoes for us this evening. Are you hungry?"

"I'm famished. Remember, I slept during most of the flight."

"Great. I think you'll enjoy dinner."

Once they were back inside, John picked up their suitcases.

"Follow me. I'll show you to the main suite."

Walking down a narrow hallway dimly lit with wall sconces, they soon entered the primary bedroom. It was once again massive in scale. Dark Polynesian furniture filled the room. An ornately carved four-poster bed adorned with sheer white netting sat beautifully located at the end of the room. It was positioned to take in the dramatic views of the ocean. Sliding glass doors brought the atmosphere of being outside into the magnificent room. Large terracotta pots containing palms and greenery sat on the tiled floor near the glass doors.

"John, this is stunning." Daniella laughed, jumping on the king-size bed. "You do everything to perfection. This bed feels so luxurious and comfortable," she remarked, rubbing her hand across the top of the elegant duvet. Gently laying back on the bed, she could have easily fallen asleep.

"Well, not everything. I have a lot of help," he added with a grin. "Let's eat. I'll show you to the kitchen. Might as well give you the grand tour."

"Sounds good. If I get any more relaxed, I might fall asleep."

Following the scrumptious aromas coming from the kitchen, it certainly didn't disappoint. It held the most refined culinary equipment money could buy. Dark cherry cabinets lined its perimeter, and a large granite island filled the center of the room. Silver warming trays held prime rib cooked to perfection and garlic roasted potatoes. Reaching for a bottle of wine, John suggested they eat outside on the patio.

Filling their glasses, John made another toast.

"Here's to an unforgettable weekend in Hawaii. But, most importantly, here's to making memories that will last a lifetime."

"Sweetheart, I couldn't ask for more," she toasted silently, hoping it might contain a proposal.

After dining on prime rib and consuming perhaps too many glasses of wine, John suggested a walk along the beach to help work off the rich food and drink. Not bothering to clear the table, John walked over and pulled out her chair. Then, removing her shoes, Daniella stood firmly, grasping his hand.

Putting his arm around her, they slowly made their way down to the shore. The beach remained warm from the day as their feet were buried in the sand. The water appeared to sparkle and dance with each incoming wave as it reflected the vivid rays of the midday sun.

"What do you think of Oahu? Think you could live here?" he whispered lovingly into her ear.

"Are you kidding? This place is incredible. What do you mean by asking if I could live here?" she asked, pausing to stare deeply into his gorgeous blue eyes. "If she could only read his mind," she thought. "What was he thinking?" she wondered.

"Well, you know, in the future, if we were married. I live a nomadic lifestyle. I get projects all over the world, including Oahu. Do you ever see yourself living here, in this house?"

"John, I swear I could live anywhere as long as I'm with you," she answered, nonchalantly biting her bottom lip to keep from becoming emotional. "John, I love you. You should know by now." Burying her head against his chest, she tried to hide the tears welling up in her eyes.

Once again, he desperately needed to hear those three little words. He had to be sure. There could be no room for doubt. Tomorrow, he would get down on one knee and propose. He had never been more certain of anything in his life. Pulling her even closer, he kissed her passionately.

"I love you too," he whispered. "Thank God, I received the bid for the project in Destiny Cove. It led me to you."

"I was alone for a lot of years after I lost Dimitri. I never expected to fall in love again. Then you came into my life, and everything changed. I no longer felt like I was simply drifting through life trying to be a great mother. You taught me how to live again," Daniella explained as tears gently moistened her face.

"No more tears, we're supposed to be having fun," John suggested, gently wiping her moist face with the back of his hand. "What was it that Ava always said you loved doing on the beach to clear your head?"

"Jogging," Daniella laughed.

"Right," he grinned, playfully pulling her by the hand. "There's an old shipwreck just a bit farther down the beach. Are you up to it? It's not that far."

"Wearing this? I can't run in a dress."

"Sure, you can, come on. Today, we sat for hours on the incoming flight, so we need physical activity. Be a good sport," John teased, sprinting down the beach. Quickly looking back for a second, it appeared she was in the game. Watching as Daniella hiked up her dress, she sprinted towards him at a fast pace. "Last one to make it to the wreck has to wash dishes tonight," he yelled.

"Really. I don't wash dishes," she screamed with laughter chasing after him.

Evidently, she was a competitive runner as she rapidly began closing the distance between them. Turning up the heat, he wasn't about to lose the bet. Determined not to lose, he began running faster and harder, giving it his all. Then, sighting the shipwreck in the distance, he only had to keep his stamina to win. Forging ahead, he picked up his pace, hurriedly reaching the wreck just seconds ahead of her. Daniella fell into his sweaty arms. They were both out of breath.

"Okay, you won," she paused, taking a deep breath. "However, the real test is to see who can run back to the house the quickest."

"Sweetheart, I'm out of shape."

"You started this, now man up, and let's finish," Daniella teased.

Not waiting to see if he would join her, she began sprinting back towards the house at a fast clip. He loved her tenacity, but there was no way he could allow her to win. Giving it his all, he chased after her. However, given the distance between them, it appeared she might easily win. Powering through, he finally began closing the gap. Catching up with her just before they reached the house, he grabbed her.

"Okay. I think you've made your point," John laughed, holding Daniella in his arms, not letting her go. Then, playfully, he pulled her into the warm water. As the next wave rolled inwards, it took them under the water. Quickly, lifting her up and out of the clutches of the next wave, he pulled her against his chest, giving her a quick kiss.

"Geez. I'm soaking wet," Daniella laughed.

Scooping her into his arms, he carried her to the house and into a warm shower.

"Stay put. I'm getting towels and bathrobes."

Coming back, he hung the towels on the shower bar, intending to give her some privacy.

"There's body wash and shampoo on the ledge in the shower."

Turning around to leave, he instantly felt her hands grabbing him as she pulled him into the shower.

"Really, Sweetheart, this is what you want," he laughed as the warm water cascaded over them. Then, taking body wash, she lathered his chest with the liquid fragrance.

"Remember those memories we're supposed to be making," she smiled.

"Yes," he grinned, pulling her close.

"Well," she laughed wickedly.

Time stood still as the two of them embraced under the sensual, warm water. A shower meant for one had turned into a romantic rendezvous for two.

Afterward, dressed only in bathrobes, John popped the cork on a bottle of champagne as they sat outside. It appeared the afternoon passed quickly.

"Daniella, this has been an amazing first day," he smiled, pouring them each a fluted glass of bubbly. "I hate to set the alarm, but we have to leave early. My housekeepers are arriving at 9:00 a.m."

"What?" she panicked. "We aren't staying?"

"Not here," he winked.

"John, this place is gorgeous. Are you sure we have to leave?"

"Trust me. You're not going to be disappointed with my plans."

"Alright, if you say so, but I truly love it here," Daniella answered, somewhat intrigued by the fact they were leaving. But, of course, knowing John as well as she did, it would have to be even better, if that was at all possible.

After her third glass of champagne, Daniella began feeling the effects of the alcohol.

"Babe, I feel kind of dizzy."

"Can you stand?"

"I think so."

Attempting to get up from her chair, she almost passed out as John caught her in his arms. Carrying her inside to the primary bedroom, he pulled back the duvet and gently placed her under the warm covers of the bed. Then, pulling her long blonde hair away from her eyes, he leaned over, lovingly kissing her on the forehead.

It had been a long day. After locking up and setting the house alarm, he quietly slipped into bed next to her. Snuggling against the love of his life, it had been a wonderful day. However, tomorrow held the promise of them being together forever.

John woke up first as the morning sun inundated the room with its soft radiance. Rolling over, he took a quick check of the time. It was almost 8:00 a.m. Shutting off the alarm, he would soon need to wake sleeping beauty who still rested peacefully beside him. Today was one of the most important days of his life. Sitting up in bed, he quietly whispered a prayer asking God for his blessings. Thoughts of his precious son, Matt, ran through his mind. His heart still ached for him. If it hadn't been for Daniella, he was sure he'd probably not have had the courage to go on with life. Now, even after the sadness that had so consumed him, sending him halfway around the world to

Kathmandu for answers, he was finally ready to get on with his life. Leaning over, he kissed Daniella awake.

"Good morning, Sweetheart, it's time to wake up," he whispered, softly kissing her once again. Finally, Daniella slowly opened her eyes.

"What time is it?" she asked, wiping the sleep from her eyes.

"It's almost 8:30 a.m. Remember, we need to leave early. I'll go to the kitchen and make us a cup of coffee. Would you like some eggs with toast and bacon?"

"Coffee most definitely and maybe some toast."

"Okay, I'll be right back. Why don't you get dressed and pack your bags while I'm in the kitchen? The maids will be in soon to clean the house."

Returning with the coffee and toast, it appeared Daniella had gotten dressed and was closing her suitcase. She looked stunning. She wore a red polka dot sundress and looked ravishing even without makeup. Her long blonde hair fell loose around her shoulders.

"Daniella, I have coffee and toast. Come over and sit down. We have a few minutes before housekeeping arrives. The limo is picking us up in about an hour."

"Okay. So where are we going?" Daniella smiled, taking a sip of coffee.

"That's still under wraps for now. You trust me, right?"

"Yes. Explicitly."

"Sweetheart, that's always been your answer for as long as I've known you. Good girl," he winked, taking a drink of coffee.

Hearing the front door opening, it seemed the maids had arrived a bit early.

"I think Mary and Betty are here," John stated, setting his coffee down to check who had entered the house.

"Who's Mary and Betty? Please don't tell me they're your old flames," Daniella laughed.

"They're my housekeepers. They've been with me for years."

John was anxious to start the day as he hurried down the hallway to greet them.

"Good morning ladies, nice to see you both. Sorry, I'm afraid I left the kitchen and patio in a mess. We'll be leaving as soon as the limo arrives. My girlfriend, Daniella, and I enjoyed the delicious dinner Chef Alton prepared last night. Would you please thank him for me? I won't be returning for a few weeks. Still, I believe one of the guys working on the Oahu project and his family will be arriving this evening. I'm sure you both will ensure their stay is pleasant. They have two small children, so please remind Alton to focus his menus around two young children. Oh, one last thing, their Springer Spaniel, Lacy, will be accompanying them."

"Mr. McDermott, you know how we feel about dogs being inside the house," Mary interrupted.

"Well, be that as it may, Lacy will be with them. I told them it was fine. Trust me, she's a lovely dog, very friendly, and she doesn't bite," John laughed.

"Is there anything else we should know?" Betty inquired.

"Not that I can think of, just ensure the Morgan family has a pleasant stay. Bill, his wife, Candy, and their two children will be the occupants. Troy is three, and Billie is almost six years old. Just make sure the patio area and outside perimeters are kept free of dog excrement," John laughed.

"Great, I'll let Mary see to that," Betty teased on her way out to the patio.

"Thanks, Betty, we'll see about that," Mary quickly countered. "Mr. McDermott, don't worry. We have it all covered. We've never let you down, and we'll ensure the Morgans are very comfortable."

Just at that moment, Daniella walked out of the bedroom.

"Ladies, please meet Daniella."

"Hello. Nice to meet you."

Hearing the doorbell, Mary walked over to answer it.

"Mr. McDermott, the limo is here," she announced.

"Great. Please have the chauffeur come inside. Our luggage is in the primary suite."

"Daniella, are you ready to go?"

"Ladies, the house is all yours. See you both on my next trip out to the islands.

"Thanks, Mr. McDermott. Have a wonderful weekend. Daniella, it was nice meeting you," Betty smiled, closing the front door.

"Wow. She's pretty. I certainly hope John finds that special someone. I think I've lost count of all the beautiful women he's entertained here. Now with Matt gone, he deserves some happiness in his life," Betty shrugged.

"Yes. You'd be right on that. But, you never know, maybe she is that special someone," Mary agreed.

Snuggling close to John in the back seat of the limo, Daniella had no idea what John had planned or where they were going. She was just along for the ride at this point.

As the limo drove through the front gate, John pulled her closer, kissing her passionately.

"So, where are we going?"

"You and your questions. Can't a guy just plan a surprise getaway? No more questions, you silly girl. You'll find out soon enough," he teased, quickly kissing her once more on the forehead.

It seemed they had driven for only a few short miles on the winding roads before approaching an airport. As the limo turned in its direction, Daniella looked over at John. Curiosity was consuming her.

"John, we're going to another airport?"

"Yes, Sweetheart, it appears that we are," he teased.

Sitting pensively in the back seat, Daniella held onto John's arm as the limo drove onto the tarmac parking next to a twin-engine Cessna owned by the McDermott Corporation.

"Are you up for a short flight this morning?"

"You fly airplanes as well as helicopters?" she questioned, becoming a bit nervous. "Do we have another choice of transportation?"

"Um, you're with me, right? No, I don't think so," he teased.

"John, you're continuously full of surprises. But as always, I trust you."

Taking her hand, he helped her out of the limo.

"Thanks, George, We'll see you on our return tomorrow evening."

Grasping her hand, he led her across the wind-swept tarmac and over to his corporate Cessna. Stowing away their luggage, he performed a checklist of routine inspections as he walked around and under the aircraft. Then he took her hand, helping her inside the plane and into her seat. Checking to ensure her seat belt was securely fastened, he handed her a headset.

"Okay. I think we're ready," John winked.

"Are you sure you know what you're doing?"

"If memory serves, I think you've flown with me before."

"Yes. That was a helicopter. But, this is a plane," Daniella questioned.

"Sweetheart, I've been flying for more than twenty years. There is no better way to see the islands than by air. So please, sit back and relax. Trust me. I wouldn't jeopardize your life, especially today," he laughed. "We're flying over to Kauai this morning," he winked.

After starting the engines and contacting the control tower, he taxied the aircraft over to the runway. After receiving clearance from the tower, he glanced at Daniella. She appeared somewhat worried.

"Don't be nervous. You've flown with me before and not once have we crashed and burned," he laughed.

"John, I don't find that amusing," she scolded.

Hopefully, the panorama of the spectacular vistas below would soon become a distraction.

As the aircraft lifted into the beautiful morning skies, it made a steep turn. They were immediately over the calm sapphire waters of the Pacific Ocean. Once again, sitting glued to her window, Daniella took in the unbelievable sights. Unexpectedly, looking down, a pod of whales could be seen swimming together. Skirting along the coast of Kauai, stunning waterfalls came into view. Water cascading over the edge of the dark green sculpted peaks was spectacular. Flying over the fog-covered summit of Mount Wai'ale' ale Crater, the dense green jungles were laden with immense waterfalls. The Na'Pali coast was stunning flying overhead. The contrast of the deep green mountainous terrain set against the dark cobalt waters of the Pacific was awe-inspiring. Suddenly, John dipped the plane to one side as he pointed out another group of large whales. Next, he flew over the Waimea Canyon, revealing its steep reddish-brown cliffs. After viewing the island from the air, John landed them safely at a local airport in Kauai.

"So, Sweetheart, what did you think of my tour?" John winked as the aircraft rolled to a stop on the tarmac.

"It was simply amazing. You're a great pilot and tourist guide. I'm sorry I doubted you or your abilities."

"Great, then next time, maybe you won't be so nervous."

"Oh, so there's going to be a next time?" Daniella smiled.

"Maybe," he winked. "Are you hungry?"

"Yes, remember we only had toast and coffee this morning."

"Our car should be here momentarily. I made reservations at a quaint little restaurant in Hanalei Bay. Their menu is quite enjoyable, and I think you'll love it. Great, our ride is here," John smiled, noticing a limo coming into view. Slowly, it stopped and parked. Picking up their luggage, John escorted Daniella across the tarmac to the limo.

Once situated inside the limo, John popped the cork on a bottle of Moet and Chandon. Then, handing her a glass, he made another toast.

"Here's to our wonderful day in Kauai and an unforgettable evening," he winked.

"Thanks, John, it has been wonderful so far. I love you."

Nestling against him, it appeared she was already feeling the effects of the champagne after only one glass.

"Geez, I've fallen in love with a pilot. Who knew?" she laughed giddily. "What other things do I not know about you?"

Leaning down, he kissed her on the forehead.

Arriving at the Sugar Cane Factory, John was once again eager to sample their phenomenal cuisine. He had dined here many times and was excited to introduce Daniella to one of his favorite eateries. It seemed their coconut shrimp was at the top of his list.

After enjoying a delicious dinner of the best foods Kauai had to offer, it was time to check-in at the beautiful five-star Hanalei Bay Resort.

Pulling back her chair, John escorted Daniella outside to the waiting limo. Once she was settled into the back seat of the car, she began questioning his next move.

"Thanks for dinner. It was incredible. So, Mr. McDermott, what's next on your agenda?"

"Oh, Mr. McDermott, is it?" he smiled. "Well, it's only a short drive. I think I'll let it be a surprise," he winked.

Slowly the car made a left turn towards the beach. He was right. Finally, they reached a gated entrance to a beautiful resort. Sitting directly on the beach, the Hanalei Bay Resort was magnificent. Parking under a stunning portico covered in lush green ivy, it was beautiful. Enormous decorative Polynesian fountains sat on each side of the tall carved double door entry. Taking her hand, he led her inside to the foyer. Walking over to the reception desk, John was anxious to check-in and receive their room key.

"Good evening, I'm John McDermott. I reserved a cabana."

Quickly checking his registry, the young man looked up.

"Yes, sir, Mr. McDermott, you're in cabana eighteen. Here is your room key. One of our concierges will be right with you. A golf cart will be provided to take you down to your cabana."

Within minutes, another young man appeared.

"Good evening Mr. McDermott. I'm Jeffrey, please follow me," he announced, picking up their luggage.

Following Jeffrey outside, a golf cart was waiting for them near the entrance.

"Hop on. It's only a short drive down to the beach," Jeffrey mentioned, quickly stowing their luggage in the seat behind them.

"I believe you're in cabana eighteen. It's the last cabana to the left."

Driving down a dimly lit path surrounded by lush tropical vegetation, it was only a short drive to the beach. Reaching the water, Jeffrey turned left onto a narrow wooden path that followed the shoreline to their cabana. Stopping at Cabana Eighteen, Jeffrey grabbed their luggage, unlocking their door.

"Welcome to the Hanalei Bay Resort. We hope you enjoy your stay. If there's anything we can do for you, please don't hesitate to let us know. Have a wonderful evening."

"Thanks, Jeffrey," John smiled, handing him a generous tip.

For all intent and purposes, the cabanas resembled grass huts from the outside. However, inside, it was exquisite. A huge king-size bed was the focus of attention entering the room. A bamboo tray sitting on the stylish silk duvet held a magnum of champagne, two fluted glasses, a cheese tray, and a bowl of chocolate-covered strawberries. The room was luxuriously furnished in dark mahogany. A sofa with matching wicker chairs and end tables sat near the front door. A huge vase of fresh flowers sat on an ornate credenza. It was five-star elegance at its best.

"This is impressive," John smiled.

"Geez, did you see the bathroom? The glass-enclosed shower is huge. The two of us could have a party in there," Daniella teased.

"Um, let me think about that one," he grinned mischievously. "Well, since you brought it up, perhaps later tonight."

"John, get your mind out of the gutter. I wasn't serious."

"Oh, but I was," he laughed, opening the magnum of champagne.

Pouring the champagne into glasses, he picked up the bowl of strawberries.

"Sweetheart, come over here. I need you to keep me from consuming all the chocolate strawberries," he grinned, taking their drinks and the fruit over to the sofa.

"John, don't you dare. Then, hurriedly, she snuggled beside him on the sofa. You know how much I crave chocolate," Daniella laughed, grabbing the bowl from his hands.

Suddenly, out of nowhere, his nerves were beginning to get the best of him. Knowing the significance of the evening ahead, he would be devastated if her answer was no. Trying to push the thoughts out of his mind, he downed his entire glass of the sparkling drink and poured another. There was no possible way her answer would be anything other than a resounding yes. He had never loved anyone more. After losing Matt, he desperately needed Daniella in his life. She had taught him the true meaning of the word love. He had enough money to last several lifetimes. Yet, he would willingly spend his last penny, seeing that she and her girls had the best of everything.

Daniella, knowing John as well as she did, sensed his uneasiness.

"John, are you okay? You look worried?"

"Yes. It's been a long day. I've made reservations for dinner at 6:00 p.m., or would you prefer to order room service?"

"If it's alright with you, let's eat in tonight. You know how I cherish being alone with you, just the two of us. I feel like shutting out the world. How about you?"

"My thoughts exactly," he winked, leaning in to kiss her passionately. The warmth of her kiss helped to calm his fears and his nerves.

"Why don't you change into something warm. We could take a walk along the beach this evening. It can get quite cool after dark. I'll run over to the lobby and pick up some dinner menus if you don't mind. I'll be right back." Giving her another quick kiss, he was out the door.

"Sure, that sounds exhilarating." Before she could even complete her sentence, he disappeared out the door like a flash.

"Something was definitely up," Daniella thought. She had a hunch. Walking over to the credenza, laying on top for all the world to see, were several dinner menus. Hiding them in the top drawer, she had to play along with his silly game. Tonight was the night. He was going to propose—every ounce of her being confirmed it. Tears welled in her eyes. Everything he had planned, the fact he brought her to Hawaii, all led up to this evening. Daniella felt ecstatic. There was no way she was wearing jogging attire or cumbersome clothes this evening. She needed to look ravishing, and she only had a few minutes to pull it off. Hurriedly, she ripped through her suitcase, pulled out a stunning red halter dress, and ran into the bathroom to change. Sweeping her long blond curls upward in the back, she held her hair in place with a silver clip. Quickly applying makeup, she accessorized with a simple pair of diamond earrings. Finally, after two quick sprays of her favorite French perfume, she was ready. "Who says a girl can't get ready in a hurry," she laughed.

Hearing the cabana door open, she walked out of the bathroom.

"Sweetheart, you look stunning," John gasped. She took his breath away. For a moment, he was speechless. "Daniella, you're gorgeous," he winked, utterly captivated by her appearance. Holding the dinner menus in his hand, his reason for leaving had practically escaped him. Then, finally, he snapped back into reality. "Babe, don't you think that dress is a little much for a walk on the beach," he seemed surprised by her attire.

"I just felt like wearing something special tonight. Do you mind?"

"No. You're beautiful. You look ravishing," John smiled, putting the menus down on the credenza as he walked across the room. Pulling her into his arms, he whispered. "How in the heck did you manage to change so quickly."

"Well," she began to answer as he stopped her short with a kiss that sent shivers throughout her entire body, giving her goosebumps.

"Geez, now I feel as if I should change clothes," he laughed.

"You're fine. You look amazing. Now, how about that walk on the beach you promised," Daniella smiled, reaching for his hand.

"It's a little windy. Do you have a wrap?"

"Yes. Wait just a moment." Then, walking over to her suitcase, she once again swiftly rummaged through its contents, taking out a black lace scarf.

"Okay. Does this work?"

"Great," he remarked, buttoning his jacket while he discreetly searched his pocket for the box containing the ring. "Let's take that walk, shall we," he winked, taking her by the arm.

The moon cast its reflection along the shore as they walked down to the beach. The incoming waves appeared translucent under the moonlight. Pausing for a moment, Daniella removed her shoes. She felt invigorated as the water washed over her feet.

Putting his arms around her to keep her warm, they slowly strolled along the water's edge, taking in the brilliance of the night sky.

"John, look up," she suggested. "Have you ever seen so many stars? They look like diamonds scattered across the universe."

"You're right. They're spectacular," he paused, turning to face her as he stared into the depths of her beautiful eyes. This was his opportunity. He had waited his entire life for this moment.

"Daniella, I've fallen madly in love with you. Every second that I spend with you makes me feel like the luckiest guy in the world. The first night I met you at the Whales Tail, I knew there was something different about you. We've been through so much together. After losing

Matt, I don't think I would have had the strength or courage to go on without you. You make my life worth living. I want to wake up each morning and feel you next to me," he smiled, dropping down on one knee. "Sweetheart, I never want it to end. Will you marry me?" he asked, taking the tiny box from his coat pocket.

"Yes. Yes," Daniella exclaimed with tears in her eyes as he slowly placed a five-carat princess cut diamond ring onto her finger. John, I love you. I love you," she repeated as tears streamed down her face. You've made me the happiest woman on earth."

Holding her tight in his arms, he kissed her with intense passion. She simply melted into his embrace, never wanting it to end.

"Daniella, you've made me the happiest guy on earth tonight. Thank God you said *yes*. But, I have to tell you, I was a bit nervous. I fell in love with you the very first time I saw you. Your presence and tenacity were alluring. I loved you then, and I love you even more tonight. Sweetheart, I want to spend the rest of my life showing you how much I love you."

"Oh John, do you know how much I love you? I've never let my guard down with anyone. I ran away with you to New York without even as much as a thought. Afterward, even with the wrath of Ava coming down on me, I never stopped loving you. I've always loved you from the moment I first saw you at the Whales Tail. We've been through so much together. I couldn't imagine my life without you."

"Let's walk back to the cabana," John winked. "I think we have dinner waiting."

Opening the door to their cabana, Daniella was utterly shocked. Tropical flowers of all colors and descriptions filled the room. There wasn't an empty space. Colorful Hibiscus, Bird of Paradise, Anthurium, and Plumeria filled the cabana. It looked like a florist shop. The fragrance of the flowers was hypnotic, and the entire room was glowing with lit candles too numerous to count.

"Oh, John, what have you done? It's gorgeous. This must-have cost a small fortune," she laughed. "I love it." Then, as more tears filled her eyes, she turned to hug and kiss the wonderful man who would soon be her husband. "John, how did I ever get so lucky? I love you."

Catering had been in and set up an elaborate feast leaving a row of silver chafing dishes filled with everything imaginable on a cart. A table was brought in completely covered with white linens, glowing candles and elegantly set with fine tableware, crystal, and silver. A bottle of Moet and Chandon sat nearby in a bucket of ice.

"Are you hungry?" John smiled.

"Honestly, I think I'm too excited to eat," she laughed.

"Well," he replied, removing the tops to the chafing dishes. "It looks too delicious to let it go to waste."

Pulling out her chair, she decided he was right. Popping the cork on the bottle of champagne, John filled their glasses.

Every morsel was delicious as they dined on a feast of steak and lobster.

"Sweetheart, lift your glass. I have to make a special toast to our engagement. You've made me an extremely happy guy tonight," he smiled. "Thanks for saying *yes.*"

"John, here's to a lifetime of happiness. I'll always love you," Daniella cried as tears of happiness ran down her face.

"No more tears. You look stunning. I think I can take away those tears," John smiled. "How would you like a couple of credit cards to plan a wedding. Oh, and by the way, there's no limit on those. However, I do expect you to keep it within reason," he laughed. "You know what, on second thoughts, I take that back. You and the girls do whatever you want. I just want you three to be happy. Shop till you drop. Isn't that what you girls say," he smiled.

"Oh, John, are you serious?"

"I believe so, but ask me again in the morning, just in case," he teased. "Yes, sweetheart, I'm serious," he laughed.

Refilling their glasses, he pulled Daniella over to the sofa.

"So, we have a lot to talk about," he mentioned taking a sip of champagne. "You know my project in Destiny Cove will be completed in the spring. Afterward, I'm out of the country and on to the next project. I'm prepared to let Jillian pick any university she would like. But, of course, Gracie is still young, and I think we should keep her with us until she graduates. What are your thoughts?"

"I totally agree. John, really, any university for Jillian?"

"Yes. Trust me. There's not a university out there that will turn down my money. Maybe Jillian would like to go to Harvard, where the boys study. I'm sure they would love that. After losing Matt, I think they share a sad connection. However, you must know it's strictly up to Jillian to decide. I'll leave all the decisions up to her. Dad will just supply the funds."

"Oh, John, where did you come from? I only wished Ava was alive to witness us making our union legal. She did love you. You do know that, right? She could be a little insensitive and rough around the edges. Still, she saw how much you cared for me," Daniella explained, wiping her eyes.

"No more crying. Drink up, Sweetheart. I remember something about a party happening later tonight in that huge shower," John smiled seductively.

Sitting together on the sofa, Daniella held onto him, not ever wanting to let go. She couldn't wait to get home and show off her sparkling ring.

"Oh, I forgot to mention, but the girls and Henry were completely informed about our weekend. Thanks to them, in a way, they made it all possible."

"So they knew?"

"Yes. Of course. You don't think I would have proposed to you without first getting the girl's blessings."

"John, you're full of surprises. I can't wait to spend the rest of my life with you."

"Finish your drink. I think I remember some promises you made earlier this evening," John laughed, pulling her up from the sofa. Then, taking her hand, he led her towards the shower.

The bathroom was filled with fresh flowers and glowing candles as they walked inside.

"John, really, flowers and candles in the bathroom?"

"Sweetheart, I aim to please," he winked, removing the silver clip from her long hair allowing it to fall loosely around her shoulders.

Slowly and seductively, their clothes slipped from their bodies, dropping to the floor. Then, taking her hand, John playfully pulled Daniella into the shower and under the tantalizing warm water.

"Doesn't this feel like heaven?" he smiled, kissing the nape of her neck.

Suddenly, the shower became hot and steamy. It appeared the best parties only required an attendance of two.

Later that night, in bed, they reflected on the day. It had been truly unforgettable. Yet, tomorrow held the promise of a new future.

Waking up to the aroma of fresh flowers, Daniella rolled over to gaze at the handsome man who still slept peacefully beside her. Looking down at her left hand, it hadn't been a dream. The ring was proof. Leaning over to kiss him awake, she smiled.

"Good morning, Sweetheart," John smiled. "Let me see your left hand. Wow. We are engaged," he teased.

"John, you're silly," Daniella laughed, smothering him with kisses.

"Sweetheart, if you continue, we may never get out of bed today."

"Sounds like a great idea to me."

Hearing his remark, she kissed him even more aggressively. Then, pulling the covers over their heads, she laughed. It seemed safe to say they were going nowhere for the moment. Once again, they simply shut out the world.

Later that morning, John ordered breakfast.

"Daniella, as unforgettable as our weekend has been, I think I remember an ongoing project that probably needs my attention," he shrugged, taking a sip of coffee.

"Do we have to leave?" she frowned.

"I'm afraid so. The guys will think I've abandoned them as well as the ongoing construction."

Getting up from his lap, she walked over to inhale the fragrance of a bouquet containing colorful yellow hibiscus.

"What are you going to do with all the flowers?"

"Well, why don't you choose a few that you especially love. I'll have them wrapped to take home. The rest I planned to donate to a local hospital," he suggested. Walking over, he kissed her on the cheek. "The limo will be here in about an hour. After that, I'll fly us back to Oahu. The jet is waiting to take us home."

Looking at her suitcase, he laughed.

"Sweetheart, your suitcase looks like an explosion in a clothing factory. Do you think you can get it closed?"

"Well, I did once. I'll figure it out," Daniella mentioned, reluctantly walking over to take care of the scattered clothes surrounding her luggage.

Glancing at his suitcase, it was only a simple matter of closing it.

"When you're packed, I'll call for the concierge," he stated, pouring himself another cup of coffee.

The next hour found them in the air on their way back to Oahu. It was only a short flight. Arriving at the International Airport in Honolulu, it was necessary to change planes before they would finally be on their way back to Destiny Cove. John's private Lear jet and crew were standing by.

"Good afternoon, welcome aboard. I hope you had a wonderful weekend in Hawaii," Stacie smiled as she greeted them.

Looking down, she noticed the brilliance and size of the diamond ring Daniella was now sporting.

"Wow. I see congratulations are in order. Mr. McDermott, I'm extremely happy for you," Stacie acknowledged. "Congratulations, Daniella," she smiled, being cordial. It was her job. However, she couldn't help being a bit jealous. It was clearly evident John was now off the market. The influential men of the McDermott Corporation, the former players whom she'd flown with all over the world, appeared to be finding another status, either engaged or married. She felt sad and disappointed. Stacie had always hoped one of the guys would find her attractive. It was the reason she had taken the job. Now, it seemed her chances were diminishing.

After comfortably settling into their seats, as usual, John asked for two glasses of champagne before they were airborne.

"Sweetheart, here's to our time in Hawaii and an amazing life together. But, most of all, here's to the future Mrs. McDermott," he winked.

"John, I love you. Thanks for an unforgettable weekend," she smiled, looking down at her ring. One day we'll share these memories with lots of grandkids."

"Did you just say grandkids?" he laughed, almost choking on his drink as he wiped his mouth, staring at Daniella. He had never imagined himself in the role of grandpa. But, of course, he wasn't opposed to the idea. All in due time, he thought.

"Geez, John, does the idea bother you?" Daniella laughed. "We're young, and I always wanted more children," Daniella smiled.

"Wow. Guess I didn't see that one coming."

"What do you think?" she blushed.

"Sweetheart, I think," he paused for a moment. She had totally caught him off guard. "If it's more babies you want, it certainly won't be a problem for me," he winked, leaning over to kiss her softly.

After finishing their drinks, John asked for pillows and blankets. Snuggling against the love of his life, he was at last completely content. Finally, they were on their way home.

Chapter Fourteen

As the limo approached the house, a huge banner hung from the garage door. In bold lettering, it read, *"Congratulations, Mom and John."* It appeared the girls knew of their impending engagement and had given them their blessings.

"It does appear the girls were informed of your plans."

"I told them before we left Destiny Cove. I would've never taken you to Hawaii and proposed without first getting them on board with my plans.

As the limo parked in front of the house, Daniella leaned over, giving him a quick kiss.

"Well, it seems you've won their hearts along with mine."

Eagerly waiting and watching from the front windows, it appeared Jillian and Gracie caught sight of them stepping out of the car. The girls were ecstatic as they hurriedly ran out to meet them.

"Oh, Mom, congratulations," Jillian screamed, giving them both a huge hug.

"Yes, congratulations," Gracie chimed in. "John told us about his plans for taking you to Hawaii. We knew."

"How did you like the islands?" Jillian inquired.

"Truly unforgettable, thanks to this handsome guy," Daniella smiled.

The girls were anxious to know all the details regarding their romantic adventure as they followed them inside.

"Oh, Henry said to tell you that he had to go down to the docks this morning. But, he said to give you both his best wishes. I think he's stopping by later," Gracie smiled.

After putting their luggage inside the living room, John asked the chauffeur to wait in the car for a moment.

"Have you girls had lunch?"

"Not really. Jillian fixed us one of her famous egg sandwiches earlier," Gracie frowned.

"Actually, I'm starved," Jillian added.

"Well, that settles it. Why don't we take these beautiful young ladies down to the Whales Tail? Sweetheart, are you up for it after the long flight?"

"Yes. That sounds wonderful."

"Great. We can give you all the details of our trip over lunch. How does that sound?" John grinned, leading his girls back to the limo.

Arriving at the restaurant, John asked for a table near the back. It appeared less crowded and quiet. He loved treating his girls to the best food Destiny Cove had to offer. After a delicious meal and endless details regarding their trip, it seemed Daniella was beginning to fall asleep.

"I think we better get your mom home. I think the trip is finally taking its toll." John suggested motioning for their waiter.

"Yes. Mom, you look tired," Jillian mentioned pushing her chair away from the table.

Once comfortably seated in the limo, Daniella laid her head on John's shoulders. She was instantly out like a light bulb.

"Girls, your mom has made me the luckiest guy on earth," John smiled, gently pulling Daniella's long blonde curls away from her face.

"John, Gracie, and I want you to know how excited we are to have you in the family. We never thought mom would remarry. We're just thankful you came into our lives, and we know you'll make her very happy."

"Well, speaking of happiness, how would you feel about helping with the wedding plans? Why don't you girls take the jet to New York this weekend and shop for dresses? I think you'll find the city offers the latest fashions in wedding gowns and bridesmaid's attire. What do you think?" John asked with a huge smile.

"Are you kidding? Really, New York?" Jillian enthusiastically asked.

"Only the best for my girls," he winked.

"Aren't you coming?" Gracie asked.

"Not this trip. I've got a lot of catching up to do on my current project. I've been away lately, and I need this project to come in on time. Besides, I think you girls can handle it all by yourselves," he laughed.

"John, I'm not sure New York fashions would fit into mom's budget?" Jillian answered. She'd always been the most conscientious when it came to money or finances.

"Sweetheart, I don't think you have to worry about that," he grinned, aware of their innocence and naivete of his net worth.

Caught off guard by his remark, Jillian covered her mouth with her hand. Then, quietly, she laughed, glancing over at Gracie. She knew he was wealthy, but this confirmed her suspensions. Jillian had never been to New York. Now, she would visit this fantastic city and shop for high-end fashions.

Arriving back at home, John saw the girls inside. Picking Daniella up, he carried her inside to the bedroom, making sure she was comfortable before he left.

"I need to go down to the site for a few hours," he whispered, pulling back the duvet. "I told the girls about my idea of you taking the jet to New York this weekend to shop for a wedding gown. I think they're excited," he winked, giving her a quick kiss.

"Oh, I'm sure," Daniella mumbled, pulling the covers up to her chin as she fell asleep.

Quietly closing the door, John hurried outside to the waiting limo.

It seemed the next few days flew by as the weekend approached.

"Are you and the girls ready? I thought I would ride out to the airport with you. I asked Captain Bradford to have you in the air by 9:00 a.m. this morning, and I'm sure the flight crew has arrived."

"Give me just a minute," Daniella replied, grabbing her scarf. It was early fall, but the weather forecaster had predicted unseasonably cooler weather for New York over the upcoming weekend.

Grabbing Daniella's suitcase, John carried it out to the front door.

"Mom, you look stunning," Jillian remarked, seeing Daniella walk into the living room. She was wearing a long black pencil skirt with a white cashmere sweater and black knee-high boots. Her colorful silk scarf matched her sweater, completing her ensemble. Wearing her long blonde hair pulled back in a ponytail, it exposed her brilliant diamond earrings. Her appearance made her seem young, giving no hint that she was the mother of two teenage daughters.

"Mom, you look beautiful," Gracie complimented.

"Yes. I have to agree with you," John winked. "Sweetheart, you're gorgeous. But, maybe, I should reconsider and tag along," he teased.

Seeing the girls outside to the limo, John entered the car after they were seated.

"I've booked you into a suite downtown at the Plaza. I think you'll enjoy their accommodations. Everything has been taken care of, and they'll be expecting your arrival around 2:00 p.m. this afternoon. Daniella, here are a couple of my credit cards. I took the liberty of having your name added to my account. There's no limit. I want you girls to enjoy yourselves but use them wisely. Here's some cash or fun money to make your weekend enjoyable," John winked, handing her a small black wallet. "Oh, you'll probably want to keep this locked in the safe in your room. Hopefully, this will ensure that you are well taken care of over the weekend. Also, one of our chauffeurs will be available if you'd like rather than using the public transit system," he explained with a grin.

Quickly opening the wallet, Daniella gasped. It contained over fifteen thousand dollars in large bills

"John, that's a huge sum of money. It's extremely generous. Are you sure you can't come with us for the weekend?"

"I would love to, but work calls. You're only in New York for three days. I think you'll do just fine. I'll call you tonight at the hotel."

Within minutes, the limo parked close to the steps of the aircraft. John escorted his beautiful young girls up the steps leading to the private jet and onboard.

"Good morning, Mr. McDermott," Stacie greeted.

"Daniella, nice to see you again. Welcome aboard. Are these beautiful young ladies your daughters?"

"Yes. Jillian and Gracie. They're both excited to be flying to New York this morning."

"Nice to meet you. Welcome aboard," Stacie smiled, showing the girls to their seats. "Mr. McDermott, we should be on time for departure at 9:00 a.m. just as you asked. The weather looks great today. Captain Bradford said our flying time would be approximately three hours. Are there any special requirements for the girls this morning?" Stacie inquired with a smile.

"Just give them a safe, comfortable ride to New York," John answered with a smile.

"You've got it. Would you ladies like a beverage before take off."

"Might I suggest a glass of chardonnay for my girl and maybe orange juice for our young ladies?" John spoke up. "Also, a lite lunch before their arrival would be great," he added. "I'm sure they're going to take advantage of the great restaurants the city has to offer once they arrive."

Daniella was somewhat embarrassed by John's assertion of making their choices. However, she knew he wanted to ensure their flight was stress-free and that he loved them.

After giving the girls a quick hug, John turned to Daniella. Pulling her close, he gave her a quick, passionate kiss.

"Sweetheart, I'm sure you'll find the perfect wedding gown. Of course, you have these smart young ladies to help with your decision. I love you," he winked, making his way towards the exit.

Stopping at the door of the aircraft, he momentarily glanced back.

"Have a wonderful weekend. I love you."

Watching as he left the aircraft, Daniella already felt lonely despite her beautiful girls accompanying her. She was now the future Mrs. John

McDermott. Just the mere thoughts of it put a huge smile on her face. It seemed she would always have the Sea Oates to thank for introducing them and perhaps a little help from Dimitri.

Ensuring her daughter's seat belts were buckled, Daniella took her seat across the aisle. Even though the girls had never flown by private plane, neither of them seemed the least bit nervous. Watching as they sipped their orange juice, they giggled quietly, staring out their window. Daniella decided to reach inside her purse for a book. She needed a quick distraction until the plane reached its cruising altitude. Noting it was Daniella's first flight without John, Stacie ensured Daniella's time onboard was comfortable in every way possible. Today's flight was short compared to her trip to the islands with John. However, looking over at the girls, Daniella was comforted seeing their smiling faces. It seemed the time passed quickly after lunch.

"Daniella, Captain Bradford wanted me to inform you that we're only about forty-five minutes out from the airport. John has arranged a limo to take you and the girls downtown to your hotel. Would you or the girls like a beverage or warm towel before we land?" Stace inquired.

"Yes. Thank you. Coffee sounds wonderful."

"We'd love soda," Jillian interjected.

"I'll be right back with those."

As the jet touched down on the runway, Jillian expressed her excitement.

"Mom, we're in New York. Can you believe it?" she eagerly announced.

Seeing the anticipation in her daughter's eyes, Daniella was thrilled to have the girls along. Even without John by her side, she looked forward to a great weekend. The city had a lot to offer besides shopping. First things first, she thought. Afterward, time permitting, she would take the girls on a quick tour of the numerous attractions.

"Welcome to New York. Have a wonderful weekend," Stacie smiled as they exited the aircraft. "I'll see you ladies on the return flight Monday morning."

A limo was waiting for their arrival as they descended the steps of the aircraft.

"Good afternoon, ladies. I'm Wilson. Welcome to New York. I'll be driving you downtown to the Plaza," the chauffeur remarked, opening their car door.

"Thank you," Daniella smiled as she and the girls entered the car.

"Wow. Mom, does John always travel in such luxury?" Jillian smiled.

"Well, as long as I've known him, he always goes first class."

Sitting back in their seats, the girls sat glued to their window during the duration of the drive downtown. Watching the expressions on their faces reminded her of the first time she visited New York with John. Traffic was moving at a snail's pace. Daniella wondered how anyone ever got used to the congested thoroughfares. Maybe public transportation was the only answer for those who lived and worked downtown.

Arriving at the Plaza Hotel, they were met by the Bellhop, who greeted them. Placing their luggage on a cart, they followed him inside to the reception desk. Daniella was awestruck by the size and magnificence of the lobby.

"Good afternoon, I'm Daniella Demos. I believe Mr. John McDermott made our reservation."

"Yes. I have it right here," the young man answered. "You're in Suite Four on the tenth floor. Your luggage will be sent up in a few minutes. I believe these theater tickets belong to you, compliments of Mr. McDermott."

"Mom, did he say theater tickets?" Gracie smiled.

"Yes. It appears John has arranged for us to see a special performance of Gigi," Daniella commented as they walked towards the elevator.

"Mom, I think I like John more than ever," she laughed.

Reaching the tenth floor, it appeared Suite Four was right in front of them. The suite was just as Daniella would've imagined as she unlocked the door. The décor and ambiance were breathtaking. It was true that John never disappointed even when reserving a suite in New York. Evening sunlight flooded through the oversized windows bathing the room in a soft glow. The furnishings were luxurious. Gold damask curtains hung from the tall windows, matching the chairs' fabric and throw pillows. A dark mahogany coffee table centered brown tufted leather sofas. However, the first noticeable item in the room was a massive vase of red roses sitting on the credenza.

"Wow. I wonder who sent these?" Jillian exclaimed, running over to read the card. "Mom, these are from John."

Walking over to look closer, Daniella smiled, finding a note attached.

"Sweetheart, I love you. I hope your weekend is wonderful. Here is a list of the most popular bridal boutiques in the city. I've taken the liberty to set appointments for you and the girls. You'll find the time and locations listed below. Enjoy. I'll call you later tonight. Love John."

"Mom, we have separate rooms," Jillian excitedly announced after exploring their suite.

"Great. We don't have to share," Gracie mentioned running off in the direction of her room.

It seemed their weekend was getting off to a great start. Maybe ordering room service was the next logical step.

"Girls, what sounds good for dinner this evening, and please don't let me hear the word pizza coming out of your mouths. I'm feeling a little tired after the flight, so I was hoping you both would go along with staying in for our first evening and simply ordering room service."

"Yes, mom, ordering room service sounds awesome. But, remember this is your weekend. It's all about you," Jillian agreed.

Daniella and the girls were ready to retreat to their bedrooms after indulging in a tasty meal of steak tenderloins, gravy, and garlic mashed potatoes. Seeking the comfort of crawling underneath the warm covers of the heavy gold damask duvet, it was simply extravagance at its best. Daniella had hardly laid her head down on the pillow when the phone next to her bed rang.

Hurriedly leaning over to answer, she heard John's voice

"Hey, Sweetheart. How are my girls this evening?"

"Oh, John, everything is spectacular. I love you. The accommodations are more than we could've possibly asked for. I only wished you were here."

"I love you too. Believe me. I wished I was there. But, I've got to bring this hotel project in on schedule. Remember, I have a project waiting overseas in the spring. So, how was the flight?"

"Not bad. Stacie ensured the girls and I were comfortable. She took excellent care of us. I certainly can't complain."

"Did you get the theater tickets?"

"Yes. Thank you. John, that was so thoughtful of you. It will be a first for the girls and me. We've never been to a show on Broadway. So I just wish again that you were here to go with us."

"I know. Next time, I promise. Sweetheart, I hate to make this short, but I need to get back to work. I'm going to be working late tonight. I'm still making up for the lost time. I love you. I hope you find the dress of your dreams. Sleep well and remember how much I love you."

"I love you too," Daniella replied, hanging up the phone. John's voice was the last thing she remembered before falling asleep.

Waking up to the morning sun as it brilliantly streamed in through the windows, Daniella looked over at the clock sitting on the nightstand. It was almost 8:00 a.m., and their first appointment was scheduled for 10:00 a.m., just enough time to jump in the shower and enjoy breakfast. Deciding to call for the limo, she didn't want to chance public transportation on their first morning in the city. Being late for their first appointment wasn't an option.

Hurriedly walking into the bathroom, she turned on the warm water. After taking a shower, she dried her hair and quickly dressed. Finally, it was time to wake the girls and order breakfast.

"Okay, sleepyhead, it's time to wake up," Daniella called out, walking into Gracie's room. We have a lot to do today, and our first appointment is at 10:00 a.m." Walking over, she lovingly kissed her youngest daughter awake.

"How do pancakes and bacon sound this morning?" she asked, pulling back the warm covers.

"Mom, can't I just sleep for a few more minutes?" Gracie revolted, rubbing her eyes.

"Gracie, we didn't come to New York for you to sleep the day away. I need you to get up and get dressed. I think a warm shower will help you wake up. Right now, please. I'm going to wake Jillian."

Walking into Jillian's room, she heard the shower in the bathroom.

It appeared she was already up. "Goodmorning, Sweetheart. Would you like pancakes for breakfast," she asked, knocking on the bathroom door.

"Yes. Mom, that sounds great. I won't take long."

"Okay. Thanks, Honey."

After enjoying breakfast with her girls, it was finally time to leave. Trying on wedding gowns was the first order of business for the day. Arriving at the first boutique, Bridal Beginnings, their window display held several stunning designs.

"Mom, these gowns are gorgeous," Jillian remarked, walking inside.

"Good morning ladies, welcome to Bridal Beginnings. I'm Jackie, and you must be our 10:00 a.m. appointment."

"Yes. I'm Daniella Demos, and these young ladies are my daughters, Jillian and Gracie."

"Nice to meet you. Please follow me. Would you like a glass of champagne and perhaps orange juice for the girls?"

"Thank you. That sounds wonderful."

Following Jackie, she led them towards the back of the shop and into a huge showroom. It was filled with numerous racks which held bridal gowns of all sizes and designs. It was a plethora of white and off-white gowns.

"Please have a seat. My assistant, Colleen, will be right with you."

After an hour of trying on different styles of gowns created by well-known designers, and another glass of champagne, it seemed Daniella was still indecisive.

"So, Mom, which was your favorite? I think you looked stunning in the heart-shaped A-line. Remember, the one that was embellished with Swarovski crystals," Jillian inquired.

"Jillian, I'm not sure about that particular gown. Why don't we continue our search at the other boutiques? I'm not quite sure I've found what I'm looking for. Besides, you girls didn't appear to like their selection of gowns for bridesmaids. So I think we should continue and keep looking."

"Mom, I completely agree with you. I didn't see anything I really liked," Gracie reluctantly admitted.

"Okay, girls, on to the next bridal shop."

After spending an entire day visiting numerous bridal boutiques, it was beginning to look as if their attempts to find the perfect gown were futile. Finally, however, there were two more appointments.

As the limo parked in front of the next boutique, Gowns by Pierre, their window display looked promising.

"Geez, mom, I think this might be the perfect place. Hopefully, you'll find what you're looking for," Jillian mentioned.

"Yes, Jillian, maybe they have what we're looking for too," Gracie added.

"I sure hope you're right. I've never tried on so many gowns before in my life." After hours of trying on bridal fashions, Daniella was becoming frustrated.

Their showroom began to look promising as they walked inside the boutique.

"Good afternoon, I'm Stephanie. Welcome to Gowns by Pierre."

"Thank you. We have an appointment at 3:00 p.m. Daniella Demos and my daughters, Jillian and Gracie, are with me this afternoon. I'm looking for something extraordinary. By that, I mean something outside your traditional designs, and my lovely daughters are also shopping for bridesmaid's dresses."

"Well, I believe you've come to the right place. Pierre specializes in gowns that are on the cutting edge of fashion. He prides himself on designing bridal fashions for women who dare to wear something which sets them apart from other brides. Follow me. May I offer you a glass of champagne or chardonnay? Would the girls like a beverage?"

"Thank you. I'll have chardonnay. I believe the girls will have a small glass of soda, Ginger Ale, if available."

Following Stephanie towards the back of the shop, they passed rack after rack of traditional long white gowns made of lace and satin. Perhaps, this wasn't going to be the right place like she had initially thought as she walked in.

"Please have a seat. My assistant, Marjorie, will be right out with your drinks. May I inquire what your dream gown would consist of as far as design and material? Also, do you have a particular price limit in mind?

"As I mentioned before, I'm looking for something a little outside of traditional, and no, there isn't a price limit."

"Is there a special color?"

"Yes. It's a second wedding, so I prefer to stay away from absolute white. I'm thinking off-white. I'm not fond of beige. Perhaps, light cream or ivory-colored gowns would look best. Also, I tend to favor form-fitting strapless gowns that accentuate the curves of a woman's body. However, on second thought, I would consider white if the design was something I fell in love with.

"Okay. I think I have your perfect gown. Marjorie will be right out with your drinks. She will work with the young ladies. I'm sure she'll find just what they're looking for in bridesmaid's attire. Give me a few minutes to check our selection. Oh, I almost forgot to ask. What timeline are we working within as far as your wedding date? If time permits, and you don't possibly find a gown you like today, we would be happy to place an order for you."

"Well, to be honest, I was hoping to find a gown today. Our wedding is a few months away. However, my trip this weekend was to specifically find a wedding gown while I'm in New York. So, I hope you'll be able to accommodate me by finding that one special gown that I've been searching for all morning."

"Certainly, give me just a few minutes to search our inventory."

"Mom, do you think they'll have a gown that you'll fall in love with?" Jillian shrugged.

"I'm not sure, but I certainly hope so," Daniella smiled.

Finally, after a few minutes, Stephanie walked out holding several different gowns in various shades of ivory.

"I've found some designs that I think you might like. Please follow me over to the dressing rooms. Marjorie is also pulling samples of our bridesmaid's dresses."

"Yes. Thank you," Jillian acknowledged following close behind with Gracie.

"Oh, you girls can bring your drinks with you."

After quickly trying on two completely different designs, Daniella became frustrated again. Finally, trying on her third design, she gasped. This was it. This dress was her reason for traveling to New York. Staring at herself in the mirror, she smiled. Turning, so her field of vision revealed every aspect of the gown, Daniella was, at last, thrilled.

"Girls, I've finally found my gown," she remarked from inside the dressing room.

"Great, mom. We can't wait to see it," Jillian answered in disbelief.

Walking out of the dressing room, the girls were amazed. Daniella looked stunning. She had never appeared more gorgeous or alluring. However, Daniella had completely changed her mind once again. Now, it seemed she had decided on a traditional design in white instead of cream. After all the hours spent looking for something untraditional, something outside the box, it appeared she would now walk down the aisle in a very traditional white gown.

She looked fabulous, wearing a magnificent, strapless, heart-shaped, form-fitting gown made of white satin overlaid with lace. Swarovski crystal buttons lined the back of the dress, making it sparkle. Sweeping her long blonde curls upward, she added a shoulder-length veil that matched identically. It eloquently completed her bridal ensemble.

"Mom. You chose white?" Jillian exclaimed.

"Yes. Completely unexpected, but I love this gown."

"Please, try these on," Stephanie asked, handing her a pair of crystal earrings.

"Wow, mom, you take my breath away," Gracie smiled.

At last, it had all come together. After hours of searching through racks of gowns at other boutiques, Daniella had finally found her dream gown. Now, only the bridesmaid's dresses remained to be chosen. Ultimately, however, it seemed a stroke of luck as Jillian and Gracie also found what they were looking for as well. After only a short time, they both decided upon long chiffon high-neck dresses in pink with matching flats. Combined with delicate gold jewelry, the girls were stunning.

"Geez, mom, I think we've finally found everything we were looking for, even after you, unbelievably, changed your color and design at the last minute. However, it was definitely the right call. That dress was made for you," Jillian smiled.

"I know. I guess I'm just a little more traditional than I originally thought," Daniella laughed.

Walking outside to the limo with their treasures, the girls laughed, knowing that cost had never entered their minds. Thanks to John, the total for today's wedding fashions was never an issue.

Glancing down at her watch, Daniella checked the time.

"Girls, we have just enough time for dinner and the Broadway performance tonight. What do you think? Are you both up to staying out late tonight and having a little fun?"

"Yes," Gracie enthusiastically answered.

"Mom, we're only in New York for the weekend. Do you have the tickets?" Jillian inquired.

"Yes. It just so happens that I do. They're in my purse."

"Well, I guess we're going to see *Gigi*. I can't wait," Gracie laughed.

After a delectable dinner at one of the restaurants John had recommended, they were ready for a night on Broadway. It would be another first for the girls from Destiny Cove. Entering the limo, they were on their way.

Gracie sat through the entire performance without saying a word. She was captivated by the music and the brilliance of the performers. The awe-inspiring experience made a significant impact on her. Daniella and Jillian both loved the play as well. However, they were not as mesmerized by the performance as she had been. After leaving the theater, Gracie made known her desire to one day work on Broadway.

"Mom, I've always loved acting in our plays at school. But, after seeing *Gigi,* I want to study acting and, hopefully, one day get a role in a musical. What do you think?" Gracie asked, stepping inside the limo for the ride back to the Plaza.

"Sweetheart, that's a pretty impressive goal. However, I believe you can do anything you set your heart and mind to do," Daniella smiled, leaning over to kiss her curly-haired daughter on the forehead.

"Yes, Gracie, you're good at acting. Every time I ask you to help me in the kitchen, you're always busy," Jillian teased.

"Jillian, please don't tease your sister. Sweetheart, there's something I've wanted to ask you. If money wasn't a problem, what university would you like to attend?"

"Mom, if money weren't an issue, I would like to attend Harvard. Matt was at Harvard. His friends Brad and Dexter are there, and I miss them so much. Honestly, I would like to be an environmentalist just like Matt. But, mom, I'll never understand why we lost him," Jillian explained, wiping tears from her eyes.

"I know, honey. Sometimes, there's no logical explanation for why tragic things happen. But, Matt bravely gave his life to save Gracie. She wouldn't be here if it weren't for Matt," Daniella reminded, giving Gracie a huge hug. Bringing up the subject brought tears to her eyes.

The rest of the ride back to the hotel seemed somber after their discussion regarding Matt. Daniella knew that John still carried the heartache of losing his only child. The loss of Matt and later Ava had greatly affected each of them. However, tonight wasn't about sadness. Instead, she needed to bring excitement and laughter back into their evening.

"Girls, why don't we stop at the Palm Court and have dessert before going up to our room. How does that sound?"

"Awesome," Gracie agreed. "Do you think they have brownies?"

"Oh, I'm sure. We've had a wonderful day. We should celebrate," Daniella added.

Looking at Jillian, she was still emotional.

"Jillian, are you alright?"

"Oh, mom, I've never told anyone, but I had fallen in love with Matt."

"Sweetheart, please don't be upset. I knew. John and I both knew. He was a great kid. If you truly want to attend Harvard, John will make it happen. But listen, don't go there just because of Matt. Only go there if it's what you truly want."

"It is what I want," Jillian stated with confidence wiping her face.

"Jillian, John loves you and Gracie. But, more importantly, I love you both very much. We'll see that you attend the university you want, even if it's Harvard. Now, no more crying. Let's get some ice cream," Daniella suggested putting her arms around Jillian.

Later that night, after devouring brownies and ice cream, the girls were finally ready to call it a night. Unlocking the door to their suite, it appeared the hurried activities of the day had begun to take their toll. Gracie and Jillian each quickly said goodnight rushing off in the direction of their rooms. Daniella walked over to the minibar. Opening a bottle of bourbon, she poured herself a small glass and sat down on the sofa. After her conversation in the limo with Jillian, it reminded her of the tragedies she had endured during the past few months. However, her life was about to change. Marrying John was not only exciting, but they were all long overdue for a little bit of happiness. She could hardly wait to get home and start planning their wedding. Just at that precise moment, the phone rang. Hurriedly rushing over to pick up the phone, she heard John's voice.

"Hey, Sweetheart, I tried calling the room earlier, but no one answered," John explained.

"Oh, we just walked in a few minutes ago. It's been a fun day but rather hectic."

"So did you find the wedding gown of your dreams," he teased.

"Yes. It's beautiful. How could I ever thank you?" Daniella cried, becoming somewhat emotional.

"Daniella, you don't have to thank me. I think you already did by agreeing to become Mrs. John McDermott," he answered.

"John, I want to come home in the morning. Could you have the plane ready?"

"Of course, but you're in New York, don't you want to stay and show the girls the sights of the city?" he questioned.

"John, I can't explain it, but I'm miserable without you."

"Oh, so, you miss me that much?" he teased.

"Please don't tease me. It's been a long day. I'm actually just finishing a glass of bourbon."

"Daniella, has it been that bad for you to be in New York without me? I thought you and the girls would have a wonderful time."

"John, we've had an incredible time. Gracie loved the Broadway performance so much that she now wants an acting career. But, as I said, I can't explain it. I simply miss you."

He knew. He could hear the stress in her voice.

"Okay. I've got you. If you want, I can have you out of New York tonight. You just say the word, and I'll have the limo pick you and the girls up and take you out to the airport right now."

"Oh, the girls are sleeping. So morning will have to do. I love you. How did I ever get so lucky?"

"Sweetheart, I think I'm the lucky one. I'll have the crew and plane ready to leave at 10:00 a.m. So you'll have time to enjoy breakfast. Please try to get some sleep. Tomorrow will arrive soon enough. I love you, and I can't wait to see you in the gown."

"Okay. I think the bourbon is finally kicking in. I'll see you tomorrow. By the way, you don't get to see the dress until I walk down the aisle," Daniella laughed. "Love you. See you soon."

Chapter Fifteen

The next few months seemed to fly by as John put the finishing touches on the elegant new Sea Oates Hotel and condominiums. It was a thing of beauty. Like a Phoenix rising from the ashes, it was gorgeous.

Daniella kept busy planning the wedding of her dreams. Even though the number of people in attendance would be small, it didn't seem to matter when it came to the eloquence of the wedding ceremony. She wanted only the best, and the McDermott Corporation was known worldwide for constructing high-end luxury hotels. John never left anything to chance when it came to the décor and ambiance of the hotels he created. His reputation had been built around the fact that his hotels never lacked sophistication or elegance. John simply constructed the best. He felt it ensured his units sold faster and kept guests coming back year after year. Daniella planned to use and incorporate his designs into the wedding of her dreams. It had finally been decided the reception would be held in the Sea Oates Hotel the following month. It was now in its final stage of completion and would encompass the theme of a Tuscany village.

Beautiful lit fountains graced the entrance to the main restaurant. The Venetian plastered walls and works of art reflected the magnificent aged décor found in buildings in Rome. The back of the restaurant incorporated a wall of glass sliding doors that opened onto tables sitting underneath bright cobalt umbrellas. The tables she planned to cover with white lace, each containing a spectacular vase of flowers along with eloquent candles. The tables would be scattered around the sizeable gray slate patio perimeter to allow an abundance of room for dancing. It was perfect. Large terracotta pots overflowing with red geraniums would be enhanced with lights. Even the long wooden walkway which led down to the beach would be lit and eloquently dressed in bows.

She had decided early on that Henry would walk her down the aisle. However, there would be no church. Instead, the ceremony was planned to take place on the beach below the back terrace of the new Sea Oates. A place that had always been close to her heart. It was the beach she had raised her daughters on, the beach she had jogged on, and the waters she swam in during the summer months. It also held her earliest memories of Dimitri. This property was also his dream when he bought the original Sea Oates. There was no other place closer to her heart than this stretch of white sandy beach she had called home for so many years.

John worked feverishly, ensuring Jillian would be accepted at Harvard. Even though she had been the Valedictorian of her graduating class at the local high school and easily had the highest grades possible, John still donated money to refurbish buildings and dormitories on the campus. He also gave money to scholarship funds. Putting his money to good use on the campus would guarantee her receiving a placement at the prestigious college. Finally, she was accepted and enrolled in the fall semester. While taking Jillian up to tour the college, John found the perfect apartment near the campus. Finally, letting her pick out the car of her dreams seemed to be the icing on the cake. Needless to say, she was ecstatic. However, before she could leave Destiny Cove, she had to fulfill her duty of standing next to her mother as maid of honor.

During the grand opening week, John and his crew were hosted at numerous gala events in and around Destiny Cove. The completion of his enormous project was an overwhelming victory for the people who lived in the community. Its completion signified growth not only to Destiny Cove but also to the adjoining towns. It would now bring in huge tourist dollars which had been missing from the local economy. Other developers were encouraged to build along the beautiful emerald shores of the Gulf of Mexico after seeing the benefits of his new hotel. The coastline was soon inundated in new construction. Hotels, condominiums, restaurants, and shopping centers sprang up everywhere. The Florida panhandle quickly became a playground for the rich and famous.

Finally, there was the matter of renting their house. After offering it to Henry at no cost, he'd made it quite clear that he intended to stay in his tiny apartment near the docks. He was a creature of habit and had no intention of moving into a large house at his age. After all, there were the memories of Ava to contend with. It simply held too many recollections of past events. So instead, Henry planned to spend his remaining days near the docks working on fishing boats. After Henry's negative response to moving in, the house was simply put on the market.

Gracie found it difficult to say goodbye to her close friends, especially those she had grown up with. However, having Truffles helped tremendously. Other than Jillian, the tiny puppy had become her one constant companion.

Now, the wedding was less than two weeks away. It left just enough time to arrange for flowers, food, and final preparations for decorating, along with packing up their belongings and listing the house for sale. It was a hectic time.

"Tracey, our realtor, wants to do an open house this weekend," John remarked, walking into the living room.

"John, can't she just wait until we're out of the house before she starts showing it?"

"Fortunately, she already has an interested buyer. Why don't we agree to let her show the house? It won't take that long. Afterward, we can take the girls to dinner."

"Fine, but I'm not moving any of the boxes that I've packed. So I hope she understands."

"I don't think she'll mind maneuvering around a few boxes."

"John, can you believe by this time next week, we'll be married."
Walking over, he held Daniella in his arms.

"Sweetheart, it can't happen soon enough for me. Are you looking forward to living in Hong Kong?" he asked, pulling her long blonde hair behind her ear as he kissed the slender nape of her neck.

"John, I'd follow you anywhere. However, I do like a few luxuries, like running water and inside amenities," she laughed.

"Daniella, I'm an architect, not a magician. So we don't go into locations like that, at least not at this time. My corporation only builds where there's the possibility of high-density residences," he chuckled. "Babe, you realize we're not going to have time for a honeymoon, right?"

"Oh, I know. But that doesn't mean we're not having a honeymoon. We're just postponing it until after we're settled in Hong Kong, right?"

"Yes. After we're all settled and you've hired a housekeeper that you trust, I promise to take you on the honeymoon of a lifetime. Just wait, Mrs. McDermott, you'll see," he winked, kissing her once more.

Deciding it would be best to vacate the house a few days before their wedding, they temporarily moved into one of the penthouses at the Sea Oates along with the girls and Truffles. It would help to expedite things. They were scheduled to leave immediately after the ceremony for Hong Kong.

As the morning sun filtered in through the drapes, finally, the day of their long-overdue wedding had arrived. The brilliance of the morning sun bathed the bedroom in a soft glow. John woke first. Looking over at his beautiful bride-to-be, he had never been more in love with her. Watching as she slept peacefully, John again felt like the luckiest man on earth. What had he ever done to deserve such a woman as Daniella? Leaning over, he kissed her awake.

"Daniella, I love you," he softly whispered. "Do you know what day it is?" he teased. "I think two people who fell madly in love are finally getting married," he said tenderly, brushing back her long blonde curls.

"That's us," she teased with a smile. Then, slowly opening her eyes, she rolled over to face him. "John, I love you. Do you even know how much?" she asked as tears began to trickle down her cheeks.

"Sweetheart, tears already. How will you ever make it through the day?" he winked, wiping her face with the back of his hand. "I love you, no more tears," he repeated. "I'll order room service."

Quickly getting out of bed, he dressed and walked over to the phone to order breakfast. Thinking of the girls who were still asleep in the next room, he decided to order a variety of breakfast entrees. Starting with pancakes, bacon, eggs, sausages, and hash browns, he ordered the entire breakfast menu along with orange juice, coffee, and a bottle of their finest champagne. Nothing was too good for his girls this morning.

Walking over, he opened the drapes. The morning sun glistened as its rays reflected off the beautiful turquoise waters of the Gulf of Mexico. So much had happened since he'd first relocated to Destiny Cove. It had only been a year, but the past twelve months had brought tragedies and heartache. However, unexpectedly, it had also given him the love of his life and a chance at a new beginning. Today, he would become a husband and the loving father of two beautiful girls. Conclusively, he would leave with more than he came with. His world had been torn apart, yet today would bring him unfathomable joy. He would leave with the woman of his dreams. Their love would sustain him for a lifetime.

Hearing a knock at the door meant the arrival of breakfast. Instantly rebounding from his deep thoughts, it was time to get the day started.

"Good morning, sir," the young gentleman smiled, pushing a cart laden with silver warming trays inside the room." The delectable aroma of bacon infused the air along with the hint of warm pancakes, scrambled eggs, everything imaginable for breakfast. Then, generously tipping the young man, he closed the door.

"Breakfast has arrived," John announced, walking into the bedroom. "Perhaps you should let the girls know."

Grabbing her robe, Daniella quickly pulled her long hair into a ponytail and walked over to the girl's room.

"Jillie, Gracie, time to get up," she whispered, drawing back their curtains. "Breakfast has arrived. You need to get up and eat before it gets cold," she added. "Today is our big day, no more time for sleeping."

"Wow. Mom, you're right. Are you excited?" Gracie asked, jumping out of bed.

"Yes. However, I'm sad at seeing Jillian leave for college."

"Oh, Mom, all kids eventually leave for college," Jillian explained. "I'm excited. Brad and Dexter arrived late last night. So we'll be driving back together. Please be happy for me," Jillian smiled, sitting up in bed.

"Sweetheart, I am happy for you. But after today, I'll be in Hong Kong, and you'll be in Massachusetts," Daniella frowned.

"Mom, please, with all the Lear Jets John owns, and you're worried about the distance," Jillian laughed. "You're welcome at my apartment anytime. Just don't come too often," Jillian added, snuggling back under the covers.

"Jillian, please get up. We have a lot to do. Breakfast is here, and soon the make-up crew will be arriving. You want to look your best, right?" Daniella mentioned.

"We'll be out in a moment," the girls laughed.

"Okay. Don't make me have to come back in here," Daniella scolded, closing the door.

John popped the cork from the bottle of champagne.

"I think we need to start this day with a toast," John suggested pouring them each a small amount of the sparkling beverage. John smiled as he gave Daniella a glass.

"Sweetheart, here's to a long and happy marriage. I love you."

"Oh, John, I love you too," Daniella smiled. Her beautiful eyes glistened with tears.

"Please, remember what I said about those tears of yours," he teased. "No more crying. Why aren't you drinking your champagne? I'll see if there's any Kleenex in the bathroom. I have a feeling they're going to be needed a lot today," he smiled with a wink.

After enjoying breakfast with the girls, John announced that he would be going over to Craig's room to get dressed. Craig was John's best man. Also, Brad and Dexter had agreed to meet the men in Craig's room. The boys were escorting Gracie and Jillian down the aisle. Now, John only hoped that Henry remembered to come over early to the hotel.

"I'm going over to Craig's room about noon. I had the men's tuxedos delivered to his room last night," John explained, lighting up a cigar.

"So, Mr. McDermott, when did you decide to start smoking?" Daniella scoffed.

"Oh that, it's only a cigar," he laughed. "It calms my nerves."

"Mom. Give the poor guy a break," Jillian laughed.

"Okay, Mr. McDermott, you're on notice. Only today," Daniella shrugged. "I really don't see what you have to be nervous about."

"Sweetheart, I've been single for a lot of years. I can't explain it," he winked. "Don't panic. I love you."

"Well, when you go over to Craig's room, you take those nasty things with you."

"No problem. Craig loves cigars."

Hearing a knock at the door," John walked over.

"I have a flower delivery for the bride-to-be," the young man stated. He was holding the most enormous bouquet of red roses John had ever seen. Quickly, giving him a tip, John took the flowers.

"I think you have an admirer," he laughed.

"Who are they from?"

"I don't know. Let me take a look at the card. Oh, the roses are from Craig and the boys. Wow. These are stunning," John mentioned sitting the massive vase on the marble coffee table.

"Be sure to thank them for me," Daniella smiled as she walked over to take a closer look and inhale their intoxicating aroma.

"They'll be at our wedding. I'll let you tell them," John suggested. "I'm going to jump in the shower before it gets too late."

The morning seemed to fly. Daniella and the girls sat on the sofa reminiscing over their earlier years of growing up along the beautiful Gulf Coast. Now, it seemed fate was pulling them away from the snow-white beaches they had grown to love.

"Well, you know what they say about our sugary white sands. Once you get the sand between your toes, it stays with you forever," Daniella commented as tears welled in her eyes.

"Mom. You are so right. Destiny Cove will always be home. We'll always come back. But, please, don't cry. John is right. How are you ever going to make it through the day without Kleenex?" Jillian smiled.

"Alright ladies, I'll see you at the alter. It's noon. I'm going over to Craig's room. First, I have to make sure Henry shows up," he winked, giving the girls a tight squeeze and quick kiss. Next, he walked over to Daniella. "Sweetheart, don't break my heart by not showing up," John teased. "I love you. I can't wait to see you in your stunning gown," he laughed, picking her up as he twirled her around. "I love you," he winked. At last stopping, he put her down. Pulling her tightly to his chest, he kissed her with such passion it made the girls blush.

"John, I love you. But, don't worry, I'll be there," she teased as he closed the door.

Quickly, just for a second, he reopened the door.

"Girls, don't forget the Kleenex," he winked. "I'm afraid your mom is going to need them."

"Mom, he really loves you. He's such a great guy," Jillian smiled.

"I know. I love him too. But just so you girls know, I never stopped loving your father. I miss him even today," Daniella admitted with tears in her eyes. "I'll always carry his love with me forever."

"We know, mom. Now, stop crying before we all start. You don't want us all to look like blubbering idiots today. Do you?" Jillian laughed.

"Girls, I'm going to jump in the shower and wash my hair. The make-up crew John hired will arrive at 1:00 p.m.," Daniella mentioned walking back towards her bedroom.

After Daniela left the living room, Gracie took the chance to speak up.

"Jillian, John's right. We can't forget the tissues. Mom is going to need them," Gracie sternly warned.

"Oh, Gracie, grow up. I'd never let Mom walk out of here without those."

Hearing another gentle knock at the door, Jillian walked over to answer it.

"Good morning, I have your bridal bouquets from Patterson's House of Flowers," the young girl announced, handing her three large boxes which smelled heavenly.

"Thank you. Just a moment," Jillian stated.

Running to get Daniella's purse, she quickly returned with money to graciously tip the young woman for the delivery.

"Thank you."

"You're welcome," Jillian smiled, closing the door.

"The flowers smell wonderful," Gracie mentioned opening the box which was marked with her name.

It revealed a gorgeous springtime bouquet of white baby's breath mixed with pink rose buds and white carnations. The flowers were entwined with greenery, and the handle was wrapped in cascading pink ribbons.

"Jillian, these are beautiful. Open your box."

Opening her box, it was precisely the same.

"These are beautiful. Do you think we should take a look at mom's bouquet?" Jillian hesitated.

"Sure. Why not?" Gracie snickered.

The flowers were breathtaking as Jillian opened the larger box. The larger bridal bouquet consisted of a beautiful floral arrangement of large white roses and miniature white Calla Lilies encased within a circle of red Anthuriums and greenery. It was exquisite. The handle of the bridal bouquet was also wrapped in white silk ribbons.

"Wow, that's stunning. Mom's going to love it," Jillian smiled.

"Yes. It's beautiful," Gracie agreed.

A few minutes later, another knock was heard at the door.

"Geez, it seems like Grand Central Station," Jillian laughed

"I have a delivery for Daniella Demos from Mr. John McDermott," the gentleman said, handing Jillian an exquisitely wrapped box with a card.

"Thank you. Wait just a moment."

Once again, running for her mom's purse, they were quickly running out of money for tips. Taking what was left, Jillian hurriedly returned to the door handing the gentleman a generous amount.

"Thank you."

"You're welcome," Jillian graciously smiled once again.

"Girls, what's going on?" Daniella asked, walking out of her bedroom with her wet hair wrapped in a towel. "I thought I heard voices."

"Mom, we received our bridesmaid bouquets, along with your bridal bouquet. You also received a gift from John," Gracie smiled.

"A gift?" Daniella questioned.

"Here's the box," Jillian grinned. She had no idea what it contained.

Sitting down on the sofa, wearing only a white bathrobe and her wet hair wrapped in a turban, Daniella read the card.

"Sweetheart, thank you for saying yes. Meet you on the beach. I love you," John.

Opening the box, Daniella gasped. It was an exquisite diamond necklace.

"Wow, this must-have cost a fortune," she mumbled under her breath.

She couldn't even begin to count the number of diamonds making up the width of the sixteen-inch necklace that was entwined with shimmering diamonds.

"Geez, mom, I've never seen a necklace with so many diamonds. It shimmers like the sun," Gracie mentioned taking a closer look.

"I'm surprised the gentleman who delivered it didn't arrive with security," Jillian laughed. "You're going to look stunning wearing those."

"Girls, this necklace isn't cheap," Daniella gasped.

"Mom, you're going to look a million bucks wearing the necklace when you walk down the aisle," Gracie added.

"I know," Daniella paused to wipe her eyes. "I know."

Hearing another knock at the door, this certainly had to be the hairdresser and make-up artists.

Walking over, this time, Gracie answered the door.

"Hello. I'm Alexis, and this is my crew. We're here to style your hair and do your make-up for the wedding. This is Cindy, Julie, and Christina. Are you ready to get started?"

"Yes. Come in," Gracie smiled. "Mom, the girls are here to style our hair and do make-up."

"Great. I guess we better get started," Daniella mentioned getting up from the sofa with the necklace safely back in the box for the moment.

"It looks as if you've already washed your hair," Alexis noticed.

"Yes."

"Great. Julie will be styling your hair, and Cindy and Christina will do the girl's hair and make-up. How would you like for us to style their hair?"

"I'd like them to wear their hair up with tiny satin rosebuds placed within the curls," Daniella suggested. "Of course, I want their make-up to be minimal at best, just a hint for the photos. My girls are natural beauties. They won't require a lot of make-up," she added.

"That will be lovely. What did you envision for yourself?" Alexis inquired.

"I would also like to wear my hair up. I would like it swept back in an abundance of curls. I don't want it to look overly done. Also, I'd like the veil simply attached to my hairband. It's sterling silver and embedded with crystals. It belonged to my mother. I think it will look eloquent. However, I'm removing the veil and the headband after saying our vows. Also, it will be a lot easier to dance in my gown without the worry of the veil attached," Daniella explained. "What do you think?"

"Great choice. I think it will look exquisite. Okay, girls, let's get to work. First, I will check on the bridal gown and the bridesmaid's dresses to see if they need to be steam-pressed."

Meanwhile, in Craig's suite, the room began to reek of cigars. The aroma coming from cigar smoke hung heavily in the air. Brad and Dexter were getting dressed as the guys anxiously waited for Henry. Bottles of whiskey and other spirits sat opened and scattered around the room. It definitely appeared to be a gentlemen's dressing room. Clothes were strewn everywhere. Finally, John heard a soft knock at the door. It was Henry.

"Henry, I'm so glad you could make it. I was beginning to get a bit worried," John smiled as he opened the door. "Come in."

"Oh, I would never upset Daniella. Especially when I'm walking her down the aisle today."

"Henry, by chance, have you ever worn a tux?" John asked.

"Nope, can't say that I have."

"Well, I guess today will be a first for you," John laughed as he lightly slapped Henry on his back. "Would you care for a drink?"

"Is that even a question?" Henry remarked.

"So, what's your poison this afternoon?"

"Oh, I'll have a glass of Jack Daniels."

"Great. I'll join you," John smiled, pouring them each a small glass of whiskey. "I believe your tuxedo is hanging on the rack," he added, quickly downing the drink and pouring them another.

Finally, the men were dressed, looking elegant.

"John, before we walk down to the elevator, I'd like to make a toast," Craig grinned, filling five small glasses with Jack Daniels. "Men, please raise your glass."

"Here's to the luckiest man I know. We've been through a lot over the past twelve years. I wish you and Daniella a long and happy marriage. No one deserves it more," Craig toasted. "Now, let's get this man married. We have another high-rise hotel to build in Hong Kong," he laughed.

"Thanks, Craig," John smiled, turning off the lights as he closed the door on their way out.

Wearing the beautiful silk satin gown, Daniella walked out of her bedroom. The gown fit her body like a glove accentuating her slim figure. The lace veil adorned with Swarovski crystals was perfectly attached to her mom's sterling silver hairband. Just the mere sight of her caused everyone in the room to gasp.

"Wow, mom, you're stunning," Gracie exclaimed.

"Oh, mom, you look gorgeous," Jillian added. "Mom, you forgot John's necklace." The expression on Daniella's face reflected sheer panic.

"Geez, sweetheart, you're right. I guess in the excitement of getting dressed, I simply forgot. But, don't worry, I'm going to get it."

Walking out with the box in her hand, she smiled, looking over at Jillian.

"Jillian, will you do me the honor of fastening it?"

"Yes. Mom, as your maid of honor, I'd consider it a privilege to assist you," Jillian smiled, fastening the diamond necklace around her mother's slender neck. "Wow, it's exquisite. Just like you."

"Girls, you both look amazing. Pink was the perfect color. It enhances your tanned face. You're both beautiful. I love you," she smiled, giving them each a quick kiss. "Okay, are we ready to go?" she winked. Pausing for a moment, she slowly inhaled, taking a deep breath to steady herself. They were finally ready.

As the elevator doors opened onto the lobby, a brilliant ray of sunshine streamed in through the huge windows surrounding the impressive hotel entrance. Daniella took it to be a good sign. She felt the closeness of Dimitri and Ava, standing beside her. Wiping her moist eyes, Daniella lightly bit her bottom lip. Hopefully, it would stop the tears she felt welling within her eyes.

Watching as she and the girls walked into the lobby, Henry, Brad, and Dexter rushed over to greet them.

"Daniella, you look like an angel," Henry complimented.

"Thanks, Henry. You don't look so bad yourself," Daniella teased.

"Geez, Daniella, you're stunning," Dexter added.

"I'll say," Brad chimed in. "You're gorgeous."

"Thanks, guys. You both look pretty handsome yourselves."

"Jillian, you and Gracie are beautiful," the boys remarked.

"Thanks, guys," the girls answered in unison.

Glancing at the clock behind the receptionist's desk, it read 1: 50 p.m. It was almost 2:00 p.m.

"Well, Henry, are you ready to take a walk down to the beach," Daniella beamed, carefully removing her satin stilettos.

"Mom, you're going barefoot?" the girls laughed.

"Remember the story I told you about getting the sugar-white sands between your toes. I want to carry these memories with me for a lifetime," Daniella smiled as an onslaught of tears flowed down her cheeks.

Watching as she removed her high heels, the girls quickly followed her lead.

"Mom, we're removing our shoes too," the girls smiled, taking off their white satin flats. Then, hurriedly, they placed their shoes near the receptionist's desk for safekeeping.

"Daniella, I certainly hope you don't mind, but I think the boys and I will keep our shoes on," Henry suggested.

"Oh, Henry, that's fine," Daniella laughed. "Okay, are you ready to take that walk," she smiled, grasping Henry's arm.

"Yes, ma'am," Henry grinned.

The day was perfect as the boys escorted Jillian and Gracie down to the beach. The weather was amazingly cooperative. The sun was warm, and a light breeze blew in from the direction of the clear, shimmering, turquoise waters. The tranquil sound of waves gently washing ashore provided the perfect backdrop.

John hired musicians who provided a string ensemble. Softly, the musicians played *Can't Help Falling in Love*. The string ensemble continued with the beautiful music as the girls slowly walked down to the beach. First, Gracie, escorted by Dexter, made their entrance. Following close behind was Jillian, as the Maid of Honor, accompanied by Brad. The peaceful, outdoor scenery provided the perfect backdrop for the wedding. Pausing at the altar, a white wooden arch covered with green ivy and pink roses, the girls and their escorts, Reverend Mac, Craig, and John, waited for the bride's grand entrance. Suddenly, John was breathless seeing Daniella for the first time in her magnificent, strapless, white lace gown and matching shoulder-length veil. Watching as Henry proudly took Daniella's arm, escorting her down the beach towards him, he was sure she had never looked more radiant. The Swarovski crystals shimmered brilliantly in the sunlight. The gown was visually stunning as she walked towards him. Daniella simplistically appeared to be angelic. No other word came to mind to describe the vision he saw before him. The diamond necklace glittered fiercely, reflecting the radiance of the afternoon sun.

Standing face to face, John took her hand.

"Wow, sweetheart, you're stunning. I love you," he whispered. "I see you received my gift," he winked.

"Yes. Thanks. I love you too," Daniella whispered with a smile.

"It's my privilege on this beautiful afternoon to unite John McDermott and Daniella Demos as husband and wife," Reverend Mac began. "John, please repeat after me."

"I, John, take you, Daniella, to be my wife, to have and to hold from this day forward, for better or worse, for richer, for poorer, in sickness and in health, to love and to cherish; from this day forward until death do us part."

"Daniella, now please repeat after me."

"I, Daniella, take you, John, to be my husband, to have and to hold from this day forward, for better or worse, for richer for poorer, in sickness and in health, to love and to cherish; from this day forward until death do us part."

"May I please have the rings. John, as you place the ring on Daniella's finger, please repeat after me."

"With this ring, I marry you and bind my life to yours. It symbolizes my eternal love, my everlasting friendship, and the promise of all my tomorrows.

"Daniella, as you place the ring on John's finger, please repeat after me."

"With this ring, I marry you and bind my life to yours. It symbolizes my eternal love, my everlasting friendship, and the promise of all my tomorrows."

The exchange of their vows and wedding rings only took a few minutes. However, the bond of love that now united them would last forever. They were now man and wife.

"You may kiss your beautiful bride," the reverend smiled.

As John playfully kissed Daniella, the guys representing the work crew who constructed the Sea Oates whistled their approval while others in attendance loudly clapped.

"I now proudly present to you for the very first time, Mr. and Mrs. John McDermott. "What God has joined together, let no man put asunder."

Firmly grasping Daniella's hand, John proudly escorted his new bride back up the aisle. Then, looking down, he laughed.

"Sweetheart, you have no shoes."

"I know. I want my toes deeply embedded in the white sands of this beach so that I'll never lose the memory of this day."

It was time to party.

John rushed over to give Jillian and Gracie a huge hug and kiss. "You both look amazing, just like your mother. I'm so proud of you."

"Thanks, John. You look pretty handsome yourself," Jillian smiled.

Thunderous applause resonated throughout the beautifully decorated restaurant as John and Daniella made their grand entrance. Watching as they entered the room, Craig rushed over.

"Congratulations," Craig smiled. "Daniella, you look gorgeous. John's a lucky guy. I guess we'll be seeing a lot of each other once we arrive in Hong Kong," he added.

"Yes. Thanks, Craig, I'm sure," Daniella smiled.

As the band began to play, *The Way You Look Tonight*, John grasped Daniella's hand and pulled her towards the dance floor. Then, holding her tight in his arms, he slowly began leading his beautiful bride with no shoes around the dance floor. Everyone watched their display of love and affection.

"I didn't know you could dance?" Daniella whispered.

"Oh, I'm sure there are a few things you don't know," he teased.

"Oh, is that so, Mr. McDermott," she laughed.

After the song ended, Daniella suggested it was time to begin the dinner service. Walking over to find Craig, she asked him to make the announcement.

"Everyone, please find your seats. We're going to begin serving dinner," Craig announced.

The staff served a delicious feast of lobster tails, filet mignon, chicken breasts stuffed with cheese and spinach, along with a variety of salads and fresh vegetables. Wine and champagne flowed freely throughout the evening.

Sitting at the front table reserved for the wedding party, it seemed Craig kept everyone in stitches. He recounted hilarious memories of his long-standing friendship with John. But, unfortunately, John felt Craig's remarks were intended to embarrass him in front of his new bride rather than be entertaining.

After their guests enjoyed dinner, Craig asked the servers to refill the champagne glasses.

"May I please have everyone's attention," Craig announced as he lightly tapped his glass with a spoon drawing everyone's focus to the head table. "I'd like to make the first toast of the evening to John and Daniella."

"Be kind," John laughed, pulling on Craig's tuxedo.

"I've known John for many years. We've traveled all over the world together and built some pretty amazing hotels, I might add. However, there's one thing I've come to love about this man. Even though he may be the boss or head honcho of McDermott Corporation, this man will get down in the trenches with you when it comes to getting things done. John, you are the luckiest man on earth to have met and married this gorgeous blonde. My sincere best wishes for a lifetime of happiness. I love you both. Please raise your glass in a toast to the happy couple," Craig smiled.

"Thanks, Craig," John smiled.

Suddenly, Henry surprised everyone by standing up to offer the next toast.

"I can't say that I've known John for a long time. But I've certainly grown to like him a lot over the past few months. Maybe not quite so much in the beginning. I think he'll understand that one. However, I've certainly known his beautiful bride for many years. Daniella is as gorgeous on the inside as she is on the outside. We lost a dear family member this past year, and if she were here tonight, I'm sure she would be standing with me to wish the very best for Daniella and John. Sweetheart, I love you. John, you better take good care of my girl. Here's to Daniella and John," Henry toasted.

"Okay, everyone, let's move this party outside to the patio," Craig suggested. "The night is young and beautiful. There's plenty of room for dancing," he announced.

The band members set up outside on the patio surrounding the pool as a stunning five-tiered wedding cake was carefully brought out. Lovingly, John grasped Daniella's hand, leading her over to the cake.

"I think we should cut the cake. What do you think?" he winked.

"Definitely," Daniella agreed.

As everyone watched, she placed her hand on top of John's. Together they both grasped the handle of the sterling silver knife, cutting their first slice of cake. Then, turning to face each other, they began laughing hilariously.

"John, don't you dare," Daniella warned a bit too late.

John gently shoved a huge piece of cake into her mouth. Then, noticing the shock on her face, he lovingly began kissing away any remains of the cake and icing.

"I had to do it," he laughed.

"Alright, Mr. McDermott," Daniella grinned. "Your turn."

Before John even realized what was happening, Daniella took another huge slice of cake. As she aimed to shove it into his mouth, he ducked, trying to avoid the cake and another catastrophe from being smeared on his face. However, his idea only made it worse. Daniella completely missed his mouth as she hilariously plastered the cake directly into his face as everyone roared with laughter.

"Wow. Sweetheart, you better be scared," John teased. "You're with me now, remember," he winked seductively, grabbing napkins to wipe his face.

"John, I'm sorry. But it would help if you hadn't ducked," Daniella laughed.

Giving him a quick kiss, she took napkins and began wiping away the remains of the cake. Finally, they both regained their composure.

As the band began playing, *You Are So Beautiful*, John grabbed Daniella. He pulled her to his chest and held her in his arms as they slowly circled the dance floor.

Daniella's eyes moistened, staring into the depths of John's captivating blue eyes.

"John, tonight has been the happiest I've ever been. I couldn't possibly love you more. I have a little surprise for you later," she smiled.

"Sweetheart, thank you for saying *yes* in Kauai. I love you," John whispered. "I promise to cherish each moment with you and give you and the girls the best life possible. So you're keeping secrets, so soon, Mrs. McDermott," John lovingly questioned.

"Later," Daniel smiled with a quick kiss.

After a few moments, everyone joined in. Even Jillian and Gracie were seen on the dance floor enjoying themselves under the brilliance of the evening stars that appeared in abundance.

The night quickly became magical as John took turns dancing with both Jillian and Gracie.

"Gracie, do you think you're going to like living in Hong Kong?" John inquired as he danced with her around the dance floor.

"I think so," she smiled. "However, I'm going to miss Jillian."

"I know. We're all going to miss Jillian. But, please try not to worry, it's only distance. I've been traveling around the world for many years now. So you'll see her more often than you think," he winked, giving her a quick kiss on the forehead.

Now, it was Jillian's turn. Catching a glimpse of her, he walked over.

"May I have this dance?" John lovingly asked.

"Certainly."

Grasping her hand, he escorted her out to the dance floor. Then, lovingly, he danced with her throughout the next song, *My Girl.*

"Jillian, I haven't had the chance to talk with you very much this evening, but your mother, and I, along with Gracie, are certainly going to miss you after tonight. I want you to know that you're welcome to come to Hong Kong any time. I know that Brad and Dexter will ride with you back to Massachusetts tomorrow morning, but I want you to drive safely. The guys can help you drive. Don't worry about your finances while you're at Harvard. I'll be depositing money each month into your account. Just use it wisely," he teased. "I want you to know that we're all very proud of you. Matt would be happy to know that you chose Harvard. I love you," John winked, kissing her on the cheek. "Oh, one last thing, don't worry about your mom or Gracie. I'll take great care of those girls," he smiled.

"I know. I love you, Dad," Jillian smiled, walking off the dance floor towards Brad.

She would never know how much those simple words meant to him. After losing Matt, he knew the importance of family, and the chance to become a father to the girls was priceless.

The night lingered on into the early morning hours as everyone danced, drank, and simply enjoyed the company of those around them.

However, John had his flight crew on standby at the airport. He needed to be in Hong Kong within the next forty-eight hours. Not much time to travel halfway around the world and be revived entirely from the flight before hosting his first business meeting.

Looking around, he quickly caught sight of Daniella talking with Craig.

"Daniella, I hate to end our lovely evening, but it's getting late. I have the flight crew on standby at the airport. They are ready to leave as soon as we arrive. So, Craig, when are you and the guys coming over?"

"Oh, we're leaving for Hong Kong tomorrow at noon. We're flying commercial for a change. I'll give your office a call as soon as we arrive."

"Great," John smiled. "Sorry, Sweetheart, I'm afraid you should begin saying your goodbyes. I see Henry nursing a glass of Jack Daniels. Let's walk over."

Grasping Daniella's hand, he walked over with her to say goodbye. He knew this wasn't going to be easy.

"Well, Henry, I guess this is so long for now. Thanks for everything, especially watching the girls so I could take this gorgeous young lady to Hawaii and make all of this possible. Whenever you feel like coming to Hong Kong, just let me know. I'll have you on the next plane."

"Yes. Henry, please visit. We're going to miss you," Daniella agreed, wiping her eyes. "Thanks for walking me down the aisle today. You know, I've probably never told you, but I've always considered you a father figure. I love you." Putting her arms around him, she became emotional. "Henry, thank you. Thank you for always being there for me, the girls, and Ava before she passed. We depended on you, and you never once let us down. Henry, I love you. Are you going to be okay? Who's going to drive you home?"

"Sweetheart, don't worry about this old fisherman. I was making it just fine here in Destiny Cove before you even arrived on the scene. But, maybe, I might just surprise you one of these days and show up at your door," he suggested with the hint of a smile.

"Well, Henry, trust me, we'd be happy to see you. Take care," John smiled, reaching out to shake his hand.

"I love you, Henry," Daniella smiled as tears trickled down her face.

"Babe, what's with you and all the waterworks tonight. I think you're coming down with something. Are you sure you're feeling okay?" John asked, glancing around for Gracie and Jillian.

"I've never been better," Daniella smiled, momentarily lost in the intensity of John's blue eyes. "I see Gracie and Jillian standing next to Brad and Dexter."

"Great. We better walk over."

"Well, girls, I guess this is where we all say our goodbyes," John suggested as he walked up to Jillian and Gracie.

"Jillian, I expect you to drive safe tomorrow. But, Brad, you, and Dexter better see to it that Jillian gets back to Harvard all in one piece. Do you understand?" Daniella warned sternly.

"Oh, don't worry, Mrs. McDermott, we're not going to let anything happen to Jillian," Dexter spoke up.

"Wow. Mrs. McDermott, is it?" Daniella smiled. "I think that's the first time someone has used my married name this evening."

"I think you better get used to it," John teased.

"Oh, Jillian," Daniella smiled, wrapping her arms around her daughter. "This is the hardest thing I've ever had to do. I love you, and I'm going to miss you more than you could possibly know," she cried, finally breaking down as she loosened her grip on Jillian, turning to bury her head into John's chest. Daniella sobbed. "John, this is so hard. I know that I'm making a complete fool of myself."

"Daniella, it's okay. Everyone understands," John mentioned trying to comfort her. "Sweetheart, please don't cry. I promise it's not the end of the world. Remember, I own several aircraft. So I think I'm well equipped to see that you and the girls are together as often as you like."

"Oh, John," Daniella cried. "How did we ever deserve you?"

"Sweetheart, I think it's more like, how did I ever deserve you and the girls," he smiled with a wink.

"Mom, please stop crying. You know that I love you. Going away to Harvard is a dream come true for me. I want this more than anything. Can't you just try to understand and be happy for me?" Jillian asked, putting her arms around Daniella.

"Okay, I will try," Daniella answered, wiping her face. "I'm sorry.

I didn't mean to become so emotional. I truly want you to be happy. If you want to attend Harvard, it's okay. We can talk over the phone."

"Yes. Mom, we can. However, not every night," Jillian looked up at John with a plea of desperation in her eyes.

"Don't worry. I won't let your mom call you every night. How would you ever study?" John whispered into Jillian's ear.

"Well, ladies, the limo is waiting to drive us out to the airport. We have a long flight ahead. Brad, Dexter, you guys take great care of my girl. You're both welcome to visit us in Hong Kong at any time. Maybe you could bring this gorgeous girl with you," he suggested kissing Jillian for the last time.

"Bye, Mom. So long, Gracie, I'll see you later," Jillian smiled. "Goodbye, Dad. I love you."

Turning to walk away, John for once felt his eyes moisten.

Rushing Daniella and Gracie back up to their hotel suite, there was just enough time to change clothes before the limo arrived.

"Make sure you're not leaving anything behind. Then, when you're finished packing, I'll set your luggage by the door," John suggested.

The limo parked close to the private jet as they arrived at the airport. Ascending the steps, Daniella suddenly stopped. Turning around, she paused for a brief moment, taking one last look at Destiny Cove. Saying goodbye to the only home she had ever known wasn't easy. She would miss the beautiful turquoise waters and sugar-white beaches. However, she knew the sand between her toes would always beckon her back to their beautiful pristine shores. With tears gently trickling down her cheeks, she was finally ready to leave the Emerald Coast. With one last glance, she whispered, "Dimitri, I love you. You'll always be with me forever."

"Good morning, Mr. and Mrs. McDermott. Welcome aboard," Stacie smiled. "Congratulations. Gracie, it's so nice to have you flying with us again this morning. What a cute puppy. He's adorable. Can I bring anyone a beverage before we're airborne?"

"Yes. I think tonight, as always, demands champagne. Our daughter would like soda. Preferably, Ginger Ale," John answered.

"John, I'll pass on the champagne. However, I would love a bottle of water."

"Are you okay?"

"Yes. Just a little nauseous."

"Thanks, Dad. You remembered my favorite drink," Gracie smiled, carrying Truffles as she walked a few rows behind her parents to take a seat.

Checking to ensure that Gracie was comfortable and had everything she needed for the flight, John walked back toward the front of the aircraft, taking a seat next to Daniella. Then, finally, he was, at last, able to relax.

"Daniella, you were certainly emotional today? Is there anything wrong?" he inquired.

"No. Everything is fine. We're all fine, all five of us," she beamed.

"Great. That's just what I wanted to hear," he winked, lounging back in his seat.

Within seconds, John bolted upright with a massive grin on his face.

"Sweetheart, did you just say, the five of us?" he exclaimed.

"Yes," Daniella smiled.

They were now leaving Destiny Cove with a future addition to their family.

Daniella was right. The sugar-white sands would always beckon her home.